**Praise for *New York Times* bestselling author
B.J. Daniels**

"Daniels is a perennial favorite on the romantic
suspense front, and I might go as far as to label her
the cowboy whisperer."
—*BookPage* on *Luck of the Draw*

"Daniels keeps readers baffled with a taut plot and
ample red herrings, expertly weaving in the threads
of the next story in the series as she introduces a
strong group of primary and secondary characters."
—*Publishers Weekly* on *Stroke of Luck*

"Daniels again turns in a taut, well-plotted, and
suspenseful tale with plenty of red herrings. Readers
will be in from the start and engaged until the end."
—*Library Journal* on *Stroke of Luck*

"Readers who like their romance spiced with mystery
can't go wrong with *Stroke of Luck* by B.J. Daniels."
—*BookPage*

"Daniels is an expert at combining layered
characters, quirky small towns, steamy chemistry
and added suspense."
—*RT Book Reviews* on *Hero's Return*

"B.J. Daniels has made *Cowboy's Legacy* quite a
nail-biting, page-turner of a story. Guaranteed to
keep you on your toes."
—*Fresh Fiction*

B.J.
NEW YORK TIMES BESTSELLING AUTHOR
DANIELS

RESTLESS HEARTS

HQN™

HQN™

ISBN-13: 978-1-335-04154-8

Recycling programs for this product may not exist in your area.

Restless Hearts

Copyright © 2019 by Barbara Heinlein

This book is for my stepdaughter Leslie
and the beautiful family she has made.

Love is where you find it. I'm glad it's brought
you back to Montana so we can share in your joy.

RESTLESS HEARTS

CHAPTER ONE

As THE SUN came up over the foothills, twelve-year-old Ty Garrison was having trouble staying in the saddle. His punishment for coming in late last night with beer on his breath included being dragged out of bed before daylight to ride fence. He should have known that the first time he tried alcohol he'd get caught. He was lucky his father hadn't taken him out to the woodshed and used the strap on him.

"I could wallop you good for this, son, but I think it's time I start treating you like a man—and you start acting like one," Shane Garrison had told him. "So you go on up to bed and we'll talk more about this early in the morning."

Except there hadn't been much talking. Just an order. "Get your butt out of that bed and into the saddle. You're riding fence this morning."

Ty was thinking that it really was high time his father stopped treating him like a kid when he saw something that set his heart off at a dead run. He reined in at the sight. Something was kicking up a whole lot of dust just over the next rise. The sound of deep snorts filled the clear November morning air, sending a chill through him.

Coming fully awake, he sat up in the saddle as he eased his horse through a patch of snow to the top of the rise. He felt his eyes go wide and reined in hard as his horse shuddered under him. He'd only seen buffalo from a distance, large dark shapes along the Montana prairie horizon next to his ranch.

Now only yards away, this one had been wallowing in the dirt but now jumped to its feet, its big shaggy head and dark eyes aimed right at him. The animal was huge, at least six feet tall at the shoulders. The beast snorted, making his horse shake again and sidestep as if wanting to run.

Ty knew the feeling. He wanted to run, as well. He'd heard stories about buffalo. How fast they were, how powerful, how destructive and, worse, what they could do to your body if you ended up under the huge hooves.

He could see where the bull had broken through the neighbor's fence and their own. It pawed the ground, snorting again, making him realize he'd startled it—just as it had startled him and his horse. His first thought was to turn tail and run home. But buffalo could clock forty miles an hour and jump six feet straight up into the air, and he could see what this one had done to two fences.

But also Ty could hear his father's words about it being time he was treated like a man. Time he acted like one. He knew what his father would do if he'd been riding fence this morning.

Carefully, he eased his rifle from its scabbard. The weapon was loaded and ready to fire. All he had to do was aim and pull the trigger. He lifted the rifle, his arms quivering, his finger resting nervously against the trigger.

As he got its big head in his sights, for some crazy reason, he thought of the buffalo head nickel his grandfather had given him. It was in the tin box where he kept his other keepsakes. He didn't want to kill this animal. In that moment, he could imagine this buffalo wild, millions of them, this prairie its home before they were all killed off. It seemed wrong to shoot it.

And yet it had broken down their fence. It could do a lot more damage if something wasn't done about it. It was one of the reasons that his father and all the other beef ranchers hated Montgomery McClintock for raising buffalo.

The huge buffalo pawed the ground again, raising a cloud of dirt in the air as it breathed hard. Early-morning steam rose from its nostrils. His horse whinnied, growing more anxious. He felt sweat run down his back. It was now or never.

The largest thing he'd ever killed was a bull elk, not something that weighed a ton. The rifle barrel swayed in the breeze. He swallowed the lump in his throat and fought to hold the gun still as he settled the crosshairs between the beast's eyes.

Through his sights, he saw with horror the buffalo lower its head and charge. He pulled the trigger. The shot went wild as his horse reared and he found himself falling through the air before hitting the ground hard.

BLAZE MCCLINTOCK ROARED down the narrow gravel road, dust boiling up behind her pickup even though it was November in Montana. The *Farmers' Almanac* was calling for a mild winter. There were only a few patches of snow around, mostly on the shady side of the hills.

She'd thought that after all these years, she wouldn't even be able to find her way to the ranch. But it was as if the way home was stamped into her DNA, something she couldn't outrun no matter how hard she tried.

The rolling Montana prairie stretched all the way to the Little Rockies. She'd forgotten how wide-open this land was and how far a person could see. It was true, the sky up here felt larger, stretching from horizon to horizon.

She slowed the pickup as she came over the rise and saw the turnoff into the ranch in the distance. She let her truck coast down the next hill. This was a fool's errand, she thought, but knew there was no turning back.

Giving the pickup more gas, she raced down the dirt road before braking for the turn. Her eyes widened as she pulled in and stopped before the stone-arched entrance into the McClintock Ranch. She'd seen plenty of the signs since she'd turned off the paved two-lane that had brought her up to this part of the state. All along the narrow dirt road to the ranches north of the Missouri Breaks, there'd been signs that read Don't Buffalo Me. Others with buffalo and a slash through them.

These were nothing new. A lot of Montana ranchers who didn't want buffalo anywhere near their cattle. It reminded her of the history of the state and how cattle ranchers had fought with sheep ranchers. Now the two lived in harmony. But it was not so with the beef and buffalo ranchers. At least, not in this part of Montana.

She stared at the dozens of signs stuck in the ground in front of the arched entrance into the ranch, no doubt compliments of her father's neighbors. The signs didn't bother her as much as the graffiti on the stone columns.

Fortunately a lot of the words scrawled in spray paint were illegible. But one jumped out at her. *KILLER*. Even that wasn't as bad as what was hanging from the arch. An effigy of her father with a rope around his neck.

For a moment, she watched it blow in the breeze and questioned what she was doing here. Her father had gone against the tide when he'd started raising buffalo. He'd known the kind of hell he was about to unleash, but once Montgomery "Monte" McClintock got something into his head, there was no reining him in.

Blaze felt angry tears burn her eyes. The father she'd been estranged from for years had been arrested for murdering a neighboring rancher. The worst part was that she suspected he was guilty as hell and yet here she was. Not that she would have been here if the judge, as they called him, hadn't asked her to come. She owed Judge WT Landusky her life. So when he'd asked her to come back here, she couldn't say no.

But she'd damn sure wanted to. She drove under the arch toward the ranch house in the distance. Memories assaulted her, especially the last time she'd left here—in handcuffs.

CHAPTER TWO

THE PLACE LOOKED exactly as she remembered it. She'd hoped that it would have changed. Instead, she felt like a rebellious teenager again. What was the retired judge thinking asking her to come back here—especially under these circumstances? She considered calling him before she got in any deeper and trying to talk him out of this.

But even as she thought it, she knew the always cantankerous Judge Landusky would simply tell her to do her job. If it wasn't for the judge, she wouldn't be a private investigator on the right side of the law instead of behind bars. It was something she never forgot. So she kept her foot on the accelerator, roaring up the familiar road toward a place she'd once called home.

As Blaze parked in front of the large rambling house where she'd grown up, she saw the ranch manager come out of the barn and head in her direction. She was surprised that Cal Sperry still worked for her father after all this time.

She could tell by his expression that he didn't recognize her as she climbed out of the pickup, stretched from the long drive and looked around the place.

She took a deep breath and let it out before turning to face the man.

Hugging sixty, Cal had the look of tough jerky. She noticed that he now walked with a slight limp. His tall, lanky body was full of authority as he stopped a few feet from her. He squinted, his face shadowed by the brim of his Western hat.

"Can I help you?" Help was the last thing his words offered as he pulled off his hat and ran a hand over his military-short graying hair.

She opened her pickup door, reached into the king cab and pulled out her suitcase. "I'd ask you to carry in my bag, but we both know how that would go." Cal had never liked her and the feeling was mutual. Like her father, he'd been disappointed that the only heir to the McClintock Ranch was female.

Didn't matter that Blaze could ride a horse as well as any man. Cal and her father considered women flighty, unpredictable, confusing and unreliable—if not entirely irrelevant. Blaze's mother had apparently proved them right when she'd taken off in the middle of the night, running as far away from Monte and the ranch as she could get, never to be heard from again.

The man's flinty eyes narrowed in his weathered face as he put his hat back on. "Like I said, you must be lost. This ain't no dude ranch."

She laughed. "You can say that again. I'd say it was good to see you again, Cal, but we both know that would be a lie."

He drew back in obvious surprise before taking her measure from her straw Western hat balanced on her thick, long auburn hair to the toes of her worn boots. "Blaze." He said her name like a curse.

"In the flesh."

Taking off his weather-beaten Stetson again, he rubbed the back of his neck for a moment before he said, "Can't imagine what *you're* doing here."

"My father's been arrested for murder. Maybe you heard."

Cal nodded slowly, studying her as if she was something he'd stepped in. "Never figured you'd come back here, given how you feel about Monte."

"You have no idea how I feel about my father," she snapped and glanced toward the house. She wondered if Monte had turned her bedroom into a gun room to wipe out all evidence of her existence. Only one way to find out, but still, she hesitated, remembering the angry words thrown around the last time she was here.

"Not sure what you think you're doing here, but there's enough trouble without you making things worse," Cal said. "Got a call this morning that one of the bulls tore out a section of fence, took out some of the neighboring rancher's fence—"

She frowned. "Is there someone out fixing it?"

"Not yet. Like I said, just heard. The rancher's twelve-year-old son tried to take care of it and got himself trampled by the bull."

Her heart rate shot up in alarm. "Is he…"

"He's in the hospital. He'll be fine. Broken arm, a few cuts and bruises." He shrugged as if it was nothing and put his hat back on.

Blaze swore, shaking her head. *"Buffalo."* Her father had been determined to raise them—even against all the protests of not just the neighboring ranchers. People in town were convinced that the animals would get out and damage everything between here and town. But a bigger fear, she'd heard, was that the buffalo would give some disease to beef that could ruin the industry.

"Monte just has to swim upstream when everyone else is swimming down, doesn't he?" she said under her breath. "Excuse me, but why are you still standing here? We need to get those fences fixed before something else happens."

Cal shook his head as if he must not have heard right. He wasn't going to like taking orders from a woman. *"Fences?"*

"Yes, fix ours *and* the neighbor's." He still hadn't moved. "Is there a problem?"

"Well," he said, scratching his jaw. "It's just that you come here, some fancy-pants private investigator, and start giving orders with this 'we' stuff after none of us have laid eyes on you in years. Isn't like you ever gave a damn about ranching, so I'm a little confused 'bout why you're here at all."

"What's confusing, Cal? My last name is still McClintock. I'm still my father's daughter, and as long as I'm here, you take orders from me since Monte is probably going to prison for the rest of his life. And as his only offspring and his power of attorney, I'll be paying your salary."

He chewed at his cheek for a moment, his eyes

dark and hard as iron. "I guess when you put it that way... I'll get the boys on those...fences. Not what Monte would do, but as you say, you *are* his daughter."

"And when they finish that, they need to see to the arch on the way into the ranch. Have them clean it up. Or maybe you'd like to take care of that yourself."

He shot her a lethal look, but said nothing as he turned and headed toward the bunkhouse.

Blaze watched him go, feeling the full weight of what she was facing. Cal Sperry was the least of her problems. She still couldn't believe that her father had given her his power of attorney. She had no idea how Judge Landusky had managed that. Apparently, the retired judge and her father went way back. She hadn't known that until recently, but she guessed it was why the judge had taken her under his wing, so to speak. That made him sound a lot sweeter than how the crusty old judge actually operated.

At the sound of a vehicle, she turned to see a pickup kicking up dust as it raced toward her. She couldn't see who was behind the wheel, but she knew trouble when she saw it coming.

She stood her ground as the truck came to a stop a few feet away from her. With the sun's glare on the windshield, she couldn't see the man behind the wheel until he climbed out.

"I thought this day couldn't get any worse." Blaze swore as she saw Jake Horn slide his sexy, lean, all-cowboy frame from behind the wheel of the pickup.

He stepped out, turned toward her, a glint in his pale eyes.

Jake was half Irish from his mother's side of the family and half Blackfoot Native American from his father's. He'd let his straight black hair grow long and kept it tied back low on his neck. The man was breathtaking from his green eyes, as inviting as Caribbean seas to his chiseled face with the high, proud cheekbones. Jake—all broad shoulders, slim hips and perfect behind, not to mention his six-pack abs under the black T-shirt he wore—here on her family ranch. This was the Jake she knew only too well.

"Whatever ill wind set you in this direction, I suggest you turn around and leave while you can," she said, hoping to remind him of the last time they'd seen each other. Only now she wasn't armed. Yet.

Jake grinned. There'd been a time when just that grin would have been an open invitation into her jeans. "The judge sent me, which means I'm staying, so you might as well welcome me with open arms."

"You wish," she said as she reached around him to grab her suitcase and wheel it toward the door of the ranch house. Looking in through the front window, she glimpsed enough of the living room to know it, too, hadn't changed. She shoved her suitcase inside before closing the door and turning back toward her pickup.

"Leaving so soon?" he asked. "I hope it wasn't anything I said." He was still grinning.

Without looking at him, she said, "There's a twelve-year-old boy in the hospital with a broken arm because one of my father's buffalo got out. I'm going to town to see if there is anything I can do for the family."

"I'd think twice before I did that."

At the sudden seriousness in his tone, she stopped walking and with a sigh, turned back to look at him. Damn the man. Just the timbre of his voice was enough to make her ache. They often agreed on little. But reason had little influence when passion came into play. Together she and Jake were a lit fuse of dynamite.

"If you came here to give me advice—"

Jake held up both hands as if in surrender, but she could tell he was far from giving up. "When I came through town, I got the feeling that the townspeople are riled up enough over the murder. Now one of their sons was hurt because of your father's buffalo? They won't be glad to see you, Blaze."

"They never were."

He nodded. "Somehow, I doubt they've forgotten you."

She groaned. "I was a teenager. I could have burned down half the town, but I didn't. Most of the stories about me aren't even true. Well, at least some of them."

He let out a chuckle. "It's the ones that are true that I think you need to worry about." His expression turned serious again. "You left. You're not one of them anymore."

Blaze looked down at her scuffed Western boots. "I'm going into town to see that boy and ask what

I can do to help. It's the right thing to do and I'm going to do it."

He shrugged. "Well, I tried," he mumbled under his breath.

"Now you can wash your hands of me," she said as she jerked open the driver's-side door of her pickup. "It won't be the first time." She'd take care of this first, then come back to face the house before deciding where to begin on investigating the murder. The judge had asked her to investigate, worried that her father couldn't get a fair shake in this county. Then again, the judge didn't know Monte like she did. Or did he?

Jake grabbed the top of the door, interrupting her thoughts. "At least let me drive you," he said behind her.

She closed her eyes, intensely aware of his body so close to hers. He smelled like sunshine even on this cold November day. Her body reacted to him as it always had, sending her heart racing. She held her breath, half-afraid of what she would do if he touched her.

"Blaze?" He said it like a caress.

"What are you doing?" she demanded on a ragged breath, refusing to turn and face him for fear that she would weaken. It had been so long and yet she remembered every whispered word, every touch, every quickened heartbeat.

"I'm going with you to save you from yourself," he said.

She counted to ten before she turned.

Jake must have taken it for acquiescence because he chuckled and said, "I can tell you've missed me. Hop in and slide over. It is always safer when I drive."

He was too close, his arm resting on the top of her open door. While her pulse thrummed in her ears, he looked calm. Maybe seeing her again wasn't throwing him off balance like it was her.

She ground her teeth and shot him an impatient look. "Seriously, Jake, I don't know what the judge was thinking sending you. I have enough going on without you here. You don't know how hard this is for me." She eyed him suspiciously. "If he really did send you. Maybe I should give him a call."

"First off, if anyone knows how hard this is on you, it's me." His voice had softened to that seductive tone that reminded her of warm nights lying naked under the stars with him.

She shook off the reminder as she felt her blood begin to heat. "Are you forgetting how we left things between us?" she asked as if reminding herself, as well.

"Not likely. I believe you had a knife to my throat."

"You're making me wish I'd used it."

He shook his head, his grin broadening. "I knew you wouldn't. Just as you and I both know you can't send me away. On second thought, let's take my pickup. You were already seen in town when you stopped for gas, so they know your rig."

She frowned. Had he been following her? "How do you know that?"

He stepped away to walk to the back of her pickup. She followed, glad to have more space between them. He pointed to the sticker pasted on the back bumper of her truck. It was almost entirely covered by dirt kicked up from her drive into the ranch, but still readable. She swore as she read Don't Buffalo Me! She reached to pull it off but Jake stopped her.

"You might be safer with it there. Come on, if you're determined to do this…" He motioned toward his pickup.

She cursed under her breath but relented. As they walked to his truck, they matched stride for stride. He'd always loved her long legs. He used to comment on them, usually when he had a hand on her thigh. Another memory she didn't need right now.

He opened the passenger-side door for her. She hesitated, but only for a moment, annoyed with him for acting like a gentleman. They both knew he was anything but. There'd been a time she would have fought his taking over like this. She hated men bossing her around—especially this one. But she liked to think that she'd mellowed since she and Jake had last seen each other. She also liked to think that she was smart enough to pick her battles.

She slid in and he closed the door. Buckling up, she watched him saunter around to the driver's side. "I still hate you."

"I know," he said as he climbed behind the wheel and started the engine. "And I still love you." He glanced at her. "Appears nothing has changed."

CHAPTER THREE

SHERIFF WILLIAM "BUD" FRASER leaned back in his office chair, folding his hands over his abundant belly as he smiled. He hated how smug he felt. He was tempting fate and he knew it. His German grandmother's words felt like a jab in his ribs. She'd been dead for years and yet at times like this he could hear her voice clear as day.

"Pride cometh before the fall." He didn't feel overconfident, though. He felt justified. Surely that wouldn't jinx things.

Montgomery McClintock was behind bars. He'd been caught standing over the victim with the murder weapon still in his hand. When arrested, the man hadn't even tried to defend himself. Nor had he wanted a lawyer. That was because Bud had him dead to rights. Monte was as guilty as hell.

So why couldn't he feel a little smug? It was an open-and-shut case. Monte was about to spend the rest of his life in prison. It wasn't the murder Bud had hoped to get the man on, but it would have to do.

Nor would it bring Bethany Reynolds McClintock back, but at least it would get her husband what he deserved. Every time he thought of Monte's wife,

who'd disappeared sixteen years ago, he envisioned
her as she'd been that day standing on the platform as
the passenger train pulled to a stop in Saddle Butte.

He had gotten discharged from the army and was
finally coming home, anxious to be back in Montana, back in the small town where he was born and
raised. When he'd stepped off the train, the first person he'd seen was Bethany.

At twenty-two, she was a vision. He'd seen her a
few times when he'd come home on leave, but only
in passing. Every time, his heart beat a little faster.
He hadn't been able to take his eyes off her. He could
admit it now… He'd wanted her since as far back as
he could remember. But she came from one of the
more well-to-do ranch families while he was the son
of the local sheriff.

But that day, dressed in his uniform, he'd felt as if
he was finally somebody. He figured now that he'd
seen some of the world as an MP in the army, maybe
she might want to go out with him.

She spotted him, recognizing him, and raised her
hand to wave. But it was her smile that gave him the
courage to head in her direction.

Unfortunately, he didn't get a chance to even talk
to her before Montgomery McClintock came off the
train wearing his big Stetson. Monte made a beeline
for her, grabbing her and swinging her up off her
feet as he spun her in the air. Bud could still hear
her laugh. As Monte set her down, saying something about having been to Chicago for some cattleman's convention, Bethany looked up into his eyes,

an enamored expression on her face. And Bud had known he would never stand a chance. Not with McClintock around.

Bud still ground his teeth at the memory. While he'd been off protecting his country, Monte had gone to college and come home to ranch after his father had died. It made Bud angry since he hadn't been able to afford college without the GI bill—unlike Monte.

Now, so many years later, they were both old men. He'd resented Monte for more than thirty-five years. Not long after Bud had returned to Saddle Butte, Monte had married Bethany. Blaze had come a few years later.

Bud always thought he could have made Bethany happier than Monte had. He recalled seeing her in town and thinking something was wrong. He'd even asked her once after he became a deputy if things were all right out at the ranch. She'd smiled and pretended that everything was fine, but he'd suspected otherwise.

When he'd heard that she'd left Monte and taken off, he'd been overjoyed to hear it. He'd always hoped she would come back to divorce Monte. He'd thought maybe he might have a chance with her then. But she'd never come back. No one heard from her or anything about her again. It was as if she'd fallen off the face of the earth.

In his imagination, he'd seen her go on to do great things, free of Saddle Butte, but mostly free of Monte McClintock. But as time went on and there was no word from or of her, he'd feared that she'd never left the county. Not alive anyway.

That was when he'd known that Monte had to have killed her. He just couldn't prove it. Rumors circulated for a while, but after sixteen years, Bethany Reynolds McClintock had been forgotten by most people in the county.

Except for Bud Fraser, who'd never been able to forget her standing next to the train that day, the sun shining in her long auburn hair and that smile on her face. It was the kind of memory that haunted his dreams.

JAKE GLANCED OVER at Blaze as they left the ranch for the drive into Saddle Butte. She had her long auburn hair plaited in a single braid that hung over one shoulder, almost to her breasts. The Western shirt she wore was blue checked and matched her eyes—and the Montana sky. Her jeans hugged curves he knew only too well. He thought she couldn't have looked more beautiful.

But worry creased her brows. He knew how difficult this was for her and doubted he was making it easier. And yet there was no place he'd rather be.

"You look good," he said. "It feels as if no time has passed since I last saw you." He laughed when she merely glared at him for a moment before she turned again to look out the side window. He'd known this wouldn't be easy given the way they'd parted, but if he was anything, it was determined.

He glanced over at her as he drove. He knew this

woman inside and out. He told himself to give it a little time and hoped he would have it, now that he was here. Turning back to his driving, he concentrated on navigating the narrow dirt road that cut through rolling hills and sagebrush-filled prairie. He could appreciate this country even though most people preferred the western part of the state with its mountains, pine trees and clear trout streams that stretched out like blue ribbons. The rolling prairie was something that grew on a person. All that wide-openness wasn't for everyone.

But for him, there was something comforting about all the space. The cloudless blue sky overhead felt huge this morning and the late-November day seemed brighter. He thought of Christmas and wondered where the two of them would be.

Being around Blaze again, he longed to be curled up in front of a fire with lights sparkling on a tree and presents waiting to be opened on Christmas morning. He remembered that feeling of expectation. The same feeling he had when he was around Blaze, he thought, and looked over at her and smiled.

"What?" she demanded as if she'd been watching him out of the corner of her eye. She turned to look at him, impatience written all over her.

"Just thinking. About Christmas."

"Christmas?" She shook her head as if unwilling to go down that familiar trail with him. "This won't take long. I'll be long gone by then." They'd been together last Christmas, curled up in bed after being thrown together on one of the judge's projects.

He hadn't realized that there were others like him, teens who had been saved and now would do anything for WT.

Then he'd met Blaze and he'd had a newfound admiration for the judge.

"We're good together," he said to her. "We'll figure this out. I'm sure that's why the judge put us together on this."

"I have no idea what he was thinking." She looked over at him and narrowed her eyes. "I'm still not sure he did."

Jake grinned. She'd threatened to call to find out if WT really had sent him. He wasn't worried that she would. Questioning the old judge was always a bad idea.

"I'm assuming you haven't talked to your father yet," he asked, trying to find some solid ground with her. Talking about why she was here, he figured, would do the trick.

"The arraignment and bail hearing are in the morning. No way is he going to get bail."

"Probably not," Jake agreed. He'd had his own brush with the law in his youth. After a string of breaking and entering charges, he'd ended up before Judge WT Landusky. He could laugh about it now, but the judge had scared him straight. Now he had nothing but respect for the man.

"From what the judge told me," he said to Blaze now, "your father hasn't said one word since he was arrested. That's got to help."

"Wait," she said, turning in the seat to stare at

him. "You think we're here to get him out of this?" She shook her head. "No, the judge was clear. He just wants to be sure that the sheriff didn't rush to judgment. Once we know for sure that he committed the crime, we walk away and let the justice system deal with my father. Which means he's going to prison for murder."

He glanced over at her, surprised by the conviction he heard in her voice. "You're that convinced he killed the rancher?"

She groaned. "My father has been fighting with Frank Anson for as far back as I can remember—even before my father decided to raise buffalo. I suspect he did it just to piss off Frank and everyone else."

"What was the problem between them before the buffalo?" Jake asked as the town of Saddle Butte, Montana, appeared on the skyline. There were only a few buildings tall enough to be seen from this distance. The water tower, the elevator grain bins next to the railroad tracks and the courthouse. Saddle Butte didn't even have a stoplight. It was what he'd heard called a one-horse town.

It was definitely a town that had forgotten its past, he thought. In its heyday, thousands of pounds of buffalo bones had been shipped from this small town for fertilizer as the free-ranging wild buffalo were killed off by the millions. He remembered seeing a photo of a pile of bones higher than any building in town. The bones were sent back East to a fertilizer plant.

"Did you hear me?"

He realized that he'd been lost in thought and mentally shook himself. "Sorry."

"Thinking about some old girlfriend of yours?" she asked.

He grinned over at her. "I'm always thinking about you."

She shook her head. "You are a terrible liar."

"Or maybe you just don't want to accept the truth. I was thinking about you, but then the town came into view and I couldn't help thinking about the wild buffalo that used to roam this part of the state in huge herds. They said it was like a dark wave over the prairie. I was wishing I could have seen that. It's hard to imagine that many."

"Buffalo? You and my father," she said with a groan. "I was saying that the trouble between him and neighboring rancher Frank Anson was his young wife, Allie. My father took a liking to her and vice versa."

"After your mother left."

Blaze shrugged. "According to my father, but maybe it was going on before that and it's why my mother left."

He heard the bitterness in her voice. Her mother had said she would come back for Blaze, but she never had. Once she'd driven away, that was the last Blaze had heard from her mother.

"Your father and Allie Anson?"

"If the stories are true, Frank said if he ever found Monte on his property again, he'd kill him."

"So you think all of this is over a woman?" Jake chuckled. "What am I saying? Isn't it always about a woman?"

She shot him a narrow-eyed glare, but then turned her attention to the small Montana town as he slowed at the city limits sign. The sign read Population 759 and 2 Old Soreheads. The *2* had been crossed out and someone had replaced it with a *1*. Next to the sign was a "don't buffalo me" poster on a stake. Welcome to Saddle Butte, Montana.

BLAZE SIGHED AND tried to ignore Jake. It was difficult. The man seemed to overpower any space he was in. She could smell the soap he'd used to shower this morning. She knew his long, straight, thick black hair was probably still damp and tied back to trail partway down his back. She had felt him looking at her most of the way into the town. What was he really doing here?

She shoved thoughts of him away and tried to concentrate on the job at hand. She already knew how this was going to go down. She would talk to her father. He probably wouldn't tell her the truth. She would investigate, and ultimately, Monte would go to prison for the rest of his life.

But then what? She'd told Cal that she was taking over the ranch in her father's absence. That was the last thing she wanted to do and her father had to know that. So why had he given her power of attorney? Didn't he realize that she would sell the place the first chance she got—and the buffalo with it?

There would be nothing he could do about it since at his age, he wouldn't ever be getting out of prison. She could wipe out his legacy with her signature. The buffalo would be gone and so would the McClintock name in this part of Montana.

She looked out the window as Jake drove through town. She remembered being a teenager driving in on a Friday or Saturday night. That seemed a lifetime ago, cruising the main street and flirting with boys.

Like the ranch, it didn't appear that anything had changed. Some of the businesses were different. Some were gone. Like so many towns in rural areas of Montana, this part of the state was losing population. Saddle Butte hung on because of the ranching. Otherwise it would have shriveled up and blown away a long time ago.

"The hospital is the next right," she said, looking out the window as they passed a few local businesses, some empty lots, a couple of older homes and a tire shop. Several people on the street looked up as they passed, but she saw no recognition on their faces when she met their gazes.

Maybe she'd been gone long enough that no one would remember her. *Right*, she thought. She'd forgotten about the bumper sticker someone had plastered on her pickup. Jake was right. She'd been spotted on her way through town and possibly followed to the gas station. She was really going to have to start paying more attention since soon she would be neck-deep in her father's mess—a dangerous place to be.

The hospital was a small one-story brick building on the edge of town. Jake parked but didn't turn off the engine for a moment.

"Are you sure about this?" he said, clearly having his reservations. "You have to know what kind of reception you're going to get in there."

She took a long breath and let it out before she turned to him. "Have you ever known me to run and hide when there is trouble? To walk away from a fight? To give up easily?"

He laughed and shook his head. "Nope. You're more of a throw-the-first-punch kind of girl. It's what I love about you."

She nodded and returned his smile as she opened her door. "And that is the problem between us. You still think I'm a girl."

She stepped out and slammed his pickup door, but not before she heard him say, "*My* kind of girl."

JAKE WAS GLAD he'd come to town with Blaze, even if she wasn't. And she was wrong about one thing. She didn't give up easily, but she'd given up on him. Now he had to figure out what to do about that.

The moment they walked into the hospital, he knew there was going to be trouble. He could feel the tension as Blaze stepped up to the reception desk and asked where they could find the Garrison boy. But before the receptionist could answer, Blaze said, "Forget it," as she spotted someone she knew and headed off down the hallway.

A cluster of people were gathered outside a partition room in the ER on the first floor. Given the number of boots, canvas jackets and Stetsons he saw in the cluster, he assumed it was the ranching family and friends.

As Blaze headed for them, he saw several of the people turn. He watched their faces and felt his stomach tense. Yep, trouble was brewing big-time. He wanted to hog-tie Blaze and keep her safe, but that would only make her turn her ire on him—and certainly not stop her since she was a woman on a mission. So he kept stride with her, knowing there was little he could do to keep them from giving her a piece of their minds.

"I heard about what happened," Blaze said when she reached the small crowd gathered there. "I'm so sorry." She seemed to ignore the stone-like stares. "I'm Blaze. Blaze McClintock. I wanted to see if there is anything I can do."

Jake saw her glance into the area where the Garrison boy lay in bed, his arm in a cast and a bandage on his head. Blaze started to step into the area, but a large rancher blocked her way.

"You have no business here," the man said. "My son could have been killed by one of your father's damned buffalo."

"That's why I'm here," Blaze said. "Shane Garrison, right? Is there anything I can do? I can't tell you how sorry I am."

"You need to leave," a woman said, grabbing Blaze's arm and pulling her back. "You just need to leave and stay away from my family."

Jake watched Blaze gently remove the woman's fingers from her arm. "Mary, I understand that you're upset."

"Upset?" The word had a hysterical edge to it. "You have no idea. My boy…" Her voice broke.

Jake stepped in. "I believe all she's saying is that she'd like to help."

"I don't know who you are, but we don't need help from the likes of either of you," Shane Garrison said.

"In that case, we'll be going, then," Jake said. He touched Blaze's arm. She jerked it away.

"I'm sorry you feel that way, but your fight is with my father, not me. And certainly not with Jake here. I'm having your fence repaired and in the meantime, I will do my best to keep my *father's* buffalo off your property."

"You do that," Shane blustered as his wife pushed past him to her son's bedside.

Jake glanced at the others standing in the hallway. Neighboring ranchers? One woman stood out among the others. Middle-aged, she had long blond hair that was pulled back with a red ribbon. Her expression was the only one that wasn't angry as she watched Blaze with sad brown eyes. The woman looked as if she wanted to say something, do something, but couldn't.

Blaze stood for a moment. He knew she wanted to say a whole lot more. He was thankful when she didn't. Her gaze took in the others, lighting for a moment on the blonde woman.

"Allie," Blaze said with a slight nod. Then, turning, she shoved her Western hat back on her head and walked, her back ramrod straight, toward the exit.

Jake chuckled to himself as he went after her. "That went better than expected," he said once they'd reached his pickup again.

"I spent my life fighting my father's battles," she said with a disgusted shake of her head. "I swore never again and here I am defending the son of a—"

"You did good in there."

She shot him a look and laughed. "I was lucky to get out of there alive and we both know it. Everyone has so much hate for my father."

"Which is why the judge is worried that the sheriff might railroad your father straight to a prison cell. Have you seen any of the evidence against him?"

Blaze shook her head as she buckled up. "Since I'm on such a roll, might as well go visit Sheriff Bud Fraser. That old goat will be delighted to see me. I used to date his son."

Jake raised an eyebrow. "Really?"

"High school. He asked me to marry him. He even bought me a ring."

"I take it you said no?"

She nodded smiling to herself. "LJ Fraser was just one of a long line of mistakes I made."

"Let me get this straight," Jake said. "You wish you'd married him?"

She laughed. "Not hardly. I wish I'd never dated him. But needless to say, it's one of the reasons his father dislikes me. I'm sure there are more."

Jake thought going to see the sheriff right now

was probably a mistake. But he knew there was no talking her out of it in the mood she was in. He started the engine and pulled out. As he did, he noticed the woman Blaze had called Allie standing just inside the hospital lobby, watching them go. "That woman—"

"Allie? Yep, she's Frank Anson's widow and the woman my father fell for."

"If true, why didn't Monte steal her from Frank?" He felt Blaze's gaze on him.

"Women can't be *stolen*. Just like men can't be stolen out of a good marriage."

"So if they were both in love, then what kept them apart?" When Blaze didn't answer, he glanced over at her.

As if feeling him watching her, she said, "Love isn't always enough."

He didn't think they were talking about Allie and Monte anymore. "Maybe it was the age difference between them." He estimated that Allie Anson was in her midforties. Montgomery "Monte" McClintock was fifty-seven.

Blaze leaned back against the seat and closed her eyes. "Not to mention that she was married to a man who kept a shotgun by his door."

Jake gave that some thought. He knew a shotgun by the door wouldn't have kept him away from the woman he loved. The only thing that had kept him away from Blaze this past year was her. The last thing she'd said to him when she'd left was that she hated him and never wanted to see him again.

He'd given her time, maybe too much, but he was here now and determined that they were going to sort out their feelings for each other. Blaze could keep denying it, but he wouldn't leave her again until he was sure she really didn't love him.

As he pulled into the parking lot at the sheriff's department, he realized what had been nagging at him since leaving the hospital. "Allie doesn't seem all that angry about your father killing her husband."

Blaze opened one eye to look at him before she sat up. "That's because if the rumors are true, my father did her a favor," she said as she climbed out. "Which makes my father look even more guilty."

CHAPTER FOUR

SHERIFF BUD FRASER had been expecting her. Blaze saw that the moment she looked into the man's face. Bud shoved back his Stetson as he met her in the hallway before she could reach his office.

"I don't have time for this right now," he said in his deep, gravelly voice. He was about her father's age, late fifties. His face was a road map of wrinkles as if from a long, tiring and rough journey to get to this point in time.

"I want to talk to you about my father's case." She glanced at the clock on the wall. "It's a little early for your dinner over at the café. Surely you can spare a few minutes. For old times' sake," she added.

He chuckled at that before breaking into a hacking cough. "Why don't you make an appointment?"

"I want to see my father."

Bud raised one grayed eyebrow. "What's the rush? You haven't seen him in years. Another day or two won't hurt."

"Are you denying me the right to see my father?"

He narrowed his gaze at her as he looked down his hawklike nose. "I heard you've become a private investigator. That doesn't give you the credentials to come in here and—"

"I'm his *daughter*. That's all the...credential I need."

The sheriff looked past her to Jake, who'd insisted that he wasn't going to let her go in alone. They'd argued on the walk into the building. She'd forgotten he'd trailed in after her. "And you are?"

"Jake Horn. I'm with her."

"Jake Horn," Bud repeated it as if letting the name wallow around in his mouth for a while before he pursed his lips and sighed. "You're that damned bounty hunter I heard about?"

"I've been known to escort criminals to court," Jake said. "I would think you'd appreciate that. But in my spare time, I'm just a simple rancher."

"Beef? Or are you one of these...buffalo people?"

"Black Angus. I hope you approve."

The sheriff shook his head as his gaze returned to Blaze. "I knew you were going to show up here bringing all kinds of trouble with you. You can see your father after his arraignment tomorrow morning. That's if he wants to see you." He settled his Stetson more securely on his head. "Now, if you will excuse me." He pushed past them and out the door.

"You all right?" Jake asked as he drove out of town, back toward the ranch.

"What are we doing here? I mean, really? This is too much like beating my head against a concrete wall. What's the point? Monte's guilty. He's hated

Frank Anson for years. He wanted his wife. Maybe he was going over the fence again and Frank caught him. Maybe—"

"That's just it. We don't know what happened," Jake said. "Let's not jump to conclusions. It could have just been a simple misunderstanding that turned violent. You know how these things happen. This whole buffalo-versus-cattle issue." He shook his head. "I just don't get it."

"Neither do most people. In Wyoming, there's no problem. Buffalo and cattle exist harmoniously. It's Montana. It's especially this part of the state. Buffalo are hard on fences. They're big and often destructive. I get it."

Jake shook his head. "I think it's more political. I know I don't worry about buffalo infecting my cattle with brucellosis, but a lot of ranchers do."

"I thought those were just the wild bison from Yellowstone Park."

They fell into a companionable silence for a while until he said, "It's like the early turf wars between sheep and cattle ranchers. I think this war will end the same way, with both realizing that the other isn't so bad."

"Those wars turned ugly, too, before it was over. My father's been buying up land, adding more buffalo. You can see how upset people are."

"Upset enough to kill one another?" He glanced over at her. "This could be about buffalo and not Frank's wife. You don't know that's what your father was arguing with the man about before Frank was killed. Or even if they were arguing. Hopefully we'll be able to get more information tomorrow. But I think we need to call in a good criminal lawyer. Your father can't get a fair trial in this county."

"Or any other county. The buffalo are why everyone in this community hates my father. But I'm not sure another county will make a difference in this state."

"They can't all hate him," Jake said. "Allie Anson, for one, didn't."

She shot him a look. "I wonder if she'll be at the arraignment tomorrow. You can bet Garrison and his bunch of rancher friends will be there."

"Which is why I'll be right by your side."

Blaze groaned and looked out as the ranch entrance archway came into view. "I actually think there are more signs out here than earlier. I asked Cal to see about getting it cleaned up. At least my father's effigy isn't still dangling from the rafters."

"I tore it down on my way in," Jake said. He felt her gaze swing on him. "No matter how you feel about him, he deserves better than that."

She said nothing, but he could almost hear her gritting her teeth. Her daddy problems were legendary. Much like Montgomery McClintock himself. The man was bigger than life. Jake couldn't imagine what it must have been like for Blaze growing up in that large dark shadow after her mother left.

But there was no doubt that it had left a chip on her shoulder bigger than Montana. The few times he'd tried to talk to her about her father had taught him that it was a subject best avoided.

He barely got the pickup stopped in the yard before she was out of the truck, slamming the door behind her. Jake parked and, grabbing his bag from the back seat, started toward the house.

"You can sleep in the barn," Blaze said over her shoulder as she strode toward the front door.

He stopped walking to stare at her slim back and that wonderful behind of hers. "You'll just have to walk farther when you get lonely," he called after her.

Her laugh followed her into the house. Jake smiled as he hoisted his duffel strap onto his shoulder and headed for the barn. It wouldn't be the first barn he'd slept in and probably not his last.

Blaze halted just inside the door of the ranch house she'd grown up in, feeling the weight of the past settle onto her shoulders. She'd hoped that the house had changed, that it would look nothing like it had the last time she was here. It was a wasted hope.

She took a breath and let it out, blinking as her eyes burned with tears. At moments like this, she missed her mother desperately. How different her life would have been if her mother hadn't left. Not that she blamed her. Living with Montgomery Mc-Clintock was no picnic. Still, Blaze hadn't expected her mother to run out on her. She'd been sixteen and had just begun to rebel. She'd always wondered if that, too, had played into why her mother had lied about sending for her as soon as she was settled.

Her father had paid a private detective to find her, but Bethany Reynolds McClintock had disappeared without a trace.

"She doesn't want to be found," Monte had told Blaze. "She had to have been planning this for some time." He'd been angry but also hurt. "What mother leaves her child? You're better-off without her."

But she hadn't been and as time when on, she'd resented her father even more, blaming him for her mother leaving. The more she pulled away from him, the more he tried to control her. It had become a vicious battle that could have only ended the way it had.

Hating to be reminded of the past, she grabbed the handle of her suitcase and started through the living room with its hardwood floor, leather furniture and Native American rugs. It was as if no one used this room. The thought made her realize that it was probably true.

As she glanced into the kitchen, she saw that there was a coffee cup sitting by the sink. Other than that, it appeared to be another room seldom used. She continued down the hallway, slowing to a stop at her father's den. There were several dirty coffee cups by his computer on the large old oak desk that had been his grandfather's. The chairs in front of the rock fireplace were worn smooth, the Navajo rug faded and threadbare, the room well used.

This was where her father lived. Alone except for Cal, she thought until she noticed the smear of pink lipstick on one coffee cup. Maybe not alone. That was the same color lipstick Allie Anson had been wearing earlier today at the hospital.

For a moment she stood there, surprised, and yet she knew she shouldn't have been. Allie and her father. Apparently the rumors were true.

At the sound of the front door opening and closing, she turned to head back down the hallway, expecting Jake. The man was incorrigible. But it wasn't Jake. A Hutterite woman wearing a long skirt, a black jacket and a polka-dot head scarf came in carrying a bucketful of rags and cleaning supplies. When she saw Blaze, she let out a cry of surprise and placed her hand over her heart.

"Hello," Blaze said, stepping into the living room. "Are you looking for my father?"

The woman shook her head. "I'm here to clean." She spoke with a German accent. "I come every few weeks. Cal said I could come for the time being with Mr. McClintock…"

"Yes, tied up, so to speak." Seeing this woman, Blaze now knew why the house had looked so clean and unused except for her father's den. "I'm Blaze. Monte is my father."

The woman nodded. "I know who you are. I've seen your photograph. You just surprised me. I didn't think you would be here."

Apparently a lot of people had thought that she wouldn't come back—even if her father was arrested for murder. "And you are?"

"Susie. So should I clean?"

Why not? Blaze thought. "Do whatever it is you

normally do." She looked past the woman to see a young Hutterite man talking to Jake out in the yard.

"That's my son. He drives me."

She nodded, having forgotten that most Hutterite women didn't drive. She started to say something more but the woman had already headed for the kitchen, where she immediately went to work scrubbing every surface down.

Blaze turned back to her suitcase and continued on down the hall. She hadn't planned to stop in the doorway of her father's room but something caught her eye. She saw the photograph beside his unmade bed. It had been taken at one of her barrel races when she was sixteen—right after her mother had left. She'd never seen the photo before and realized her father must have taken it. She hadn't even known he'd been there.

Blaze stared at the photo so prominently displayed as she tried to swallow the lump in her throat.

At the sound of the woman cleaning in the kitchen, she moved on down the hallway to the far end of the house. Her room was past the laundry room. This door was closed. She stopped in front of it for a moment, afraid of what she would find once she opened this door. The room would be used for storage now. Taking a deep breath, she let it out, turned the knob and pushed. The door swung in. Her breath caught as she stared in surprise.

Her room appeared to be exactly as she'd left it. Her father hadn't turned it into a gun room or a junk storage area. He'd even had Susie clean it, from what she could tell. Her barrel racing awards were still on the shelves along with her collection of ceramic horses.

She pulled her suitcase in and moved to the closet, surprised that her throat had closed up on her again. Opening the closet door, she saw the clothes she'd left behind and shook her head. Her father had probably just shut the door and left it. Because he'd known that one day she would come back? Or had he thought she'd be like her mother and never return?

ALLISON "ALLIE" ANSON stood in the middle of her kitchen, trying to remember why she'd come into this room. The house seemed strangely quiet without Frank. Not that she saw that much of him when he was home. He spent his days outside tinkering with the tractor, hauling hay, feeding cattle, hanging out in the barn.

She looked around the kitchen, feeling lost. She wasn't hungry, hadn't been all day, even though she knew she needed to eat. She walked to the refrigerator, opened the door and looked inside.

Foil-covered casserole dishes were stacked like bricks on the shelves. She caught the scent of a Tater Tot casserole and quickly closed the door. On the counter there were plastic-wrapped trays of home-made dinner rolls, cinnamon rolls, pies and cookies. Her neighbors had begun showing up not long after Frank had been taken away in the coroner's van.

The memory of the black body bag sent a chill up her backbone. She could still see Monte being led away in handcuffs, his gaze holding hers right until he was forced into the back of a patrol SUV.

Shaking off the memory, she moved to the stove to put the kettle on. Normally she would have had a cup of coffee, but she was trying to limit her caffeine, so she'd been drinking some kind of tea her doctor had suggested that wouldn't hurt the baby. It was tasteless.

She placed a hand over her stomach. Forty-two was old for her to be having her first child. She wondered what people would say. No one knew yet. But it wouldn't be long. She was starting to show. She wouldn't be able to keep it a secret much longer.

The kettle began to whistle. She turned off the flame and took the pot over to where she had her cup from this morning, the tea bag still in it. Her hand trembled as she poured hot water into her cup. Seeing Blaze McClintock this morning at the hospital had come as such a shock. She was surprised how much the young woman looked like her mother, Bethany. It reminded her of those first lonely, isolated months after arriving on the ranch as a newlywed.

Bethany McClintock had been her first friend, her only friend. Allie didn't think she would have survived that year if it hadn't been for her. Living this far from everything had come as such a shock. Frank had played down the distance from town, the distance from other ranch houses, the vastness with so little on the horizon.

They'd met in Bozeman at Montana State University. She'd just come out of a bad relationship with a young man who'd broken her heart. Frank had been much older, more mature. He'd been in town as part of a cattle study through the university. His eyes had lit up when he talked about the family ranch. He'd made it sound so enchanting.

She'd been a junior with a plan to become an elementary teacher. She loved children. Frank had promised her a half dozen of her own if she would marry him, quit school and come to live with him on the family ranch. He'd said she could go back to school if she wanted to, but to give it a year before she made up her mind.

He'd professed his undying love for her, and at that moment in her life, being loved was something she'd desperately needed. She'd lost her mother her freshman year in college. Her father had remarried and moved away. She'd felt abandoned, and then her boyfriend had broken up with her and she'd been devastated.

She remembered the first time she'd seen Frank. He'd looked so uncomfortable in the new jeans and shirt, his hair slicked down with water, his calloused hands, big and awkward. She'd found it endearing. He'd been nothing like the man who'd broken her heart. Frank had been shy when he'd kissed her. After a few dates, she'd let him get to first base.

Even now she had to smile at the memory of him trying to unhook her bra, his clumsy attempt to caress her breasts with his overlarge fingers, his embarrassment when he'd come in his pants the first time she'd let him get to second base.

When he'd gotten down on one knee to ask her to marry him, she'd said yes. The diamond had been small, the ring too large, but it had been in a velvet box and Frank had had tears in his eyes. She couldn't have said no even if she'd wanted to.

But nothing had been like Frank said it would be once they'd reached the ranch. He hadn't wanted her to go back to school when she'd realized that they weren't going to have even one child of their own. She'd hated living so far out of town, in country that was so alien to her. She'd grown up in the mountains with pine trees. The wind blowing across the prairie at night was like a haunting moan. She'd thought she would lose her mind from the sound of it.

Worse, Frank was much coarser with her than he'd been at college. She'd hated the way he smelled when he came in from the pasture. She'd hated the way he grabbed her, rubbed her nipples raw before he climbed onto her and off just as quickly.

She'd always loved to read, but found herself hiding her books when Frank came into the house. He ridiculed her for reading so much, saying she could help more around the ranch, telling her that she wasn't pulling her weight.

But the biggest surprise was to find out that Frank's mother, Hilda, would be living with them. The woman had died of heart failure fourteen months after Allie and Frank married and moved in. But they were torturous months. From the moment Allie walked in the door, the woman told her just how worthless she was.

When Allie had complained to Frank, he'd informed her that his mother would teach her what she didn't know. Which appeared to be a whole lot. It became clear that his mother had done everything for him and now he wanted her to do it exactly as his mother had. Unfortunately, she'd never been able to meet his mother's standards while she was alive and even less so after she was dead.

Now she picked up her cup of tea and looked out the window at the prairie she'd come to hate and finally to love. She'd been miserable until she met her neighbor Bethany McClintock. Living with Frank had become more bearable after that. Bethany was also a reader, so they often talked about books they were reading while Allie darned Frank's socks. Frank never threw anything away. His mother had taught him not to be wasteful, he'd often said. In truth, Frank was cheap.

Those years had flown by. Then her only real friend, Bethany, had disappeared without a word. Winter had come early that year. The cold, the snow building up against the side of the house, the dark days making her feel trapped. She hadn't been able to stand being closed in to a life that she hated. The only thing that kept her sane was plotting to leave Frank and their marriage in the coming spring.

But then one day she looked up and there was Montgomery McClintock.

CHAPTER FIVE

"SHE'S GOT THAT bounty hunter staying out there at Monte's place," Shane Garrison said to the ranchers and deputy who'd gathered outside the hospital by his pickup. "The sheriff just called me. Told me that they showed up down at his office. The daughter's a private investigator. Bud's worried that they're going to stir things up by putting their noses into his investigation."

"What can she do?" One of the older ranchers pulled off his hat and raked a hand through his thinning brown hair. "Everyone knows that Monte killed Frank. He hasn't even denied it. I think we should let the sheriff handle this. Monte's in jail, probably going to prison for the rest of his life. Why not just let nature take its course?"

"I agree with Floyd," another rancher said. "I know you're upset over your son's accident—"

"Ty could have been killed," Shane snapped. The other ranchers all nodded and looked down at their boots. "Something has to be done. Cal Sperry out at the ranch won't be a problem. He'll make himself scarce, but I can't say the same for this Jake Horn.

Bud told me that he has a reputation for butting into other people's business."

"What are you thinking of doing?" one of the younger ranchers asked, excitement in his voice. "If the sheriff is worried, then these two are going to be trouble."

Garrison nodded. "McClintock's been buying up land and talking to East Coast developers about some fool plan he has to let the buffalo roam free. I'd like to wipe that ranch off the map before it's too late."

"I'm with you," the young rancher said. "We should have stopped him the minute we heard about him bringing in buffalo. Now with his daughter back, who knows what she might do. Maybe bring in more buffalo."

"I really doubt that's going to happen," Floyd said. "She hasn't been back here in years. Once her father is convicted—"

"How long will that take?" Garrison demanded. "I can't wait that long. What if she sells the place to one of those East Coast developers? We'll never be able to get rid of the buffalo if that happens. No, we have to make sure there isn't much left to sell."

"What are you talking about?" a rancher asked. "Shane—"

"It would be a damned tragedy if something happened out there to make them leave," the younger rancher interjected.

"It certainly would," Garrison said with a grin.

Another rancher held up his hands and took a step back. "I want nothing to do with this."

"We won't get caught," the cocky young rancher said. "Anyway," he joked, "I'm good friends with the sheriff's son. Hell, if I talk to LJ, he'll probably want in on helping us."

"Count me out, too," Floyd said and turned to walk away. The other rancher followed after him along with several others who'd been standing around listening.

Garrison swore but then looked at the young rancher. "We don't need them but when it happens, they'll keep their mouths shut. They don't want buffalo in this county any more than we do. They just don't have the balls to do anything about it. You really think the sheriff's son will join us?"

JAKE HAD THROWN his duffel along with his saddle and gear into the tack room when he heard a vehicle pull up, and he looked out to see the Hutterites. The young man who'd arrived with the woman headed out to the barn when he saw him. Jake introduced himself. Thomas explained that he'd brought his mother to the house to clean.

Then the young man sat down on a log by the sunny side of the barn, pulled out his pocketknife and a piece of wood he'd been working on. Jake saw that he was carving a bird. He looked toward the house, thinking of Blaze. He knew better than anyone what a toll all of this must be taking on her and wished there was some way to make it easier for her.

The thought made him laugh. Blaze wouldn't accept comfort, especially from him, even after everything they'd been through. Or maybe because of it. He'd seen her vulnerable and that was all it had taken for her to push him away. She'd blamed it on something else, but he'd known. She must get tired of always being so damned independent, he thought. Or maybe not. Maybe that was what kept her together.

"I'd ask what you're doing here," said a deep male voice behind him. He'd heard enough about Cal Sperry to know at once what kind of reception he was going to get from the man. Turning, he gave the ranch manager a smile.

Cal shook his head. "First her, now you? Are you two trying to get us all killed?"

"I beg your pardon?"

"The county's in an uproar over Frank's killing. I'm surprised the ranchers haven't stormed the jail and dragged Monte out to string him up—just like they used to do back in the Old West."

"Strange attitude, given that the man has paid your wages for years," Jake commented.

"Just tellin' it like it is. That woman showing up here thinking she's somethin' she's not, and you…" Cal shook his head. "You're just askin' for more trouble."

"That woman is his daughter."

"You think I don't know that?" The ranch manager spit on the ground at his feet. "What's she think she's going to do anyway?"

"I believe she wants to make sure her father gets a fair trial."

Cal chuckled at that. "Given how Monte felt about Frank Anson—and Frank's *wife*?"

"I get the feeling you're enjoying this."

"Well, you'd be wrong. Monte goes to prison, I'm out of a job because I sure as hell ain't workin' for her." He jabbed a finger toward the house.

"Her name is Blaze. Blaze *McClintock*. And unless you want to be unemployed even sooner, I suggest you treat her with respect."

The ranch manager chuckled. "I already seen the writing on the wall. You and *Blaze* just brought it home for me. I'll be packing up my stuff and moving off the ranch this afternoon. The ranch hands are going with me." He smiled, his teeth dark with tobacco. "You know anything about running a buffalo ranch, son?"

Jake considered telling him that it couldn't be that hard if Cal could do it, but he decided to keep that to himself.

"Well, you best learn, and fast." With that, the man turned and walked back toward the small cabin he'd called home for years. Past him, Jake saw the ranch hands packing up their gear and spilling out of the bunkhouse, as well. He suspected that Cal was behind them all leaving. It unnerved him a little. Rats jumping ship? Or was there more to this?

Either way, it meant he and Blaze would be alone on the ranch tonight. Just the two of them. Almost like old times.

BLAZE HAD JUST returned to the living room when she saw Jake and Cal talking outside by the barn. The conversation seemed agreeable enough, but she could tell by Jake's handsome face that whatever the ranch manager was saying, Jake didn't like it. Normally, he was good at keeping his feelings hidden—unlike her.

As Cal walked away, Jake headed for the house. She braced herself, expecting bad news, because that was all she'd gotten since the judge's call about her father. Down the hall, she could hear Susie running the vacuum. The woman's son appeared to be whittling a piece of wood over by the barn.

It surprised her that her father would hire Hutterites. They lived communally, all working for the good of the colony. Socialists, some said. They didn't vote, they didn't join the military and, while the men drove new vehicles and the best farm machinery that money could buy, they tried to hang on to the old ways. The women wore dresses and cooked, cleaned and sewed. The men wore suspenders and worked the fields. They tried to maintain an independence and culture that Blaze had always admired.

She heard Susie move deeper into the house, the sound of the vacuum almost comforting this far from civilization.

"Cal giving you a hard time?" she asked as Jake came through the door.

He shook his head. "Nothing he could say can rile me."

She heard what he hadn't said. "But he said something that's going to rile *me*."

"He's quitting and taking the ranch hands with him."

That didn't come as a complete surprise. She

knew he'd quit before he'd work for her. But she hadn't expected it so soon. And, of course, he'd talk the ranch hands into leaving with him. She hated to think what he'd told them. Then again, people in these parts had been talking about her from as far back as she could remember.

"He suggested I learn about buffalo ranching, and quickly. Don't worry, I can handle it. I've fed and watered my share of animals before. I have a friend taking care of my small spread while I'm here. I'll see to the buffalo."

She wasn't worried. She knew that Jake could handle most anything. "I can help, too." She met his gaze. "You can tell me what needs to be done." Cal and the rest of them were trying to force her out. It only made her dig her heels in even more, although the last thing she wanted to do was raise buffalo. She watched a string of pickups drive past on their way out, stopping only to let a car come in. What now?

As the car came to a stop and a woman stepped out, Blaze swore under her breath. Tawny Brooks.

"That's my clue to leave," Jake said. "I'll go see what shape they left the bunkhouse in. Unless you'd prefer I stay in the barn."

She waved him away. "Take Cal's cabin or stay in the bunkhouse," she said as she watched her once-best friend head for the front door. "Sleep wherever you like."

"If that were the case, I'd be sleeping with you." He quickly ducked out before she could chuck the sculpture she'd picked up to throw at him. He tipped his hat to Tawny as her old friend stepped in the door and left. Blaze waited, already knowing why the woman was here. She knew what had been going on in Saddle Butte, thanks to the internet. She'd seen all the gossip—and the big news.

Tawny looked after Jake for a moment. The man couldn't help being noticed. Then she seemed to remember why she'd driven out here and rushed to Blaze.

"I was so glad to hear you were back," Tawny said as she threw her arms around her. "It's been way too long." As if feeling Blaze's resistance— and not just to the hug—the woman let go of her and stepped back.

Blaze remembered how her friend had deserted her the night they'd accidentally set the fire in the old theater in town. Blaze had later been arrested out at the ranch. She'd never told anyone that Tawny was with her or that it was her once-best friend who'd started the fire. They'd both been trespassing.

But neither had Tawny come forward, letting Blaze take the blame. After that, Blaze had gotten into more trouble and Tawny had distanced herself from her.

"You must have heard," Tawny said now. "Yes, LJ and I are engaged." She said it as if thinking that was why she wasn't getting the warm reception she'd hoped for.

Tawny held out her engagement ring, wiggling her fingers so the diamond caught the sunlight coming through the window.

"I heard. My sympathies."

Tawny made a disapproving face and walked around the living room for a moment before plopping down in a chair as if planning to stay for a while. "Don't tell me that you're jealous. *You* broke up with *him*. That made him fair game."

Blaze sighed, refusing to sit down since she had no desire to prolong this and just settled on the arm of a chair. "Is that why you drove all the way out here? To tell me about your engagement?" She hated to bust her bubble and tell her that she already knew.

"I came out to give you my condolences about your father." Tawny shook her head and tsk-tsked. "Everyone says he'll probably never see the outside of a prison cell again. That's if they don't execute him."

"That's assuming he's guilty."

Tawny laughed. "Of course he's guilty."

"How do you know that?" Blaze asked, more out of curiosity about where the woman got her facts than anything else. The same internet comments she herself had read.

"He was found standing over poor Frank's body holding a smoking gun."

That was pretty much what the judge had told her. "Is that what everyone is saying?"

"LJ heard it from the sheriff when they brought Monte in." Of course the sheriff's son had heard it straight from the horse's mouth, so to speak. Tawny took a breath. "I suppose you've heard that your father is refusing to say anything. He's even refusing a lawyer."

That last part was new. "Since when?"

She shrugged. "He'll have a public defender with him at the arraignment tomorrow. I thought you knew that."

Blaze shook her head. The news just kept getting better and better. "How could I know that? The sheriff wouldn't let me see him."

Tawny pursed her lips. "Everyone is upset by all this. Murder?" She wrinkled her nose. "And we all know why he did it."

"Do tell."

The woman rolled her eyes. "Allie Anson, obviously."

"Not buffalo?"

Tawny sat back and looked confused. "Why are you acting like this? You hate your father and always have. You know he ran your mother off. You used to say that you would never forgive him."

She realized that was probably what she did say back then, back before she was arrested. Back before she met Judge Landusky and he turned her life around.

"People change."

Tawny laughed again. "You? Or your father?"

Blaze got to her feet. "Thanks for stopping by with your condolences, but until I know exactly what happened that day…"

The woman gave her a sympathetic look as she rose from her chair. "I'm sorry about…everything. We used to be best friends. I suppose you have to say nice thing since he's your father. People are wondering what you're going to do with the ranch once he's convicted." She seemed to catch herself. "*If* he's convicted."

So this was really what Tawny had driven all the way out here for, Blaze thought. "That's the thing about people in these parts—they do love to wonder," she said and smiled. "Let's let them keep wondering." She walked to the door and held it open.

"It was good to see you again," Tawny said. "If there is anything I can do—"

"I'm afraid there isn't. Thanks for the thought, though, and good luck with your…engagement."

The woman studied her for a moment before she nodded. "I'll tell LJ hi for you."

Blaze laughed. "Please, don't bother. He's your problem now. Not mine." She shut the door behind Tawny a little too hard and turned to find Jake standing at the edge of the kitchen. He'd obviously come in the back way. Because he was worried about her? Or just curious?

"How long have you been listening?" she asked, knowing from his expression that he'd probably heard it all.

"Long enough. You were kind of tough on her. Because she's engaged to your old boyfriend?"

She laughed and shook her head.

"I know LJ let you down."

"He wasn't the only one. And now the two of them are getting married." Blaze shook head again. "Tell me there isn't any justice in the world."

Jake moved to her, concern in his expression. "Looks like your past is coming out of the woodwork."

"Lots of curious people," she agreed.

"*Have* you thought about what you would do with the ranch if your father is convicted?"

Blaze gave him an impatient look. "Not you, too."

He reached out, his warm fingertips skimming her cheek before he cupped it. "Whatever you decide to do, I'll back you all the way."

She looked into those tempting green eyes. It would be so easy to let herself go. She felt herself being drawn in. How easy it would have been to step into his arms and let him keep her from thinking about any of this for a while. But even as she thought it, she knew it would only complicate things more for both of them.

"It's too early to worry about what to do with the ranch," she said, stepping away and breaking eye contact. Her blood thrummed just under her skin. Desire burned inside her. She could feel his gaze warming her back. "I need to find something for my father to wear to the hearing." She glanced at her phone. "Then I'm going to take a hot bath and go to bed with a good book. The arraignment is fairly early in the morning. I need a good night's sleep."

She wondered if she was trying to convince herself—or him. She heard him chuckle as she walked him to the door.

"If you need me—"

"I won't."

"I'll drive in the morning." He seemed to be waiting for her to argue and looked surprised when she didn't.

"See you in the morning, then," she said as he stepped out.

"Sweet dreams," he said as he met her gaze for a moment before he turned to walk away.

His words brought back the ache inside her in an instant. Damn the man. He knew too well the effect he had on her.

She closed and locked the door behind him before going to her room, where she again closed the door and locked it. She knew she was locking herself in—not locking Jake out. He wouldn't come back—not unless she invited him.

For a moment, she leaned against the door, asking herself why she was fighting it. Jake could make all this better—at least for a little while. But that was the problem. If she climbed back into bed with him, she knew how hard it would be when they separated.

Her poor heart couldn't take that. Not again.

She pushed him out of her thoughts as she walked toward her bath. Was it true that her father had refused a lawyer? Because he was guilty? If so, what was she doing here?

CHAPTER SIX

WHEN THEY BROUGHT her father into the courtroom the next morning, Blaze felt her heart drop. He'd aged. His hair was peppered with gray and curled at his neck, much longer than he used to wear it. There were deep-set lines around his eyes in a face weathered by the years and the sun and a life on the back of a horse.

He was still a large man with broad shoulders, a straight if not rigid back. When he looked up, she met his familiar blue eyes—eyes so much like her own—and felt a knot form in her chest. He was still handsome, still larger-than-life, still the implacable father she'd known.

He met her gaze for only a moment, but she saw surprise before he looked away. Her pulse leaped. Had WT not told him she was coming to Saddle Butte? Of course, her father would have known. He'd turned his power of attorney over to her. At least, according to the judge.

She felt off balance as if her normally firmly planted feet were on unstable ground. Her plan to soak in the tub, read one of the books she'd brought and go to sleep early hadn't worked out. She hadn't been able to keep her place in the book. Her mind kept wandering to the fact that Jake was only a stone's throw from her bedroom. When she was able not to think about him, she found herself thinking about her father, remembering those years after her mother left.

Now Jake reached over and took her hand. She hated that he knew how vulnerable she was at this moment, but she didn't pull away. Her cold hand disappeared into his large warm one. He squeezed gently without looking at her and she thought about what he'd said last night. Whatever she decided to do, he had her back.

"All rise," the bailiff called, and she stumbled to her feet as Jake released her hand and they both watched Judge Elmer White take his seat.

Blaze listened as her father and who appeared to be a public defender rose to their feet as the judge informed her father of the charges. Deliberate homicide.

As the judge notified Monte of his right to a criminal defense attorney, her father said he didn't need one and that he didn't need the public defender, either.

The judge peered at him over the top of his reading glasses. "Are you saying you're waiving your right to an attorney?"

"I am."

The public defender made the argument that Mr. McClintock owned a large ranch south of town with a few hundred head of buffalo that needed to be tended to and asked that the judge grant bail.

"Bail denied," the judge said and slammed down his gavel. "At this point, would the defendant like to enter a plea?"

"Not guilty," the public defender said and tried to quiet her father, who was attempting to talk over him.

But Monte wasn't having it. "I'm guilty."

The judge studied him from over his reading glasses again. "Mr. McClintock, do you have any idea what you're doing?"

"I do."

Shaking his head, the judge said, "I would like to accept that your plea is being entered knowingly, but I can't until you have an opportunity for access to a…criminal attorney who can explain the situation to you and we can assess if you are mentally capable of making such a plea, given the severity of the charge."

Her father started to argue, but the judge slammed down his gavel and the hearing was over almost as quickly as it had begun. Monte had been remanded over to the county jail until further notice.

Blaze rose on wobbly legs. No lawyer? He'd pled guilty? "I have to see him."

"Let's make it happen," Jake said. He took her arm as if he knew how shaken she was by what she'd just witnessed. As they were leaving the courtroom, she saw Shane Garrison and some of the other ranchers. LJ was with them. He gave her a smirk as if to say he expected as much from both her father and her. She noticed that of the ranchers who'd been at the hospital yesterday, only LJ hung back with Shane. She saw the two whispering to each other until they saw her watching them and stepped apart.

BLAZE CAUGHT UP with the prosecutor, a man she'd gone to high school with named Dave Graber. "I need to see my father."

"I hope to talk some sense into him myself." Dave stopped walking to look at her. He frowned. "You haven't been able to visit him yet?"

"No, the sheriff wouldn't let me."

Dave cursed under his breath. "Come on, I'll see that you get in. I know this judge. He isn't going to let your father plead guilty until Monte first talks to a criminal lawyer. Your father needs to know what's at stake here."

"I want to see the evidence against him," she said as they hurried down the hallway toward the attached county jail.

"I'm sure you've heard that he was found standing over Frank Anson holding a gun."

"You already have the ballistics back on the gun?"

"No, but—"

"So you don't know it's the gun that killed Frank." She couldn't help sounding surprised.

"Your father pretty much admitted it when a ranch hand came riding up."

She stopped walking. "Pretty much?" Dave stopped, as well. He raked a hand through his hair. "Until I see that ballistics report…"

He looked at his shoes for a moment as if fighting for patience. "The last thing you want to do is drag your father and this community through a long, expensive trial."

"Would you say that if it was your father?" she snapped. "A decent lawyer would ask that the venue be moved so Monte can get a fair trial."

"A change of venue isn't going to help. This is Montana. If you could get it moved maybe to Wyoming..."

"So what you're saying is that this is about buffalo and my father has already been convicted."

The prosecutor sighed. "Blaze—"

"I have my father's power of attorney and I will do whatever it takes to see that he isn't railroaded over some damned buffalo." With that, she stormed down the hall, leaving both Dave and Jake in her wake.

JAKE WATCHED HER go as he joined the prosecutor.

"You're a friend of hers?" the man asked.

"Something like that." Their relationship was a little hard to nail down at this moment. He didn't even know what he was doing here. He certainly hadn't been much to help her.

"Try to talk some sense into her," the prosecutor said.

Jake laughed. "If you know Blaze at all, then you know she makes up her own mind about most things."

"She's making a mistake. Her father doesn't want to go through a long trial any more than the rest of this county does. Truthfully, I'm not sure he's up to it. I've seen what it does to men like him who've lived life outdoors in wide-open places. Going through the scrutiny a trial demands… Any secrets he has, they'll come out." He met Jake's gaze and exchanged a warning look.

"What kind of secrets are we talking about here?" Jake asked.

The man looked embarrassed. "Just that according to scuttlebutt, this might not be Monte's first murder. His wife… Well, there were rumors that she never left that ranch. Not alive anyway. In sixteen years, no one has seen or heard from her. If she's buried out there…"

"What are you saying?" Jake demanded.

"My father was prosecutor back then. He might have backed off the case because he knew Bethany. He'd dated her before Monte and he knew that she'd always wanted to leave here, make something of herself, and he liked Monte."

They'd reached the county jail. Blaze had already burst in and was arguing with the sheriff when they stepped inside the door.

"Bud, let her see her father," Dave said impatiently.

The sheriff looked as if he wanted to argue, but finally sighed and said, "I'll have him brought out to an interview room." With that, he added over his shoulder, "Have a seat. I'll call you when he's ready."

"The SOB is going to make us wait," Blaze said. "You're right, Jake. I need to find a good criminal lawyer." She looked at Dave, who held up his hands and backstepped away.

"Clarkston Evans," Jake said. "I did some research last night. I'll text you his number. He's supposed to be the best in the West unless you prefer to do your own research or hire a lawyer from Montana."

She shook her head, her gaze holding his for a long moment. In her blue eyes, he saw gratitude. It wasn't what he'd hoped to see, but for now, he'd take it. He texted her the attorney's number and took a seat.

Unlike her, he knew the sheriff would make them wait. But in contrast, he'd learned patience—the hard way. He'd spent years with a chip on his shoulder because of the way he was treated by a lot of people. It had gotten him thrown behind bars—a place he never wanted to go again. Fortunately, Judge Landusky had saved him from a life of confinement.

But the judge had also taught him to stop daring people to try to knock that boulder-size rock off his shoulder, because life wasn't fair. And instead to accept reality and use it to become stronger. He'd been schooled on ways to fight other than with fists. Blaze, though, was still learning that lesson.

THE MOMENT BLAZE was led into the room where her father was waiting behind a metal desk, she was almost too angry to speak. "What the hell is wrong with you?" she demanded.

Her father looked up at her, his blue eyes softening. "It's good to see you, too. But what are you doing here?"

She stared at him. "Judge Landusky didn't tell you I was coming?" She saw from his expression that WT hadn't told him. Because the man wasn't sure she would actually return? "He said you've turned over your power of attorney to me."

Her father nodded. "You will be able to do whatever you want with the ranch. Just because I gave you my power of attorney, though, it doesn't mean I want you involved in this."

"Too bad," Blaze said as she pulled out a chair across from him. "I can't let you do this."

"Peanut—"

"No." His nickname for her felt like a stab to her heart. "Don't call me that." He hadn't for years. It hurt too much because he'd called her Peanut back when they'd been a family, when her mother had been a part of it.

"I'm sorry."

"I need to know the truth."

Her father smiled at that. "Is that why you're here?"

"I'm here to make sure you get a fair trial."

"There isn't going to be a trial."

"Because you killed that man?"

Her father looked away. "It doesn't matter."

"The hell it doesn't." She waited until his gaze returned to her. "Yes or no."

He snorted and looked at Jake. "Mr. Horn. We haven't met, but I've heard about you."

"All good things, I'm sure," Jake said and started

to shake Monte's hand, only to see that he was still shackled.

Blaze shoved back her chair and stormed to the door, pounding on it until a deputy appeared. "Why is my father shackled like that? I want his restraints removed."

"Sheriff was very specific about the shackles not being removed."

She slammed the door in the man's face and turned back to the table and her father.

"I know why my daughter is here, but why are *you* here, Mr. Horn?"

"Please call me Jake. Hopefully one day we'll be family."

Blaze shot him a deadly look and sat down again.

"I'm here as moral support for your daughter," Jake answered.

This time, her father laughed heartily. "We both know Blaze doesn't take any kind of support well, maybe especially moral support." His gaze returned to her. "I appreciate you coming here since something needs to be done about the ranch."

"Cal quit and took the ranch hands with him."

He nodded. "I figured that's what he'd do. You need to put the ranch up for sale and leave town as soon as possible."

She stared at him. That was the last thing she thought he would say. "That's why you gave me power of attorney? To get rid of me? Because you're worried about *me*? You're the one behind bars this time."

He sighed. "I've always been worried about you because you're so much like me."

Blaze wanted to argue that as well, but held her tongue. She liked to believe she was more like her mother, lie or not. "What is it you think is going to happen that I need to get out of town quickly?"

"I've made enemies," he said simply.

"That's putting it mildly. You think they'll come after *me*?"

He glanced at Jake. "They'll come after both of you." His gaze returned to her. "Please. For once, do as I ask. I know what I'm doing."

She actually saw that he believed that and said as much. "I'm hiring a criminal attorney." Before he could argue, she rushed on, "Judge White has made it clear he won't take a guilty plea from you until you've talked to a criminal attorney." She was buying time and she figured he knew it and didn't like it.

"Blaze—"

"You know," she said as she got to her feet again, "I came back to Montana believing that you were guilty. But you've now convinced me that something is not right. Otherwise why rush to plead guilty?"

"You don't understand."

"I think I do," she said. "You're covering for someone and I'm pretty sure I know who." He tried to interrupt her again, but she continued, "I came here to get to the truth and I will."

"Even if I beg you to leave it alone?" he demanded as she headed for the door.

The plea in his tone made her turn to look back

at him. As she did, she realized that the balance of power between them had shifted. There'd been a time when she'd adored him. Then her mother had left and she'd blamed him and went from idolizing the man to hating him. Now she felt a well of love for her father that she hadn't felt in years. She knew he had to be innocent and covering for someone, and she was determined to find out why and stop him.

"Sometimes we do things that are best for those we love even if they don't like it," she said and met his gaze. "Isn't that what you said to me the last time I was arrested, and you left me in jail?" With that, she walked out.

Behind her, she heard her father say to Jake, "Stop her. If you love her, save her from herself."

Before the door closed, she heard Jake chuckle. He was still shaking his head when she turned to look back at him as he came out of the interview room.

"He's lying," she said, hating to hear her voice break with emotion.

"Probably. But why, given the consequences?"

"That's what I'm going to find out."

Jake smiled and nodded. "I expected nothing less."

She eyed him suspiciously. "What did you just say to my father when he told you to save me from myself?"

He tilted his head, holding her gaze with his emerald green one for a long moment. "I told him I do love you and I'll die trying to save you."

Blaze shook her head at him, his words hitting her

at heart level. She opened her mouth to say something smart, but nothing came to mind. "I better call that lawyer," she said at last and turned toward the door.

CHAPTER SEVEN

JAKE SMILED TO HIMSELF. Blaze never could take a compliment. But he knew it was more than that. She didn't want him dying for her. If she could have done what needed to be done up here on her own, she would have. It was partly stubborn pride. Mostly it was not letting anyone get too close. When her mother had left, Blaze had put up a wall around her heart. He knew because he'd been trying to tear it down from the moment he met her.

As he reached to push open the outer door for her, the sheriff stopped them. "Dave left this for you." He handed Blaze a manila envelope. "I'm not sure what you're up to but I'd be real careful if I was you."

"That almost sounds like a threat," Jake said as Blaze took the envelope.

"You stay out of this," Bud said without looking at him.

"My father's lawyer is on his way," she said. "Meanwhile, isn't there a ballistics test that needs to be run?"

The sheriff sucked at his teeth, his eyes hard as stones. "Let him plead guilty and do this county a favor. He killed Frank. The sooner you sell that ranch, and you and your buffalo and your…boyfriend clear out—"

"You know, if I hear that one more time, I just might decide to stay and work that ranch, and my personal business is none of yours," Blaze snapped.

The sheriff let out a grunt. "No one will work for you."

"Maybe no one from around here," Jake said. "But I can get workers."

"I thought I told you to—"

"Sheriff…" Blaze said. "You're starting to sound awfully vindictive for a lawman. I can't help but notice how you want to rush this case through. Why is that? Because, like us, you know something is wrong with all this? Or will you do anything, even break the law, to get rid of my father?"

Bud shook his head. "Just remember, I warned you." With that, he turned, walked down to his office and closed the door behind him.

When they stepped outside, Jake looked over at Blaze. "Am I your boyfriend?"

She shot him a look. "That's all you got out of that entire conversation?"

"Just making sure."

Blaze shook her head.

"Short of clarifying your intentions, I agree with the sheriff. You're in danger."

"Because they're going to try to run me off?" She laughed. "Let them try."

He shook his head. "The sheriff knows about it, or suspects. And we both know he isn't going to do a damned thing about it. I don't like this. These ranchers get together and adopt a mob mentality... It's hard to say what they'll do. I think you should give some thought about what to do next."

They'd reached his pickup. She stopped to face him. "I already have. I'm betting that Cal never fixed that fence," she said as she opened the passenger side of his rig. "I'm going back to the ranch and mend it." When he said nothing, she gave him a pleading look. "That's a place to start. I can't keep these ranchers from coming after me. So I'm going to do what I can do. I can fix a damned fence." With that, she climbed into the pickup, leaving him nothing more to say or do but drive her home.

BLAZE GROANED WHEN she came out of the house after changing clothes to find Jake saddling up two horses. "I don't want you going with me."

"Too bad. The judge sent me here for a reason. And right now, it seems it is to mend fences. So to speak."

"I doubt that was the reason, but I'd love to know exactly what it was," she said as she took a set of reins from him.

"Just to help you any way I can."

She scoffed at that. "I just might call the judge and see if that's what he said."

"He was worried about you and your father. He thought I might be of help."

She studied him for a moment before she swung

up into the saddle. "I see you've filled a couple of saddle bags with what we need to fix the fence."

"It won't be my first fence," he said with that charming grin of his as he swung a leg over and settled into his saddle.

He looked good on the back of a horse. Hell, he looked good no matter what.

"I have no idea where we're going."

"I know where Garrison's ranch connects to this one. I thought we'd ride along the fence until we find the opening. Ready?" Jake was like her, at home in the saddle. They both needed this, and in truth, she didn't mind having him along.

They rode out across the pasture toward the northwest corner of the ranch through rolling prairie. The snow had receded except on the north side of the hills, leaving the ground bare and warm from the sun. Blaze breathed in the day, happy for a reprieve from winter weather. It wouldn't last. Eventually a storm would roll in and blanket the prairie with fresh white snow that would last until April.

As she looked out across the land, she felt a strange sense of pride. This was all McClintock property. Her father had worked hard, adding more land as it became available, expanding the ranch almost to the Little Rockies. She thought of the hours she used to spend riding this ranch. After her mother had left, she spent every hour she could away from her father and on her horse.

"It's beautiful here," Jake said. In the distance, she spotted where the fence had been destroyed by the buffalo. On the McClintock Ranch side, the fence was solid-sided and seven feet tall. One of the largest expenses when her father had decided to raise buffalo was replacing the fences. Plain old barbed wire wouldn't do.

Not just higher and solid-sided, the fences had to be sturdy with five strands of tensile wire along the top—often electrified. All to keep the buffalo in. Supposedly if you kept the animals watered and fed, they wouldn't try to escape. But even then, they often tended to push against fences or anything else around, doing damage because of their size and weight. Another reason a lot of ranchers didn't like them.

So how had one gotten out?

As they topped a small rise, Blaze reined in beside Jake to stare at the buffalo herd spread out across the prairie. Their dark furry bodies dotted the land for a good mile. She'd had no idea her father had purchased so many buffalo. She'd often tried to imagine what it had been like when they'd run free on this very land before so many were killed.

"It's breathtaking, isn't it?" Jake said as if awed by the sight.

"I forget what magnificent animals they are."

"My great-grandfather used to tell stories about the herd," he said. "I remember the reverent way he talked about the buffalo."

She looked over at him. To his Native American side of the family, the buffalo had been much more than food.

"I love to hear about your heritage."

He smiled at her. "It's a part of me. Just like the Irish side." He shrugged as he spurred his horse and she followed. She hadn't gone far when she saw the dead bull was lying in a mound some distance from where it had broken through the fence. Of course Shane Garrison had shot the big bull. Not that she blamed him. He'd shot it on McClintock property, though, when the bison was no longer a danger to him or his family. Still, she knew killing the massive animal hadn't calmed his need for retribution. Probably far from it.

The incident with his son proved everything the ranchers had been saying about buffalo. Now they had a cause. She knew Jake was right. There would be trouble.

Jake swung down from his horse. She sat for a moment, emotions warring each other before she dismounted.

JAKE SAW AT once how the bull had gotten out. He swore under his breath as he heard Blaze dismount behind him. "It wasn't an accident."

She stared at the fence where someone had purposely cut through it, weakening it. "Why here?" she asked but answered her own question. "The dirt on the other side. It's a perfect wallowing place. They'd known that the bull would bust the rest of the way through to get to it."

Buffalo loved to roll around in soft dirt, usually in a slight hollow. All the bull had to do was hit the corrupted fence and it would have given way. Getting through the barbed wire fence on the other side was just a matter of walking through it for the massive bull.

"I don't think any of the others have gotten out," Jake said. "They seem to be staying away from the dead bull."

"Who do you think did this?" she asked as she saw him studying the cuts in the fence.

"The damage was done on Garrison's side."

"What? He cut both his fence and ours? Why would he…" She met Jake's gaze. "He could have gotten his own son killed." Blaze looked away, but not before he'd seen the pain in her eyes. "I don't understand any of this."

"I can fix the fence enough until I can get a contractor up here to repair it properly. We also need to hire someone to come in and haul away the dead bison. I can take care of that, if it's all right with you." She nodded. "The least Garrison could have done was to let us know he'd killed the bull. The animal is starting to bloat. We could have maybe saved the meat and taken it into the local food bank or had someone from one of the reservations pick it up. It just seems like such a waste."

Not one to waste time standing around complaining, Jake went to work. He unpacked the materials he needed to make the repairs first to Garrison's barbed wire fence, then the buffalo fence. He wasn't surprised when Blaze fell in to help. It was late afternoon before they finished, with her working next to him until they were both sweaty and dirty. He was reminded of how they'd worked together before.

"We still make a pretty good team," he said.

She stopped to wipe the back of her hand across her forehead. He didn't see anger in her blue eyes. But what he saw was even more worrisome. She looked overwhelmed, as if all of this was going to be too much for her—just as he'd feared. She was too personally involved. He could see a roller coaster of emotions traveling too close to the surface. He feared it wouldn't take too much to derail her.

He wanted to tell her that everything was going to be all right, but he knew better than to offer platitudes. Instead, he stepped to her, grabbed the back of her neck in his hand and pulled her into a kiss. He'd caught her by surprise and it took her a moment before she pushed against his chest with her palms. She didn't push hard, but he knew better than to ignore the gesture. He stepped back. For that moment, she'd kissed him like she used to, verifying what he already knew. What they'd had was still there.

"What was that about?" she asked, sounding tired.

"It was a kiss."

"I'm aware."

"You looked so good standing there. I wanted to kiss you to see if you still tasted sweet." She held up a hand as if to stop him from saying any more—as if that was all it would take. He grinned. "You do still taste sweet, in case you were wondering. And for a moment there, you forgot how much you hate me."

Blaze shook her head, the fire back in those blue

eyes. She was always stronger on the fight. "We aren't getting back together. If that's what you're doing here—"

"The judge—"

"Right, the judge sent you. Did I mention that I tried to call him when I was in the house changing?" She smiled. "You look worried." He shook his head in denial. "He didn't answer but I left him a message to call me." Jake shrugged as if it was no concern to him. "You better pray that he says he sent you and that this isn't some kind of...of—"

"Seduction?" He couldn't help but laugh. "Both of us hot and sweaty from mending the fences, standing downwind of a dead buffalo? You seriously think that?"

"I know your idea of seduction," she snapped.

He grinned. "So you *haven't* forgotten."

Blaze shook her head in obvious irritation with him and swung around to reach for her reins. But as she did, he saw her touch the tip of her tongue to her upper lip. He felt heat race to his loins. She hadn't forgotten how good they were together any more than he had.

As he started for his horse, he sensed something on the wind and turned to see riders coming across the prairie far below them and headed their way. All that was between the riders and them were hundreds of buffalo. At first the riders appeared like a mirage, their horses kicking up snow and dirt. But this was no mirage. The riders were real and they were headed for the buffalo herd.

His heart leaped to his throat. "Blaze, saddle up. Now."

She turned to follow his gaze and froze for only a moment, before she swung up into the saddle and he did the same.

The masked riders fanned out, riding fast, circling the herd. The sound of gunfire filled the air moments before it was drowned out by the roar of hooves as the buffalo began to move in a wave of a huge dark mass.

"They're stampeding the buffalo right at us," Jake said with a curse. "We're going to have to try to outrun them." He reached over and slapped the rump of her horse, making it jump forward. "Go!" he yelled. "Go and don't look back!"

CHAPTER EIGHT

JAKE'S HORSE REARED as if hearing the thunder of the hooves headed toward them. He reined in, calculating how long he had. Blaze had taken off toward the ranch house at a fast gallop, leaning over her horse, the two almost as one. But he knew she would never be able to outrun the herd of buffalo. A horse could get up to thirty miles an hour at a fast gallop. But a buffalo could clock forty when riled, and these cowboys were making sure the herd was riled.

He also knew herd mentality. The buffalo began to react to the threat as the riders continued to fire shots into the air. Once a few of the animals had taken off, more joined them in a chain reaction that now had the whole herd running in his direction.

The once-scattered herd tightened up ranks until it was a clustered moving group. The buffalo came in a dark wave, leaving behind a cloud that rose into the clear November air.

He looked to see Blaze top a rise. He knew he had to move. He'd given her a head start, but with the buffalo thundering in this direction, it wouldn't be long before they caught her, as well. Did the riders hope to kill them? Force the buffalo through more fence to destroy it? All he knew was that he had to turn the herd. He knew the animals would avoid obstacles if possible since when on the run, buffalo preferred open spaces.

Taking off his hat, he began to wave it as he rode across the front ring of the herd. Some of them began to turn, but others continued running toward the ranch house. At least he'd been able to divide the group.

He swung back, finding himself in the middle of the herd. Riding at an exhilarating breakneck speed with the huge animals all around him, he pulled his pistol and fired it into the air, but the sound was drowned out by the pounding of hooves. Still, more of the buffalo began to break off from the collective as he continued to divide them.

When he had a chance to look over his shoulder, he saw that the riders had turned back and were now racing toward the corner of the ranch where they'd come through one of the gates to get inside the fenced area.

He wanted to go after them, but he knew he couldn't stop the buffalo run and chase down the men. He cut more buffalo from the herd. The numbers dwindled, and the animals slowed and turned back as they neared the ranch buildings.

By the time he saw Blaze and the ranch house in the distance, only a small group of bison were still running in that direction. He fired his gun as he rode at them and turned them back as well before he slowed, too, and his heart rate settled back to normal.

He felt flushed and couldn't help grinning. He couldn't remember the last time he'd had to ride like that. He hadn't had a day like this in a very long time, he thought, remembering his and Blaze's earlier kiss. Actually he hadn't had this much fun since the last time he and Blaze were together—and in trouble.

BLAZE WATCHED JAKE ride toward her with the same sense of awe that she'd experienced the first time she'd seen him on the back of a horse. It had been at a county fair. He'd been riding in a horse relay race between tribes.

The Native Americans rode bareback, making a loop around the arena to leap from a racing horse onto the next one until, several horses later, the winner crossed the finish line first at an amazing gallop. She'd never seen anything more thrilling.

It had been love at first sight. She hadn't been able to take her eyes off the man. At some point, he must have sensed her, because he'd looked up into the stands, his pale eyes zeroing in on her. She remembered his grin. And his wink. He'd known even then that she was going to be his.

She looked at him now, seeing how completely content he was sitting astride his horse after being caught in a buffalo stampede. "You enjoyed that," she accused him. "Do you realize how terrified I was for you?"

He gave her that knowing grin and slid off his horse to come to her. "Once I knew you were all right…"

She wanted to slug him for scaring her. Kiss him because he made her want him even more. Make love to him just because being naked in his arms was the one place she felt safe.

"I can't deal with you right now," she said and, grabbing her horse's reins, turned toward the gate that led to the barn. He rushed to open it for her before standing back, his hands raised in surrender, but that damned grin still warmed his handsome face. "Why don't you let me take care of your horse? It's the least I can do after upsetting you."

She shot him a look, about to argue, but fearing she was also about to cry tears of relief that he was safe, she thrust her reins into his hands and stormed away. Tears burned her eyes nonetheless. She had to swallow down her feelings, especially the fear she'd felt watching him ride into that herd of buffalo and the fear that she would never love anyone the way she did Jake Horn.

THE SHERIFF RUBBED the gray stubble on his jaw as he took in the tracks. "Looks like the buffalo stampeded. Good thing you got them turned when you did or they would have wiped out everything between here and town."

Blaze groaned. "The point is that five riders purposely stampeded the herd."

The sheriff poised his pen over his notepad. "Who were these riders?"

"They wore masks," Jake said.

"I see," Bud said. "So you don't know who they

were." He put away his pen and notepad. "Could have been anyone."

"Wasn't just anyone," Blaze argued, "and you know it. Why don't you start by questioning Shane Garrison and his buddies?"

"They knew what they were doing," Jake said. "They rounded up the herd and ran them at us."

"That must have been something, that many buffalo headed right for you," the sheriff said. "I can see why you might be upset."

"What are you going to do about it, Sheriff?" Blaze demanded.

"Well, you say they were wearing masks? So you can't describe them."

"One of them was riding an Appaloosa," Jake said. "If I can find that horse, then I can tell you exactly who that man was."

The sheriff chuckled. "You say you were caught in a buffalo stampede and yet you could recognize a spotted horse that one of the men was riding? Doubt that would stand up in court."

"It wouldn't have to," he said. "I would take care of this myself."

Bud narrowed his gaze. "Now, that would be a bad idea, son."

"I'm not your son."

The sheriff sighed heavily. "I'm sorry as hell that your buffalo stampeded, Blaze, but we all know how dangerous they are. Sounds like some kids decided to have some fun with you."

"The riders weren't kids." He met Bud's squinted

gaze and held it for a long moment, meeting the sheriff's warning look with one of his own.

"I'd be careful, Mr. Horn," Bud said quietly. "You don't want to end up in my jail, trust me." He broke his gaze and stepped away. "I'll write up a report. If you think of anything else, you just give me a call." He headed for his patrol SUV.

Blaze started to go after him, but Jake laid a hand on her arm.

With a shake of his head, he said, "You're wasting your breath."

"It's my breath to waste," she said, pulling her arm free but staying where she was. "That man…" She fumed for a moment. "I'd like to tell him what I think of him."

"Haven't you done that already?"

She turned to look at him. "On several occasions."

"Did it help?"

"Made me feel better."

He smiled. "Then have at it." He waved an arm in the sheriff's direction as the lawman started to climb into his rig.

Blaze shook her head. "We all know who those men were, or at least can take a reasonable guess."

"At least a couple of the ones we saw at court today whispering together," Jake said. "Your old boyfriend was one of them. Any chance he owns a big Appaloosa?"

"I don't know. And what would be the point even if we found the horse?" she asked. "It isn't like the sheriff would arrest him. They're trying to get us to leave."

"That would be my guess."

"Well, I'm not leaving," she said with the stomp of one boot as the sheriff drove away.

Jake laughed. "I guess it's you and me, then, baby."

She shot him a look but merely sighed. "This could get us killed, you know."

"I know," he said, watching the patrol SUV kick up dust as it roared out of the ranch. They'd been lucky today. He feared what the men who'd managed to get away with their stunt today would do next.

"WHAT THE HELL were you thinking?" the sheriff demanded when his son answered. He could hear the television in the background, almost smell the stale beer. It was LJ's day off and if his son was anything, he was predictable.

"What?"

"Causing a buffalo stampede out at the McClintock Ranch. Ring any bells?"

"I don't know what you're talking about."

"Like hell you don't. You were seen."

"Not likely from that distance since we were wearing masks," LJ said.

Bud tried to control his temper, but it was damned hard. "Sometimes you don't use the good sense that God gave you. Jake Horn recognized your horse."

"My horse?"

"The Appaloosa. It kind of stands out."

LJ laughed. "So he thinks he saw a horse that looks like mine. Like he could tell the difference."

"I suspect he can. That was a fool thing to do and what was the point?"

"Maybe we just wanted to put a little fear into them."

"And if you'd killed them?" Bud demanded.

"You said they were going to be trouble. I just thought—"

"You didn't *think*. You're a sheriff's deputy. You're supposed to uphold the law, not break it. You want to lose this job?"

"No. Someday I want to be sheriff."

"That's a scary thought." He considered things for a moment. "This isn't about Blaze, is it? About getting back at her now that she has a new boyfriend?"

His son scoffed. "I've been over her a long time. Hell, I'm marrying Tawny. I couldn't care less about Blaze and who she is with."

Bud ground his teeth. He could hear just the opposite in his son's voice. "LJ, you can't—"

"I just told you. We did it to scare them, that's all. It had nothing to do with Blaze except for the fact that she's trouble, just like you said."

He sighed. "Listen, no more of this, all right? And keep that damned horse of yours hidden. This will blow over as long as you and your…friends don't do anything stupid again, understood?"

"I hear ya. But you have to admit her coming back like this with that… It's like she's trying to rub it in my face."

In the background, Bud heard his son open a can of beer and swore under his breath. "She probably thinks the same thing with you being engaged to Tawny. I'm sure she's seen the ring you bought your fiancée, so I'd say you're even." He let that sink in for a moment. "Stay away from the McClintock Ranch and Blaze. You hear me?"

"I hear ya." Silence, then, "All I want to do is make you proud."

"You do, son," Bud said, shaking his head. "Might be a good idea if you stayed close to home for the rest of the day."

CHAPTER NINE

As JAKE ENTERED the house later that evening, he heard the sound of Christmas music. Earlier, he and Blaze had made sure there was plenty of water and hay for the buffalo herd. He'd seen to the horses as well before heading for the house.

Now he stopped and frowned, surprised by what he was hearing. Walking into the den, he found Blaze curled up on the leather couch in front of the television. She paused the picture on the screen when she saw him.

"You're watching a Hallmark Christmas movie?" he said.

"Don't judge."

"I'm not. If I make popcorn, can I join you?"

She narrowed her eyes at him. "If you're planning to make fun—"

"I wouldn't dream of it." He headed for the kitchen before she could argue further. He returned ten minutes later with a bowl of popcorn just the way she liked it—mixed with Hot Tamales candies.

She took it, still suspicious. "Thanks."

"Stop looking at me like I have an ulterior motive," he said as he sat down on the couch next to her. "I like Christmas movies and popcorn."

"Since when?"

"Since this is our second Christmas together."

"We aren't together."

"Really? It certainly looks like we're together," he said, reaching over to help himself to the popcorn in her bowl.

"You aren't going to know what's going on," she said. "The movie is half-over."

"Don't worry. I'll catch up. It's about love and the spirit of Christmas, right?" He could feel her gaze on him. "I'm no stranger to love *or* the spirit of Christmas."

She scoffed at that and hit Play again. He settled in, watching her out of the corner of his eye. Damn, she was adorable sitting there in a pair of what looked like new flannel pajamas, hugging a bowl of popcorn.

He squinted at the fabric. "Are those buffalo on your pj's?" he asked in surprise.

She hushed him and whispered, "It seemed appropriate when I realized I would be staying on a buffalo ranch. It was one of those impulsive purchases, all right?"

"You look cute in them," he whispered back and helped himself to more of her popcorn and candy.

"Why didn't you get your own bowl?"

He grinned. "I like sharing with you."

She sighed but gave up her tight hold on the bowl. He snuggled into the couch next to her, smiling to himself. She felt warm against his side. He liked the smell of her and certainly the feel of her. He realized that he was also a huge fan of life's simple pleasures, like watching a movie with Blaze on a cold November night.

He even found himself interested in the plot and by the time the credits rolled, he found himself almost choked up. He was the kind of man who could appreciate a happy ending. In fact, he was hoping for one himself, even though he knew it was an uphill climb given that he wanted it with Blaze McClintock.

"Go ahead, say something rude," Blaze said as she turned off the television and handed him the empty bowl to take to the kitchen.

"It was a good movie."

She turned her gaze on him, studying him as if she'd heard the break in his voice or seen that his eyes were shiny with emotion. "It got to you," she said, sitting up straighter to study him.

He started to deny it, but then he chuckled and said, "Okay, what if it did? It reminded me a little of us."

She flopped back on the couch. "And then you go and ruin the movie for me. They were nothing like us."

"Star-crossed lovers finding their way back to each other. Tell me you didn't notice the similarities."

She shook her head. "They loved each other the first time around."

"So did we."

"Jake—"

He sat up so they were face-to-face again. "You cannot possibly doubt that."

She chewed at her cheek for a long moment. "You hurt me."

He nodded soberly. "I did that and I have been sorry ever since. If I had it to do over—"

She pushed off the couch. "Well, you won't get the chance. I'm going to bed."

He knew better than to try to change her mind by simply apologizing again. It was going to take a whole lot more than that—just like in the movie, where the hero had to prove himself. Wasn't that why he was here?

Jake sat back on the couch and then called over his shoulder as he listened to her pad barefoot down the hallway, "I really do like your pajamas." She didn't answer but he thought he heard her chuckle. She didn't believe that he could like baggy flannel pj's on her any more than she believed how sorry he was about hurting her.

Rising to his feet, he took the empty bowl to the kitchen, grabbed his coat from where he'd left it by the door and then headed for the bunkhouse. As he stepped outside, he felt the cold air circle around him to steal his breath. Snuggling down into the collar of his coat, he tromped on the crusty frozen ground toward the bunkhouse.

The night was cold and clear, and stars dusted Montana's big night sky. To the north, he saw light shooting up in spectacular colors. The northern lights. He couldn't let Blaze miss this. Like him, he doubted she'd seen them since they'd both left Montana.

Turning back, he spotted her standing outside the back door of the house. Her face was turned up to the lights. He saw that she was as taken with the sight as if it were her first time. He'd seen that expression on her face before during their lovemaking.

He smiled as he studied her in the ethereal lights, feeling that familiar ache to tear down the wall she'd built around her heart. He'd gotten a pretty good start on it the last time they were together—until things had gone awry.

But now, he'd caught her in the magic of the moment, and it gave him a thrill that raised goose bumps over his flesh and sent a shiver through him that was both wonder and desire.

She seemed to sense she was being watched, her gaze shifting in his direction. He held his breath, freezing in place, feeling guilty for this intimate moment he'd witnessed and at the same time, blessed.

Blaze hugged herself before stepping back inside, the moment lost. The sky seemed less spectacular as he turned and walked on to the bunkhouse. As he did, he became more aware of the ice crystals dancing in the air and the scent of snow on the slight breeze.

It was late November, so it wasn't as if he thought they could get away without having a snowstorm. But he'd hoped it would hold off a little longer. This far out of town, it would be difficult to come and go.

The lawyer would be driving in tomorrow and

staying at the only hotel in Saddle Butte. Blaze was anxious to talk to the man, even more anxious for her father to talk to him. She wouldn't let a snowstorm stop her, no matter how much it put down tonight.

He reached the bunkhouse, slowing just outside to take one last look at the sky before turning in for the night. He felt himself riding again with the stampeding buffalo as he lay down and closed his eyes. He'd thought he'd have trouble sleeping, but, pleased with the day he'd had, he dropped right off.

Waking with a start at daylight, he found Blaze standing over him. His first thought was to grab her and pull her down onto the bed with him, but the look in her eyes made him think better of it.

"What time is it?" he asked, blinking at the light coming through the bunkhouse window. The dream he'd been in the middle of still hung around him. He'd been racing across the prairie in the middle of a thousand buffalo, his hair blowing back, the air cool on his bare chest as he straddled the fastest horse he'd ever ridden, Blaze with her arms around him, daring him to go faster.

"The attorney just called. We're meeting him in town for breakfast," Blaze said and turned on her heel to leave.

Against his better judgment, he reached for her, his fingers barely skimming hers as she left. He groaned. "I'll get a shower and be right there."

BLAZE STARED OUT at the prairie as it swept past the truck window. It had snowed just enough last night to dust the landscape in white. Cold air pressed at the pickup's cab, while inside it felt almost too comfortable.

It made her think of Jake this morning, curled up in the bunkhouse. She'd watched him sleep for a few moments before she'd awakened him. He'd looked so tranquil. She suspected that he'd slept like a baby.

That was the difference between them. She'd lain in bed last night reliving the stampede and her fear seeing Jake in the middle of those thundering buffalo. Her heart still pounded at even the thought of it. She wanted those men caught and punished, even as she knew that was never going to happen. Judge Landusky often warned her against wanting things that were impossible.

Like her and Jake. This morning as she'd looked down at him sleeping so peacefully, she'd wanted to pinch him. Or throw ice water on him. Worse, climb in beside him and soak up his male warmth radiating from under the covers.

"What if you can't change your father's mind?" Jake asked as he drove.

"I don't even want to think about that right now," she said. "After we talk to the lawyer…"

"If we have a heavy snow, it's going to be harder to feed the buffalo. I can handle it since your father has a barn filled with hay. With that artesian well on the property, I can also get them watered. But I think you need to consider the long term. Even if your father pleads not guilty and goes to trial…"

Blaze shot him a look. "We really need to talk about this right now?"

"No," he said, unruffled. "We could talk about you and me instead."

"I know what you're getting at."

"You do?" He sounded surprised as he looked from his driving to her.

"What am I going to do with the ranch and animals if my father pleads guilty and goes to prison for the rest of his life?"

Jake let out a chuckle. "Blaze, I'm fine with being your hired ranch hand for as long as this takes with your father, but after that…" He glanced over at her again.

She swallowed the lump in her throat as she looked into his eyes. She knew damned well what he was asking and quickly looked away. "Fine, if I can't sell right away, I'll hire help." She could see that he was about to argue that she hadn't been able to keep the help she had. What made her think she could just hire someone given the problems with the neighboring ranchers?

"You're making me wish I'd taken my own pickup," she said grudgingly.

He grinned but said nothing as he drove, and she leaned back, closed her eyes and fought tears. Why did she have to treat him like this? Because he wanted more than she could give. She'd surrendered a huge piece of her heart to him only to have him break it. She refused to chance that again. Even if they hadn't been all wrong for each other. She knew him, knew that he wanted that happy ending from the movie last night, complete with kids. He wanted her and a family.

How could she have a family being a private investigator? Her job often took her out of state. It was often dangerous. He was asking her to give that up to do what? Marry him?

What was she thinking? Jake didn't think in long-term anything. He lived for the moment. He'd never mentioned marriage. She reminded herself what had happened last time. He'd wanted her, but their intense relationship had scared him—just as it had her. That was where the other woman had come in. An old friend he had to help? If that didn't sound like a made-up story, she didn't know what did. He hadn't even put up a fight when she'd packed her things to leave. The memory still hurt.

She mentally shook her head, trying to clear her thoughts. It was like he said—the judge had sent him. That was all this was and when it was over, they'd go their separate ways. Just like last time, she thought as the small Western town of Saddle Butte appeared on the horizon.

JAKE STEWED ALL the way to town. Blaze McClintock was the most stubborn, contrary woman he'd ever met. And the most captivating, smart and sexy. Damn, but she was amazing. He'd let her go once. For her own good, not that she understood that. But he'd never gotten over her and now he knew he never would.

That was why he'd begged the judge to let him help her on this case with her father. The judge had planned to send someone else.

"What's going on with the two of you?" Judge WT Landusky had demanded in his no-nonsense tone.

"Right now, she's not happy with me, but—"

"Whose fault is that?"

"Mine, but—"

"You sincerely want to help her, or do you have another agenda?"

He'd cleared his throat, surprised how much emotion came to the surface when he even thought of Blaze. "I know her. This is going to be really hard for her. She'll need me."

"How noble," the man had ground out. "What are you really after?" It was so like the judge to cut past the bull to the heart of the matter.

"I want her back."

"*Back?* What does that even mean? You can't be talking marriage because you're not the marrying type. Your words, not mine."

"People change."

The judge had grunted. "We wish. You'd better be sure of what exactly you're after and that it is in Blaze's best interests. Do I have to tell you how unhappy I would be if you hurt her again?"

"Did she—"

"Talk to me about it?" The judge had let out a sharp bark of a laugh. "You just told me that you know her. Do you really think she would tell me anything about the two of you? I saw her when she came back from the last project the two of you worked on. That was enough to know what happened."

Jake wasn't in the habit of pouring his heart out. "She's all I think about. I haven't been able to get over her. I know you don't approve, but—"

"I never said that. I just don't want you to hurt her again or this will be the last time I let you work together."

"I won't hurt her. I promise you. If she'll take me… I want to grow old with her, raise a passel of children, spend the rest of my life loving her."

"And you told her this?"

"Not yet. I'm hoping to find the right time."

"With Blaze, there won't be the perfect time." The judge scoffed. "Good luck. You're going to need it."

Jake parked in front of the local eatery, The Cattleman Café. As they climbed out, he said, "Gotta love the name."

Blaze merely grunted. She was definitely in a mood this morning. He wanted to ask how she'd slept, but thought better of it, suspecting she hadn't and that was part of the problem.

Clarkston Evans was waiting for them in a back room of the café with a cup of coffee in front of him and the local newspaper spread out beside the cup. He was writing on a legal pad as they walked in.

He gave them only a passing glance before he said, "I'm starving. Signal the waitress so we can place our breakfast orders. While they're cooking it up, we can talk. You want coffee? Have her bring in a carafe and some cups." He told them his order and turned his attention back to what he'd been writing down.

Jake had heard that the man was no-nonsense on the verge of rude, but he'd also heard that he was damned good at his job.

"I'll take care of it," Jake offered. "The usual?" he asked Blaze.

She hesitated, looking momentarily annoyed that he knew her so well. But she nodded as she sat down across from the lawyer. "Thanks. Tell the waitress to make that coffee hot and black, real strong."

Clarkston looked up at her, smiled and continued his writing until Jake returned with the cups and carafe filled with coffee.

BLAZE HAD BEEN sipping her coffee, trying to get enough caffeine in her that she could face this day without scowling. She'd definitely woken up on the wrong side of the bed.

"So, Ms. McClintock," the attorney said.

She looked up in surprise that he had finally acknowledged her presence. Patience was not her long suit.

Clarkston Evans had finally quit writing on his notepad. He pushed it aside. "Tell me what you know about the case."

"Only what I read in the file, which isn't much." She handed him the manila envelope Dave had left for her at the jail yesterday. Last night, when she couldn't sleep, she'd finally opened it and looked through the evidence against her father. It was pretty

cut-and-dried—if the gun her father had been holding had killed Frank Anson. She had no reason to
believe it wasn't the murder weapon.

"Tell me what it says," Clarkston said as the waitress brought in their breakfast platters. "I'll read it
later." He had picked up his fork and was shoveling
in his food. She took a bite of her own breakfast and
glanced over at Jake.

He was sipping his coffee and watching her. When
she met his gaze, he gave her a reassuring smile. It
didn't help. She felt anxious and worried. Right now,
it felt as if getting a criminal lawyer all the way up
here had been a waste of time.

"My father was found standing over the victim,
a gun in his hand."

"By whom?" the lawyer asked.

"A ranch hand on the Garrison place named Everett Banks. Banks said that he'd heard a couple of
shots and came riding. He said Monte dropped the
pistol as he approached. He saw Frank dead, asked
my father what had happened, but all Monte did was
shake his head. Everett called the sheriff's office."

Clarkston chewed, swallowed, wiped his mouth
and asked, "Where did this happen?"

"Just inside the Anson property next to our ranch."

"In sight of the Anson house?" the lawyer asked
with what seemed like renewed interest. "Did Mrs.
Anson witness the shooting?"

"I don't know."

"You've seen your father. What did he tell you?"

"Nothing. He wants to plead guilty."

That didn't seem to surprise the man. He finished his breakfast, pushed away the plate and dumped the contents of the envelope she'd given him out on the table. "I don't see the ballistics report in here."

"I got the impression it wasn't back yet."

The lawyer raised a brow. "So we don't know for sure that the gun he was holding was the murder weapon."

"I believe the sheriff thinks it's a done deal."

"Hmm," Clarkston said, then drank his coffee before he added, "let's go see your father."

By then, she'd eaten what she could of her breakfast while answering his questions. Jake had put away his egg sandwich without any trouble. He always slept and ate like a man with a clear conscience, she thought with irritation as she pushed her plate away and rose.

"I'll take care of the check," Jake said quietly as he, too, got to his feet, "and meet you at the jail."

JAKE FOUND BLAZE and the attorney sitting in a visiting room, waiting for Monte to be brought in. He could tell she was nervous and impatient. Her father had made it clear yesterday that he wanted to plead guilty and that he wanted her to stay out of it.

When Monte came through the door, he didn't seem surprised to see the lawyer sitting on the opposite side of the table, waiting for him. He put a hand on Blaze's shoulder for a moment before he pulled up a chair. The shackles he'd been wearing the day before had been removed. Jake figured that was the attorney's doing.

"This is a waste of money," Monte said to Blaze while looking at the lawyer. "I'm sure she's told you, I want to plead guilty. I'm sorry you've wasted your time coming up here." Jake realized that Monte had recognized the attorney and knew he'd gotten a reputation for winning murder cases much larger than his own.

Clarkston seemed to study the man for a long moment. They were close in age. He seemed to be sizing up Monte. "I won't let the judge move ahead on this until I see the ballistics report on the gun."

Monte swore and turned to Blaze. "I asked you not to do this."

"The judge isn't going to sentence you in a case like this until all the boxes have been checked off," Clarkston said. "I'm one of those boxes. You seem worried about the ballistics report. Is that because you weren't holding the gun that killed Frank Anson?"

Jake watched the rancher lean back in his chair and clamp his mouth shut.

Blaze was staring at her father in shock. "If you didn't shoot him..." She frowned. "I was right! You're covering for someone?" she cried. "Allie. *Allie killed her husband?*"

Monte rose so abruptly that he knocked over his chair. "I've had enough of this. Let me plead guilty. I just want this over with. I know what I'm doing."

"What *are* you doing?" Clarkston asked. "It's my

job to tell you what will happen if the judge accepts a guilty plea from you. You will go directly to prison, no trial, no chance of seeing freedom for the rest of your life. You're not a young man, but you're not that old. You're talking a lot of years behind bars. I suggest you give that some thought."

Monte had turned his back and, stepping to the door, pounded it to be let out. A deputy appeared and took him away.

"Who is Allie?" the lawyer asked.

BLAZE STORMED INTO the prosecutor's office after leaving the confines of the visiting room at the sheriff's office. Dave was on the phone, but he quickly hung up and rose, hands in a gesture that was apparently supposed to calm her down.

"Where are the ballistics results?" she demanded.

"These things take time," he said.

She shook her head. "Don't try to snow me."

He smiled. "Take it easy."

"My father's pistol isn't the murder weapon, is it?"

Dave sighed and sat back down in his chair. "They're running the test again, but just because the gun he was holding wasn't—"

Blaze slammed her palm down hard on his desk, making everything on the wood-smooth surface vibrate. "He didn't kill Frank." She said it with some amazement because she now realized it was true. "He didn't kill Frank."

"We don't know that. We're trying not to jump to conclusions."

"You mean like arresting my father without evidence that he was the one who shot the man?"

"He was standing over him with a loaded gun."

She shook her head. "And if your second test proves that Frank wasn't killed with the gun my father had been holding?"

Dave sighed again. "Then we are asking for a warrant to search the ranch for other weapons."

She felt all the air rush out of her. "You can't be serious."

The prosecutor leaned back in his chair. "Blaze, there's a reason your father isn't talking, why he wants to plead guilty. Why would he do that if he wasn't guilty? Maybe that pistol wasn't the gun he used. Everett heard two shots. One of them was a rifle."

She felt her eyes widen. "*A rifle?* Is that what you're telling me? Frank was killed with a hunting rifle, not a pistol?"

Dave was holding up his hands again. "I'm not saying that. Just that it's possible your father shot him from some distance, ditched the rifle and walked up to him holding the pistol in his hand because he planned to finish him off if he wasn't dead."

"That is a lot of supposition for a man who just said he was trying not to jump to conclusions."

"Frank's dead. Your father wants to plead guilty to his murder. There isn't a lot of room here for confusion."

"What if he didn't do it? What if he is covering for the person who did?"

"You have someone in mind?"

They both knew whom she had in mind. "You'll let me know when the ballistics results come back. Clarkston Evans is handling my father's case. He's waiting for those results." She tossed Clarkston's card down on the desk.

Dave groaned. "Called in the big guns, did you?"

"He isn't going to let the judge move ahead until he sees the ballistics test results."

"I'm afraid you're going to be disappointed if you think your father is innocent."

She chuckled. "I've never said he was innocent. I'm just questioning if he killed Frank Anson. You should be questioning the same thing. Unless you want to put Monte away because it would be good for your career, considering how people in this county feel about him."

"I hope you know me better than that."

Blaze scoffed. "I know you're under pressure to put this one away."

"You're right about that, but not for the reasons you think," Dave said as he leaned forward to look her in the eye. "Sentiments in this county are against your father. With you throwing yourself into this, you've upset some people."

"Spit it out, Dave. What are you trying to say?"

"That I'm worried you're in danger."

She laughed. "Apparently the sheriff didn't tell you that Jake and I could have been killed on the ranch yesterday because of some…locals starting a buffalo stampede?"

"My point exactly."

"So I should back off? How about you get on the sheriff to find those men and prosecute them before they do something worse?" With that, she stormed out, slamming the door so hard it rattled the windows.

She looked around for Jake. Earlier as they were leaving the jail, Jake said he would wait for her outside. She hadn't asked why or even cared. She'd been furious and had wanted to talk to Dave alone anyway.

Now, though, she saw Jake standing outside the door. He pocketed his phone as she approached him. Had he been giving Judge Landusky an update? He smiled at her, obviously having overheard at least the final part of her tirade.

Like him, she desperately needed fresh air and space. She was so angry that she feared she would break down and cry. Judge Landusky had been right to ask her to come here. Something was terribly wrong, and the prosecutor knew it.

CHAPTER TEN

ALLIE DROVE FRANK'S old International into town that afternoon. She hadn't been into Saddle Butte since Ty Garrison had been injured. Before that it had only been to go to the funeral home to make arrangements to have Frank buried once his body was released.

He'd already bought a plot for himself next to his mother and father in the town cemetery. As a wedding present, he'd bought Allie one on the other side. One she had no intentions of ever using. The last place she wanted to be laid to rest was near his mother.

Hilda had resented her from the first day she set eyes on Allie. Nothing Allie could do met with the woman's approval. It wasn't until Hilda was on her deathbed that she finally said something nice to her daughter-in-law.

"You are better than what I expected him to bring home," Hilda had said, taking Allie's hand in her bony fingers. "Promise me that you will take care of him as long as he lives."

Promise kept, Allie thought as she drove into Saddle Butte.

With arrangements already made, the funeral to be set after the autopsy was complete and his body turned back over to her, she drove on past the funeral home to the bank. She didn't need much since, living on the ranch, she had her own canned fruits and vegetables along with at least half a beef cut and wrapped in the freezer next to elk, venison and antelope.

Frank had always prided himself on living close to the land. He hated being even a little dependent on the town. A neighbor had a couple of dairy cows and kept them in milk, cream and butter. Flour and sugar were bought when they went to what Frank called the big city so they could hit a big-box store. Simple living, he'd called it. That wasn't what Allie called it.

After pulling into the bank parking lot, she sat for a moment, trying to settle her nerves, as well as her stomach. She'd had morning sickness—what a misnomer that was, since she'd had it all day for months. She waited for her stomach to settle down before she climbed out of the rig and entered the side door. Frank had never let her have a checkbook.

He'd handled all the finances, giving her cash when she needed it but always demanding to know what she needed it for. If it wasn't something he thought necessary, he'd talk her out of buying it. Or if she insisted, he'd pout for days after. She was fine putting up with his pouting. It was when his mother was alive that she couldn't bear the two of them ganging up on her. Back then, she'd just give up, telling herself to bide her time. One day she'd be free of them both.

The bank president, Abram Curtis, saw her and waved her into his office. "Mrs. Anson," he said, coming around his desk to take both of her hands in his. "My condolences."

"Thank you." She retrieved her hands from his damp ones.

"Please have a seat and tell me how I can be of help." He took his chair behind his desk and leaned forward, the elbows of his shirt on the shiny, clean surface.

She cleared her voice, her stomach doing tiny flips. "I need to know how I stand financially."

"How you stand?"

"Frank handled all the finances."

"Oh, I see." He moved to his computer and began to type. She watched him, nervously expecting the worst. At college, Frank had talked about how much land his family owned, how many cattle they ran. It wasn't until she'd arrived on his so-called spread that she realized that the ranch was small, the house old, the outbuildings dilapidated and everything needed work. The first thing he'd told her was that money was hard to come by so he expected her to make do without it.

Abram stopped typing, stared at the screen and then swiveled around to look at her. She tried to read his somber expression. He seemed hesitant to tell her just how bad it was.

"It's bad, right?" she asked, bracing herself. She'd already figured that if she could sell the ranch and the cattle—not nearly as many as Frank had led her to believe—she might have enough to start over somewhere. That was if anyone wanted to buy the place. And if she had enough money to live on until it sold.

"At the end of last month, you had a balance of $2,113.97 The payment on the loans your husband had came out the first part of the month, leaving you with $743.19."

It was even less than she'd expected. She gulped back the angry sob that rose in her throat. "Is there a savings account?"

The banker shook his head, making her eyes burn. She would have to sell the ranch and cattle as soon as possible to survive. That didn't bother her as much as the thought that there would be nothing left once she paid off the loans the banker was referring to— let alone Frank's burial costs.

"These loans," she began but had to clear her voice. "How much is owed against the place?"

"Well…" He squinted at the screen for a moment before looking up at her. "It appears those have been paid off as of a few minutes ago."

"What?" He didn't answer. He was staring at the computer screen as if trying to make sense of what he was seeing. "How is that possible?"

Abram coughed. "Not only was the loan against your place paid off, but a bank transfer just came in a moment ago, bringing your current balance up to $50,743.19."

She blinked, leaning forward because she knew she hadn't heard correctly. "I'm sorry? Are you telling me someone paid off my loans and deposited money into my account? That has to be a mistake."

She had a sudden thought. "Was it like a life insurance policy or something?" She knew it couldn't be life insurance. Frank hadn't believed in it, thought insurance men were all crooks.

The banker shook his head.

Allie stared at him. "Then who would…?" She'd barely gotten the words started when she saw Abram make a few taps on the keys and stiffen.

"Montgomery McClintock had the money moved from his account across the street at our competing bank into your account." Abram turned off the screen to look at her. "Is there anything else I can help you with, *Mrs.* Anson?" he asked, his voice colder than the November day outside.

"MY FATHER DID WHAT?" Blaze moved about the kitchen of the ranch house as she listened to Clarkston Evans on the other end of the line.

"I just spoke with the sheriff. Apparently, he got a call from Abram Curtis at one of the banks. He's trying to read something into this. Were you aware that your father had his banker transfer money to the widow of the dead man? He gave her fifty thousand dollars and paid off the loans against her ranch."

"He's in jail. How could he—"

"He had Martin Shores take care of it. Is that his banker?"

She groaned. "Yes." Did her father really not know how bad this looked, giving money to Allie? "Have you spoken with my father about this?"

"I plan to see him again tomorrow. I'm hoping the

ballistics tests results will be back by then, but I will definitely ask him about this money changing hands. Forgive me for being indelicate, but—"

"Were they having an affair? I have no idea. I haven't been back here for years." She didn't add, though, that almost a year after her mother disappeared, she'd seen his father coming back from a ride from the direction of the Anson Ranch. Her father had looked so young, so vibrant, so…happy. Which had only made her angrier at the thought that he could be any of those things with her mother missing.

"I'll discuss it with your father."

"Won't this make him look more guilty?" she asked.

"You're forgetting that he wants everyone to believe he *is* guilty."

"But if he *was* having an affair with Allie…"

"I'd rather hear it from him before I consider any consequences. I'm thinking of talking to this woman as well tomorrow. Would you like to come along when I do since you apparently know her?"

"Sure." He suggested a time and she hung up and looked at Jake.

"I hate to even ask," he said.

"He gave her fifty thousand dollars."

"Allie Anson, the dead man's widow? That could be seen as guilt."

She laughed. "You think? What it sounds like to me is premeditated homicide. Doesn't Montana still have the death penalty?"

"It hasn't been used in twenty-one years. The last

time they hanged anyone was 1943. Lethal gas was adopted in 1983 but was never used."

"You researched it?" The realization made her feel even worse. Like her, he'd assumed her father was guilty, given everything she'd told him about Monte. "You checked because you're worried, aren't you?"

"There are only two people on death row. It would be very unusual for the prosecution to ask for the death penalty in a case like this."

She shook her head. "But Montana still *has* the death penalty," she argued. "This judge just might sentence him to death."

Jake got to his feet. "That's why your father has a lawyer." He put his hands on her shoulders and looked into her eyes. "Don't buy trouble. Just because he gave this woman money... Maybe he was merely being kind."

Blaze scoffed. "Try selling that to a judge." His palms were warm against her shoulders. She yearned to be in his arms, to feel safe and warm and protected for just a few moments.

"Didn't you say you felt sorry for her?" he asked as he removed his hands.

"I didn't think she was happy and that was a long time ago. If I'm right, she's the one who shot her husband and my father is taking the rap for it. The money just makes him look more stupid."

"Stupid? Or in love?"

"Please," she said, moving away from him out of

self-preservation. Being close to him only made her ache inside for what they once had.

"People do stupid things for love," he said behind her, his voice soft, seductive. She closed her eyes, drawn to what he was offering. Why fight it? Why not enjoy the time they had together? It wasn't like he could hurt her again. She was too smart for that.

She turned toward him and started to say… She didn't know what she might have said because his cell phone rang. She watched him check it, then excuse himself, saying he had to take the call.

"What's up?" he asked into the phone as he headed for the front door.

Her heart dropped like a rock as he stepped outside. She was such a fool. Had she really been thinking about climbing back into his bed?

Blaze watched him pacing a little in the cold outside, his breath coming out in puffs as he talked in the dark to whoever was on the other end of that call. She turned away, unable to watch, her heart aching as much as her body. Damn Jake. Damn her body for wanting him, needing him, aching for him. And damn that weak moment only seconds ago when she'd almost fallen into his arms—and his bed—again.

Behind her, she heard him come back into the house. He brought with him a gust of Montana winter wind.

"Brrr, it's cold out there," he said. "I was thinking we could watch another movie and I'd make—"

"I'm tired. I'll go to bed and read," she said without turning around.

A heavy silence fell between them. He knew her. He knew she was hurt and angry and suddenly trusting him even less, if that was possible.

"Blaze, if it's about that phone call. It wasn't—"

"I couldn't care less." She didn't wait for the lie he was about to tell her. "Lock the door behind you." She walked down to her bedroom and closed and locked that door, as well. She leaned against it, letting tears trail down her cheeks unheeded for a few moments. Hastily, she wiped at them, angry with herself for letting Jake get to her again.

JAKE HEARD HER lock her bedroom door and swore under his breath. He shouldn't have taken the call. But even if he hadn't, Blaze would have thought the worst. He considered going after her and what? Pounding on her door? Trying to reason through the locked door?

He stared after her, cursing himself. They were getting closer earlier. But the moment had been lost when he'd taken the phone call. Sighing, he knew it was because she didn't trust him. Could she ever again? If she couldn't then they would never survive together. She would always be waiting for him to prove again what a bastard he was.

Even though it was pitch-black outside, it wasn't late. Montana in winter, he thought as he headed for the bunkhouse. He wasn't going to be able to sleep and, unlike Blaze, he didn't have a book to read.

He'd packed too quickly to get here, to be with her. He thought about going back to the house to see if there was one in her father's den that might hold his attention. Also, he'd forgotten to lock the door as she'd asked.

As he started back, he caught the glow of a set of headlights on the road past the ranch. The roar of what sounded like a pickup engine reached him about the time the vehicle dipped down a hill and the lights blinked out. He listened, but it appeared the pickup had gone on past.

Standing in the dark, he reminded himself just how dangerous this mission could get. The buffalo stampede was still fresh in his mind. The men had wanted to scare them off. Their attempt had failed. So what would they do next?

He listened for the pickup engine until he heard it in the distance. No late-night visitor. At least not tonight.

He glanced toward the house. He could see that Blaze's bedroom light was on. He caught glimpses of her shadow moving around behind the drapes. He realized that she would be fuming and probably wouldn't be able to sleep again. He'd prefer to talk to her in the morning, but he feared she would only work herself up more if he didn't tell her tonight.

Making up his mind, he stormed back to the house. They needed to have this out, and right now was as good a time as any. He walked into the house, glad he hadn't locked himself out and stalked down the hallway to pound on her bedroom door.

"We're going to talk about this," he yelled.

"Go away, Jake."

"I'm not going to do this with a door between us. I think you know I will break down this door if you don't open it." Silence. He took a step back and was about to put his boot into the door when he heard her unlock it. The door slowly swung open.

She stood, arms folded, still dressed in jeans and a Western shirt. Her blue eyes fired with anger. She hadn't even tugged off her boots. He took some satisfaction in the fact that she hadn't already been in bed reading. He knew this woman. Like him, she was still too stirred up.

"Let's talk in the living room," he said and went back down the hall, not completely sure she'd follow him. He threw more logs onto the fire and closed the screen. When he turned he saw that she'd made herself comfortable in one of the leather chairs.

He took one across from her, the coffee table between them. Blaze looked a little less angry with him. But sometimes it was hard to tell. She still had her arms folded and that distrusting glint in her eye. She was giving him a look he recognized only too well. Damn, but the woman was full of wild spirit. It was one of the things he loved about her.

"What's it going to take for you to trust me?" he demanded.

She shook her head. "Give me one reason I should ever trust you again."

Reaching into his pocket, he pulled out his cell phone and slid it across the coffee table. When she still hadn't moved, he took back the phone, called up the last call and slid the phone over where she could see the number. "You can see the last number that called and when."

She didn't pick up the phone.

He nodded toward it. "Did you ever consider that I might need to talk to someone privately who isn't some secret lover? Call the number if you don't believe me."

She looked down. He saw her eyes widen before they lifted to his again. "Why is the judge calling you?"

He let out a bark of a laugh. "The last problem he asked me to look into wasn't quite finished when this happened, so he's been letting me know how it's going."

"You dropped it to come here?"

He met her gaze, holding it. "Nothing was more important than helping you."

She scoffed. "That certainly wasn't true the last time we saw each other."

"Okay, you want to go there, fine." She started to argue, but he spoke over her. "You were right about one thing. Cara Ramsey was an old friend and a former lover. She was in serious trouble and she came to me for help."

"Before you start sugarcoating it, I saw you kissing her."

"You saw *her* kissing me. She wanted you out of the way almost as much as I did. But not for the same reasons," he said before she could jump on what he'd just said. "She was jealous of you. *I* was worried about you. Cara's trouble was bad and so were the people she was involved with. I didn't want to get you killed. So when you misinterpreted the kiss, I saw it as a way to get you out of there fast without any argument."

She shook her head. "You seriously expect me to believe this?"

"It just happens to be the truth. I've never lied to you, Blaze. I've never given you any reason to mistrust me. If you're honest with yourself, you used that kiss as much as I did. You were scared of what we had between us. You were looking for a way out."

She opened her mouth but then closed it. He could see that she wanted to argue the point, but then her gaze moved past him toward the front of the house about the time he heard the soft tap at the door.

"It's Allie," she said as she rose to her feet. "I think it would be best if I spoke to her alone."

"This isn't over, Blaze."

She met his gaze. Hers had softened. She swallowed. "No, I don't believe it is."

As she went to the front door, he let himself out the back.

ALLIE RUBBED HER arms as she tried to warm up. It was warm in the house, but she was chilled to the bone. After she'd left the bank, she hadn't wanted to go home. She'd gone to the grocery store and bought anything that caught her eye, filling her basket and then putting most of it back. Her refrigerator was full of food and she couldn't keep anything down, so what was the point?

She'd thought about going to the small department store, seeing if they had maternity wear, but then the news would be out before she could reach home. So she'd just driven around, taking roads she'd never been on before and finally ending up at the McClintock Ranch.

"Come sit by the fire," Blaze suggested, not seeming surprised to see her—even this late at night.

Now that she was here, she didn't know where to begin. She warmed her hands in front of the fire before taking the chair she was offered. "I'm sorry."

Blaze looked at her and asked, "What are you sorry about, Allie?"

She had to look away from those intense blue eyes so like her father's. Just the thought of Montgomery behind bars... "He didn't kill Frank."

"How do you know that?"

"Your father isn't a killer."

Allie could feel the woman's sharp gaze on her. "Are you?"

She shook her head, but she could see that Blaze didn't believe her.

"Then who killed Frank?"

"I don't know. Honestly." Her voice broke. She'd told herself that she wouldn't break down, but being here in this house without Montgomery...

"Then how do you know it wasn't my father?"

"Because Montgomery wouldn't. He might have

wanted to…for me. But he wouldn't. He couldn't. He's not that kind of man."

Blaze looked as if she wanted to argue the point. It reminded Allie how much Montgomery's daughter had blamed him when her mother had left. It broke her heart, the pain he'd gone through with Blaze. He'd never thought he'd see her again. She'd written him off, he said, and blamed himself for it.

When Blaze finally spoke, all she said was "You have a lot more faith in my father than I do." She cocked her head, those eyes intent again. "What exactly is your relationship with him?"

She'd expected the question and yet it still took her a moment. Relationships weren't that easy to classify or clarify. For example, if she'd been asked what her relationship had been with Frank at the end, she would have had trouble expressing how little they had known each other or how much she had resented him.

"Your father and I are friends."

Blaze started to rise as if she'd had enough.

"We are also lovers." She said the words, knowing that not even *lovers* covered what they'd been to each other. They'd saved each other. Out here in the middle of the prairie, far from town, far from civilization, they'd comforted each other through the hardest times.

Blaze lowered herself back down into the chair. "For how long?"

"Years, beginning after your mother left."

"Which could explain why he paid off your ranch notes and gave you fifty thousand dollars in cash."

"I had no idea he was going to do that," she cried. "I was shocked when I went to the bank and found out."

"The judge will see it as guilt money for killing your husband. If he did kill him. I think he might be covering for someone. I suppose you wouldn't know anything about that."

"No, I—" She felt sick to her stomach. "May I use your restroom?"

"Third door down the hall," Blaze said. "But I'm sure you already know that."

Allie left her and rushed away, barely making it before the juice she'd drunk earlier came up. She ran cold water. Blotted her face with it and then used one of the towels to dry before she returned to the living room. The moment she walked in, she felt as if something had changed.

Blaze didn't let on that anything had happened in her absence, but Allie sensed it. She spotted her purse lying on the couch where she'd dropped it. Had it been partially open when she'd left to go in the restroom? Her heart began to pound a little harder as she sat down next to it, moving the bag so the opening wasn't visible across the room. But it might be too late. Blaze might have already snooped.

"The two of you must have talked about the future." Blaze seemed to study her openly for a long moment. She felt herself shiver under the woman's intent stare. "What was your plan?"

She shook her head. "We… That is, he wanted me to leave Frank but I couldn't. We couldn't have stayed here, not with Frank's ranch right next door. I couldn't do that to your father. He loves this ranch. He wants to leave it to you. To give you something tangible."

Blaze made a disgusted sound. "You had an affair with my father for years and yet you couldn't leave your husband? Allie, why did you come here tonight?"

"To tell you that Montgomery didn't kill Frank and that I don't want the money. I will pay you back as soon as I sell the ranch."

"It's not my money and clearly my father wants you to have it." Blaze stood and Allie did the same, gathering up her purse and holding it close. For a few moments, they merely stood staring at each other.

"You look so much like your mother. She was the best friend I ever had."

Blaze looked as if she'd slapped her. "And you couldn't wait to get into her bed."

"That's not true." Her voice broke again and she had to fight tears. Her emotions were all over the place. "Your father was so lonely. You weren't talking to him. His heart was broken. He adored your mother. At one point, I thought…"

"You thought what?" Blaze demanded.

"That he might take his own life. He missed Bethany so much that he didn't want to go on and he blamed himself for her leaving."

"And now he's in love with you."

She could feel Blaze's gaze go to her protruding stomach and, willing herself not to, she still covered it protectively with her free hand.

"Oh my God." Blaze let out a cry. "Tell me you aren't—"

"I am." She lifted her chin, refusing to feel guilty about the child she was carrying. "I'm pregnant with your father's baby."

BLAZE COULDN'T SPEAK for a moment. "Does my father know? Of course, he knows." Her eyes widened. "Frank. If he found out—" She felt fury course through her. "I knew my father was protecting you. Now I know why."

"I love your father." Allie sounded close to tears. "I don't want him going to prison for a murder he didn't commit."

"Then tell the sheriff the truth."

"I tried to, but he wasn't interested."

"What are you talking about?" Blaze snapped. "All you've told him from what I've seen of the evidence is that you didn't fire the shot that killed your husband and that you didn't see anything."

"I didn't."

Blaze shook her head. "What is really going on? You're pregnant, you're carrying a gun in your purse…" Allie's eyes widened as if she'd known Blaze had looked in her purse while she was in the bathroom. "And not just a gun, but your passport. Planning to skip the country?"

"I'm not going anywhere without your father."

She thought at least that might be true. "If it wasn't you or my father, then who? Frank was your husband. You have to know something."

Allie pulled her purse closer to her side and for a moment looked worried. Or was that fear? "Frank had been acting strangely for months."

"Strange how?"

"He would get cleaned up and go into town in the evenings, something he never used to do. He'd make up stories about why he had to go in, but I never believed them. When I questioned him, he became angry. He'd been getting more violent. There were times I was afraid for my life."

She stared at the woman. "That all sounds like a motive for murder and a pretty good defense, as well."

"I didn't kill him. There were times I wished him gone, but not dead."

"Does my father know that? Because I think he's pleading guilty to protect you and your baby."

"No." Allie shook her head adamantly. "He knows I didn't do it." But she didn't sound completely convinced of that.

Blaze thought about Frank and his change of character before his death. "Where do you think your husband went on those nights?"

"I have no idea." Her tone said she didn't care, either.

Blaze had a sudden mental picture of Frank, short, squat and neither handsome or wealthy. But still she had to ask, "Another woman?"

Allie shrugged. "I have trouble believing that. Frank wasn't all that interested in the one he had."

Blaze knew that never stopped a man from seeking out another woman. She couldn't help but think about Jake and what he'd told her tonight. Dragging her thoughts back to the woman in front of her, she asked, "Did Frank know about you and my father?"

Allie dropped her head for a moment. "I don't think so."

"But he suspected."

She lifted her head. "Maybe. It could explain the change in him. A while back, I rode into town with Frank during the day. We split up to run separate errands. I saw him across the street arguing with Hutch Durham. They looked like they might come to blows before Hutch's wife, Rita, stepped between them. Later, when I saw Rita in the post office, she tried to avoid me."

"You think Frank might have been seeing Rita?" They would have been about the same age, mid-fifties.

"Frank always swore he couldn't stand the woman, but I suppose anything is possible. Also some nights Frank came home with money. I have no idea where he got it. I thought he might have sold some hay or something. On those nights, he was in a good mood. When he didn't come home with money, he was often drunk and mean."

"Did Frank have a gambling problem?"

"A man who squeezed a dime so hard it squeaked?"

Allie said. "Not just that. Frank often spoke out against gambling, as well as drinking."

Blaze chuckled. "If what you're telling me is true, then there might have been someone else who wanted Frank dead—especially if he'd lost money to that person and hadn't paid him."

"He did seem worried, but then again, he was always worried about making ends meet on that hardscrabble land of his."

"Well, it's yours now. You're going to sell?" Allie nodded. "Then what?"

"That's just it—I don't know." Her hands went to her stomach again.

"If you're waiting to see what happens with Monte… Does he know how you feel about him?"

Allie nodded, tears in her eyes. "If I'm wrong and Montgomery killed Frank…" She looked up until her pale eyes met Blaze's. "Then he did it for me, which means this is all my fault." She began to sob, raising her hand to her face.

Blaze hesitated for only a moment before she stepped to the woman and put an arm around her. Allie turned to cry into her shoulder.

If Blaze believed anything, it was that Allie loved Monte and wouldn't let him go to prison for something she'd done.

After a moment, the woman got control over herself again. Blaze handed her a tissue, offered to make her a cup of tea, but Allie declined.

"I should go."

"Allie, when I first came back, I was convinced

my father was guilty. But more and more, I think he just might be innocent. I'm going to find out who killed Frank. In the meantime, we have to keep Monte from pleading guilty. If you have any influence over him…"

CHAPTER ELEVEN

LONG AFTER THE woman left, Blaze stood in front of the fire, chilled by what Allie had told her. Her thoughts were all over the place. Allie was pregnant. Pregnant with a half brother or sister to Blaze. If Frank had found out… It was one more reason why her father might have killed the man.

She pulled out her phone, unable to let this go until morning, and dialed the attorney.

"Sorry to call so late, but I need to know who has visited my father since he's been in jail," Blaze said.

"I wanted to know the same thing. Hold on. I have the list." She could hear him rustling through some papers. When he'd answered, she'd gotten the impression he'd been working instead of sleeping. He read off the list.

"Allison Anson, Martin Shores…"

"His banker, right," she said before he could continue. "That explained the transfer of funds."

"…Rita Durham, Pastor Westlake, Luella Brown—"

"Who—"

"Luella works at the local café. I believe she's a waitress there."

Why would she come visit Monte? Blaze wondered. Why would any of them?

He continued, "Ron Pierce."

She frowned.

"He owns the Cowboy Bar," Clarkston was saying. "And Lonny Dean."

"Lonny Dean?"

The lawyer consulted his notes. "Married to Sandra Westlake." He looked up. "The preacher's daughter."

She sighed. "Quite a mix." A lot more than she would have expected. "Did you ask my father about his visitors?"

"I did."

"What did he tell you?"

"That is was none of my business. Your father is a difficult client."

She figured that was putting it mildly. "Still no ballistics report?"

"I'm told that the slug was misplaced but found again and another test is being run."

"What?" she demanded. The only reason the slug had disappeared and another test had to be run was because it didn't fit the sheriff's story about who killed Frank Anson. She said as much to the lawyer but he didn't respond. She had a feeling that he'd dealt with small-town officials in the past.

"So we will have a little time to keep Monte from pleading guilty?" she asked.

"Some. I'll be speaking with him again in the morning, but if he is still adamant, all I can do is try to convince the judge that he doesn't know what he's doing and that there isn't enough evidence against him to let him plead guilty."

"Did you know that you can tell a lot about a woman by what she has in her purse?" Blaze asked.

"Pardon?" the attorney asked.

"Allie stopped by earlier. She carries a handgun in hers. Along with her passport." She heard his intake of breath. She had his attention now. "I told you that my father is covering for her. Also, she's pregnant with his child. It all adds up to one thing. He's getting her out of the country before the truth comes out."

"Thank you for the information," Clarkston said. "I'll take it up with him in the morning." So would she.

She thanked him and disconnected. As she did, she looked toward the front window and the dark outside between her and the bunkhouse. She'd thought Jake might come back over to continue their earlier conversation when he heard Allie leave. But Allie must have walked over because Blaze couldn't remember hearing a vehicle start up.

After a while, she realized that Jake wasn't coming back. He would know that she needed time to mull over what he'd told her. He was right about one thing. She hadn't trusted the chemistry between them. Nor did she trust that it would last. So maybe she had used the kiss between him and Cara for her exit.

Could she ever trust Jake enough to trust her heart with him again? She had no idea. But tonight, she'd felt herself weakening.

She thought about going over to the bunkhouse, but they'd pretty much said it all and it was late, and if she went over there and found him in bed... Blaze shook her head as the image of him lying on his bunk flashed in her mind. The man slept naked as a jaybird. That thought did not help.

Nor did the aching need she felt. No man had been able to fill it since Jake. She feared no other man could. She thought about the last time she'd seen Jake before he drove up in the ranch yard. She'd put a knife to this throat.

"You need to get your temper under control, young woman." It was the first thing Judge Landusky had said to her in his gravelly, blunt tone.

She was still working on that. She'd been angry for a long time. Ever since her mother had left, promising to send for her, and hadn't been heard from again. She'd lost trust in not just her mother after that. She hadn't trusted that her father had told her the truth about why her mother had left. So yes, she had an anger problem, she admitted to herself. A trust issue, as well.

She went back to her bedroom; this time she undressed, climbed into bed and closed her eyes. She thought she wouldn't be able to sleep, but when she opened her eyes again, the sun was shining.

Showered and dressed, she wandered out to the kitchen to find Jake making breakfast. Not just breakfast, but her favorite: buttermilk pancakes and bacon.

He motioned her to a chair at the table and served her a plate and fixed one for himself before he joined her. She was already digging into her pancakes slathered with butter and chokecherry syrup when he asked, "What happened last night?"

She took another bite.

"Blaze, we're doing this together, remember?"

How could she forget? "I'm hungry and you know this is my favorite breakfast." She took another bite of pancake followed by a strip of bacon before she told him what she'd learned from Allie Anson and her father's lawyer.

"She could merely be afraid," Jake said. "After all, her husband was recently killed."

"That could explain the gun," Blaze agreed. "But the passport?"

Jake seemed to consider that. "Maybe your father will tell Clarkston something when they talk."

"Maybe." She couldn't help feeling doubtful. "It's almost like Monte is up to something. I want to talk to Rita Durham and find out why she visited my father in jail. If she was involved with Frank…"

"That sounds like a long shot."

She nodded. "Given the argument Allie witnessed? I would bet it involves money, not adultery."

"Okay, I'll approach this from another angle. Shall we meet somewhere in town when we're through? Maybe go have dinner at the steak house?"

She met his gaze. Weakened by just the sight of him, let alone the breakfast he'd made her, she felt all warm and cozy inside and he looked so darn good this morning. "Why not?"

They decided to take two vehicles to town. As she

started toward hers, she called over to him, "Hey, thanks for breakfast. It was great."

Jake smiled for the first time that morning. "I still know what you like." His gaze locked with hers. Heat rushed straight to her center. Jake definitely knew what she liked.

She cleared her throat as she broke eye contact. "I'll give you a call later."

AFTER WHAT BLAZE had told him about her conversation with Allie, Jake agreed that Frank Anson's problem might be gambling. Most small towns had a poker game going somewhere. He was determined to find it. As an outsider, though, getting to the table could prove to be much harder.

He headed for the bank to get as much cash as he could out of the ATM machine, then looked around for possible places to hold a game. His cell phone rang and he saw it was the judge.

"How are things going?" WT asked without preamble.

"We're following up on some leads. There could be others who wanted Frank Anson dead. He might have been gambling and in debt to some ranchers who might have wanted their money."

"What about Blaze's father?"

"He still wants to plead guilty, but we've hired a criminal lawyer. Her father's lover is Frank Anson's wife, and she's pregnant. Also, the slug taken from Frank's body got misplaced. They are apparently running the ballistics test again."

The judge made a disgruntled sound. "I was worried about the sheriff up there. How is Blaze doing?"

"You know Blaze. But she seems to be holding up fairly well, all things considered."

"All things, including you?"

"I'm giving her space."

"I see." Jake figured the judge did see. "Be careful. You're stirring up a hornet's nest. I heard about the buffalo stampede." He wondered how the judge had heard but didn't ask. "I know you'll keep Blaze safe. As safe as is humanly possible since—you're right—she is her own woman."

He chuckled. "Yes, sir, she sure is."

As he disconnected, he headed for the nearest bar. It was probably his best bet when it came to finding out the poker game location. But it was also a great place to get the shit beat out of him if he wasn't careful.

BLAZE TRIED TO get in to see her father, but was told she'd have to come back later in the afternoon.

When she exited the courthouse, she stopped for a moment to take a breath and tried to curb her anger. Tears burned her eyes. She hated that they were making it difficult to see her father. There was nothing worse than feeling powerless. She wiped at the tears and when she looked up, her heart dropped.

Wade Cameron was standing in front of her, holding a toddler who was the spitting image of him. "Blaze?" He looked surprised to see her, but not as surprised as she was to see him. She'd heard that he'd moved away. If there had been one person on earth she hadn't wanted to run into, it was him.

A young pretty woman joined him on the sidewalk. Blaze saw with another heart drop that she was very pregnant.

"Blaze, this is my wife, Missy. Maybe you remember her from high school."

Melissa "Missy" Frederickson was two years younger than her and Wade. She'd been raised in town, the daughter of the now senator. Missy and Wade looked like the perfect family, Blaze thought with a tug of jealousy. Wade had been her first love, so there'd always been a special place in her heart for him.

"Yes," she said, surprised that her voice sounded normal. "I remember Missy. How are you?"

"Right now I feel like an elephant," the young woman said with a laugh, her hand going to her very large belly.

"We're having twins," Wade said, sounding proud and excited. "Identical baby girls." He grinned over at his wife. "And this is Conner, our son."

"Hi, Conner." Blaze felt as if the smile on her face had been glued there. Wade had everything that she'd once wanted with him. Then her mother had disappeared and her life had imploded, taking those dreams with it.

"I bet you even have a dog," Blaze heard herself say. The whole package, just as she'd once imagined it.

"Goldie," Conner said and grinned just like his father.

"Goldie. A golden retriever." She nodded, fighting tears. Wade had gone on and made that perfect life that they'd planned when they were together. With someone else. Not that she could blame him. She'd gone on to jail and would have ended up in prison if it hadn't been for the judge.

"I'm happy for you." Her voice wobbled.

"I'm sorry to hear about your father," Wade said as if knowing that wasn't what was making her so emotional. It was just like him to cover for her.

"Yes, that's why I'm in town. So, are you living here now?"

"Just visiting," he said. "We moved to North Dakota to be closer to Missy's grandparents. They're quite elderly and need the help." He looked at his wife. "We'd better get going." His gaze met Blaze's again. "It was good seeing you. Take care." He reached out and touched her hand, squeezing it for a moment before they moved on.

Blaze stood there, surprised by the warring emotions that rushed through her. Jealousy, regret, and yet, when he'd touched her, she'd felt nothing but a warm hand on hers. She let out a laugh filled with relief.

Seeing him reminded her of what she'd once wanted more than anything. A husband, children, a family and a damned dog. She'd always wondered what had happened to Wade and if he had been The One. Now she knew. She couldn't help smiling. She was happy for him as she headed for her pickup, and happy to realize that he wasn't the man for her, probably never had been, even if he'd been available.

She thought of Jake and sighed. No man, not even Wade back in the day, had made her feel the way Jake did. If she wanted a husband, children, a family and a dog, then the only man she wanted it with was Jake.

Blaze was almost to her pickup when she saw him. Jake. He was standing over by the hardware store. The moment their gazes met, she knew that he'd seen her talking to Wade and his family. Jake looked... concerned for her. She cursed herself for telling him about her first love. Now he would think that she was heartbroken and still in love with Wade, when there was only one man she wanted like her next breath.

JAKE HAD JUST come out of the first establishment after drinking a beer and getting nowhere with the bartender or the regulars bellied up to the bar. As he started to enter the next bar, he saw Blaze across the street.

The moment he saw her talking to the cowboy, he knew it had to be Wade Cameron. Blaze had told him about the rancher's son, her high school love. It had been serious. They'd talked about marriage. Blaze had thought he was the one she would end up with. Maybe she still had—until this moment. He felt for her. There was nothing like having your dreams crushed. His heart went out to her.

He couldn't see her expression, but from her body language she was uncomfortable seeing her old boyfriend and his pregnant wife and child. Then again, was marriage and a family what Blaze wanted anymore?

Jealousy made him nauseous as he watched. Blaze had always said what a great guy Wade was. A regular Boy Scout when it came to honesty and loyalty. Jake knew he couldn't hold a candle to the cowboy. He started to turn away when he saw Wade reach for Blaze's hand—and then witnessed her reaction as the man and his family moved away.

It was like a swift kick to his gut. She was smiling, laughing, and then she saw him and scowled. Jake tried to understand her reaction as he watched her walk to her pickup. She didn't seem heartbroken after all. At least, he hoped not. He didn't want that for her. He didn't want Wade for her even if the man had been free.

He simply wanted her for himself, and seeing her with Wade and his family, Jake knew he had to step it up before some other old boyfriend appeared. He had to make Blaze see how much he loved her and that he was as serious as the ring he'd been carrying around in his pocket.

BLAZE QUICKLY PUT Wade out of her mind and drove the few miles out of town to the Durham Ranch. If only she could put Jake Horn out of her mind as easily.

She had thought about calling first to make sure Rita was home but decided against it. Better to surprise her. When she drove up, she saw that there were several rigs in the yard. She didn't really want to see Hutch and hoped, if around, that he was out feeding cattle. She wanted to speak to Rita alone.

When the woman answered the door, Blaze saw that she had indeed surprised her. Rita blinked a couple of times. From her expression, she was sorry she'd opened the door. "Blaze? What are you doing—"

"We need to talk. Mind if I come in?" It was clear that Rita did mind, but after a moment's hesitation, she stepped back to let her enter.

The house was typical of most in the area. From the floors to the furnishings, it had the lived-in, worn look of at least a couple of generations of family leaving their mark on it.

"I can't imagine what we have to talk about," Rita said, closing the front door and standing by it.

Blaze had walked to the middle of the living room and, not being offered a chair, turned to look at her. Montanans were famous for hospitality when even strangers happened by the ranch. So Blaze knew at once that there was a good reason Rita Durham wasn't happy to see her.

Rita was a typical hands-on ranchwoman dressed in jeans, a flannel shirt, her graying hair cut short, her skin wrinkled and worn from living a good part of her life outside in the elements. "Let's talk about my father."

"Monte? Why would you think—"

"You visited him at the jail."

"So?" Rita said with a toss of her head. "I was just being neighborly."

Blaze scoffed at that. "I know about the argument Frank Anson had with your husband. Was it over you?"

The woman looked shocked that she would even ask such a thing. "*Me and Frank?* You can't be serious."

Blaze said nothing, waiting.

Rita tried to wait her out but eventually failed. "If you must know, I went to see Monte because I'd heard that he gave that woman money."

"That woman being Allie Anson?"

Crossing her arms and looking prim, Rita said, "That money should have gone to my husband."

"Why is that?"

"Frank owed him! That's what they were arguing about. Frank said he didn't have it, couldn't get it. He'd reneged on his debt. To some, he'd have been strung up for that."

"Instead he was merely shot and killed."

Rita blanched. "You can't think we had anything to do with that."

"Why not? You're angry enough. Frank had no way to pay and you and Hutch knew it. So one of you killed him. I've seen you shoot at the fair, Rita. You're quite the markswoman."

"That was years ago," she snapped. "You don't know nothing about me or my husband or what it's been like since you left."

"Why don't you tell me?"

The woman shook her head but said, "Times have been hard. Last winter…" She waved an arm through the air. "You don't want to hear about my troubles and I'm not interested in yours, either."

"So Hutch took up gambling?"

Rita snapped her lips shut tight.

Blaze didn't have the patience to wait her out this time. "I'm sorry that you've had a rough go of it. But Monte can give his money to anyone he likes."

The woman raised a brow and looked down her nose. "Seems like there was something goin' on between 'em. Or are you going to deny that, too?"

"Whatever the deal is with Allie and my father, it has nothing to do with this."

Rita huffed. "He killed Frank for her and then got to feeling guilty and paid her off."

Blaze had figured that would be the local consensus. "You had more reason to kill Frank than my father did. Also, I suspect Hutch wasn't the only person Frank owed money to."

The woman pursed her lips for a moment and Blaze thought she wasn't going to open them to speak again. "Frank had enemies. After all, he's the one who sold that extra land to your father, and look how that turned out."

"You blame Frank for my father raising buffalo?"

"Monte couldn't have done it without that extra land," Rita said stubbornly.

"Who else did Frank owe money to?" Blaze asked.

The woman shrugged. "I wouldn't know anything about that."

She just bet. "Well, right now, you and your husband are the prime suspects. Want to give that a little more thought?"

The back door opened and closed, followed by the sound of boots thumping across the floor, headed in their direction. Hutch was back. Which meant this conversation was over.

Blaze turned to look at the man as he came into the room and stopped dead.

"What the hell are you doing here?" Hutch demanded. He was a large man with a known bad temper.

"She thinks one of us shot Frank," Rita cried.

"*What?* That's the stupidest thing I've ever heard. Everyone knows who killed Frank Anson."

"He owed you money," Blaze pointed out.

The rancher's angry gaze shot from Blaze to his wife and back. "That is none of your business. I think it's time for you to leave." He took a few threatening steps toward her.

She couldn't have agreed more. Turning, she headed for the door. Rita stepped aside to let her leave. But at the door, Blaze stopped and turned back. "Did you know that your wife visited my father in jail?"

She saw Hutch's surprised expression and heard Rita say, "It isn't what you think."

Blaze would have loved to have known what Hutch thought as she left and headed for the jail to see her father. That was if the sheriff let her. She just hoped Monte would be more forthcoming than Rita had been.

IT HAD TAKEN going to four bars, nursing a beer at each and flashing around a wad of money before Jake had found the poker game. There was one tonight in the back room at the hardware store. He'd left the bartender a nice tip.

As he left the bar, he saw Blaze's pickup parked over in front of the jail and headed there. Walking in, he saw her waiting impatiently. Fortunately, a deputy came out just then to say that she could go in to see Monte.

Jake signed in and followed her down the hallway. They took seats in a small room after being searched. A deputy had also been stationed right outside the door.

Monte didn't look glad to see them when he was brought in. "Blaze, I told you what I wanted. Why are you wasting money on this lawyer?"

"Because you didn't kill Frank Anson."

The man sighed and looked as if he was going to leave. Instead, he slowly pulled up a chair and dropped into it.

"Listen to me," Blaze said. "I talked with Allie." Monte's gaze instantly became alert. "She got the money you had transferred to her. She's going to put the ranch up for sale. The only thing is she doesn't know what she will do after that. It all depends on you." She paused to take a deep breath. "Dad, the woman's in love with you. She didn't kill Frank. If you're taking the blame to protect her…" Blaze seemed to suddenly realize she hadn't called Monte Dad since her mother disappeared; he knew.

She then gave what appeared to be a mental shake and rushed on. "She wants a future with you and your baby." Monte's eyes widened. Jake couldn't tell if she was getting through to him. "If I'm right, someone else killed Frank and is letting you take the fall for it because you are so stubborn. Tell me that you'll change your plea to innocent. Then help me figure out who did it."

Monte looked up at her, his blue eyes sad. "I didn't want you involved in this."

"Well, I am. Jake and I both are," she said, for the first time acknowledging his presence. "I need to know what happened that day."

"There isn't anything to tell. I was down by the stock tank. I saw Frank riding in my direction. He looked upset. Then I heard a shot. I saw him fall off his horse. I got over there as quickly as I could. I'd drawn my pistol because I had no idea where the shot had come from."

"You didn't see anyone?" Her father shook his head. "Then he had to have been shot by a rifle. That should show up when they do the ballistics test. They'll know he wasn't killed with your pistol."

"Then what happened?" Jake asked.

"When I reached him, I heard another shot. This one whizzed past my head, so I dropped down next to Frank. I checked his pulse. He was gone. About then, I heard someone come riding up. I thought at first it was the killer. It was the hired hand from the Garrison Ranch, Everett Banks. When he saw me, he drew his gun. I dropped mine and put my hands up as he made the call to the sheriff."

"You didn't bother to tell him that you hadn't fired the shot that killed Frank?" Blaze demanded.

Her father shrugged. "I had no idea what was going on."

She sighed heavily and looked at Jake before turning back to her father. "You must suspect who might have killed Frank other than Allie."

Monte shook his head. "Frank didn't get along with a lot of people, but I'd have no idea who might have wanted him dead."

"Other than his wife?"

Her father met his gaze. "She didn't want him dead, either."

The deputy opened the door to say that time was up. "I'm going to get you out of here," Blaze told her father. "But you have to change your plea. Promise me."

He sighed. "All right, but be careful. I didn't want you in this." With that, he rose and let the deputy take him back to his cell.

"We need to find out what's holding up that ballistics report," Jake said when they were outside again.

Blaze nodded. "Yes, we do."

He smiled over at her, glad to hear her say *we*. "Let's get some dinner. I found a poker game I'm going to tonight. Will you be all right without me?"

She shot him a look, but it lacked her usual snark as they headed down the street toward the steak house. "You know, I am glad you're here."

He chuckled. "And I know how hard that was for you to admit."

Blaze laughed. "I actually feel better about all of this. I was so sure he was guilty, but I believe him. He didn't kill Frank. I'm just hoping the ballistics results prove it."

They hadn't gone far when a pickup-load of young ranchmen roared past. Several threw half-filled beer cans and yelled slurs.

Jake grabbed Blaze and shielded her from the beer raining down on them, as well as the thrown cans.

"You okay?" he said as the pickup raced away.

"Jerks."

He put his arm around her, realizing she was shivering.

"Jake, let's skip dinner and go home and wash off the beer in the shower."

He cocked his head at her and looked into those amazing blue eyes. *"Together?"* He was only joking.

But when Blaze met his gaze, he saw the desire shining in her eyes. "Don't you think that would be more fun?"

Jake laughed. "Absolutely." He figured she'd come to her senses before she reached the house and change her mind. But he was smiling as he followed her out of town, although he was a little worried those fools in the pickup might double back. So far, he hadn't seen them and was glad that there was no traffic on the dirt road to her ranch other than the two of them.

Ahead, her taillights became even more distant. The woman loved to drive fast. He smiled to himself, thinking that with Blaze you had to appreciate the whole package.

As they came over a rise, he saw her touch her brakes about the same time that he saw smoke billowing up against the dark sky and caught the acrid scent on the air leaking into the pickup from outside.

Swearing, he saw her speed up again. It took him a moment to realize where the smoke was coming from. His heart dropped. The McClintock Ranch.

CHAPTER TWELVE

BLAZE HAD KNOWN the moment she saw the smoke. The ranch. Of course her father's enemies would hit again. The buffalo stampede was just a warning. Now they'd gotten serious. They wanted to run her and her father out. Apparently it wasn't enough that Monte was in jail and probably headed for prison even though he hadn't killed Frank.

But whoever was behind this had gone too far this time. As she drove she dug out her phone to call 911. By the time someone answered she was at the gate and could see that it was the smaller of the two barns burning.

"This is Blaze McClintock. My barn is on fire," she said into the phone when the dispatcher came on the line. The area had a volunteer fire department, but she wasn't even sure they would respond. Nonetheless, she had to try. The dispatcher said she would notify them.

Disconnecting, she roared into the yard. Jake was right behind her. She parked some distance from the flames and jumped out. Jake was even faster.

"I'll get the water truck," he yelled over the howl of the fire. "You water down what you can of the large barn with the garden hose." He ran off to disappear into the dark cloud of smoke.

When she reached the faucet she had to screw on the hose since everything had been drained for the winter. She could feel the heat at her back and was relieved when she finally got the water going and could begin spraying the flames that had already leaped to the larger barn. If they lost that… She thought of the horses, but before she even looked toward the pasture, she knew that Jake had already released them from the stable. He wouldn't take any chances with the animals in case the fire got away from them.

Turning the hose on the side of the main barn, she let the icy water stream down to form icicles. It was late November and freezing cold outside. So why would the barn catch on fire? She knew it wouldn't. Not without help.

When she heard the sirens and saw the flashing lights, she felt a lump form in her chest. The volunteer fire department *had* come—even given the way people felt about her father. She brushed at her sudden tears and kept watering down the side of the barn, shooting the water as high as she could onto the roof. Her back burned from the heat while the front of her, wet from the icy spray, was freezing. She could no longer feel her fingers. They couldn't save the small barn, but maybe they could save the larger one.

She could hear the steady thump of the pump as Jake did his best to keep the fire from spreading. As the fire trucks pulled in and the volunteers went to work, she realized they just might be able to save the main barn.

She'd been so focused on what she was doing that she hadn't heard the fireman come up behind her. It wasn't until he tapped her on the shoulder. She started and turned to look into Shane Garrison's face beneath the shield on his helmet. She met his gaze, knowing she must look shocked and yet so intensely grateful.

He motioned for her to put down the hose and stand back. She mouthed "Thank you," and turned off the water to move away as the firemen went to work.

Ice crystals mixed with smoke in the air as the huge hoses began to douse the flames. She watched for only a moment before she went into the house to make something for them all to eat and drink.

HOURS LATER, the fire finally out and the main barn saved, Jake turned on the shower for an exhausted Blaze. She'd served all the firemen chili she'd whipped up along with corn bread and cold beer. He'd wondered if it was the first time many of them had been on the McClintock property. He was sure few of them had ever been inside the house. Blaze had invited them in, but they'd all declined, saying they'd only track it up.

So she'd brought everything out to the main barn and they'd stood around, eating and drinking and talking about the fire before packing up and heading back to town to their own homes. Jake had helped her bring in everything from the barn, though there wasn't much food left. He could tell that she was dead on her feet, but that she'd been touched by her neighbors' generosity and help.

Now she could barely keep her eyes open as he stripped off her clothes and guided her under the warm spray. He did the same, joining her only long enough to soap her down, rinse her and wrap a towel around her before pushing her in the direction of her bedroom. He finished his shower, thinking about the long, exhausting day, and yet he felt good. He didn't mind physical labor. They'd saved the main barn. At least for now. A fire investigator would be brought in.

But Jake knew what the investigator would find. Arson. He and Blaze had alibis since they'd been seen on the street at the time the fire was started. He doubted the culprit would ever be caught, but maybe the county's feelings toward Blaze would soften. The ranchers might argue and fight, but they wouldn't burn down each other's barns.

So whom did that leave? He shut off the water and grabbed a large towel. Wrapping it around his waist, he went out into the bedroom, already knowing what he would find. He stopped in the doorway, listening to Blaze's gentle breathing. The only reason she'd let him undress her and push her into the shower was that she'd been too exhausted to do it herself.

She'd fallen asleep spread across the bed. He pulled down one side of the comforter, then rolled her onto the sheet and covered her up. She sighed but didn't wake. He watched her sleep for a few moments, thinking this was probably the only time she'd been at peace in days.

Retrieving all the smoky and dirty clothing from the two of them, he headed down the hall to the washer and dryer. He put in a load and considered making a run for it out to the bunkhouse in only a towel. Even he wasn't that crazy given that the night had turned more frigid.

Back in Blaze's bedroom, he climbed into the side opposite hers and pulled the comforter over himself. The moment he closed his eyes, he was out. The bad dreams came later, just before dawn.

CHAPTER THIRTEEN

BLAZE ROLLED OVER, her arm going out to the opposite side of the bed. It was warm. Her eyes flew open. Warm and empty. She breathed in Jake's scent and was reminded of all the mornings she'd awakened to find him next to her in bed. The reminder sent a wave of disappointment through her along with that old ache.

She rolled onto her back and stared up at the ceiling. Sunlight shone in the window. She couldn't believe she'd slept through the night for the first time in a long while.

For a few moments, she'd forgotten about the fire, about her father being in jail for murder, about the uphill battle she was waging to prove his innocence. He was innocent, wasn't he? At least not guilty of killing Frank Anson.

Blaze touched the other side of the bed again. It wasn't quite as warm, his scent also no longer lingering on the air. He hadn't left her bed very long ago, but she knew he wouldn't be back. Not unless she invited him.

She thought about the invitation she'd made him in town. It had been at a weak moment, but once out of her mouth, she hadn't been about to take it back. She shook her head.

She wanted Jake, needed him, ached for him. The thought of mindless sex with Jake… She knew what she'd wanted was to lose herself in him for a while but had a feeling that wasn't what Jake wanted. He was right about the last time they'd been together. Had she taken advantage of the situation after seeing him kissing his old girlfriend? She'd known that Jake wanted more from her. He had used the *L* word. He'd been waiting for her to tell him that she loved him, knowing what that would mean. *Love* wasn't a word either of them threw around easily.

Jake loved her. Wanted her. For keeps.

IN THE KITCHEN, Jake heard the sound of the shower down the hall in Blaze's bedroom. He'd hoped she would come looking for him this morning. He was disappointed and yet not surprised. But he'd known in the light of day, she would keep her distance. He flipped the pancakes he had going on the stove and checked the bacon. She'd be starved. It was why he'd made breakfast for her again this morning. She would want the same thing she'd had yesterday. He knew this woman too well.

His cell phone rang. "I heard you were looking around for a card game?" the male voice on the other end of the line asked. "Thought we might see you last night." Whoever was at the other end of this call was disappointed that the group hadn't been able to fleece him last night. They thought they'd found a sucker.

"It's a high-stakes game," the man was saying. "Not sure if you're—"

"I'm up for it," Jake said as he slid the pancakes into the oven to keep them warm until Blaze was ready. "Had a fire out here at the ranch so I missed last night's."

"Not to worry. There's one this afternoon at five in the rear of the hardware store. Come in the back way. Cash only."

"I'll be there." He disconnected and looked up as Blaze came into the room. She was dressed in jeans and a sweater that hugged her lush body. Her face looked paler, which made her hair look redder this morning. But her blue eyes were clear and bright. She looked ready to take on the world.

"Mornin'," she said almost sheepishly.

He grinned, wondering if she remembered him putting her into the shower—alone—or knew that he'd spent the night lying next to her, both of them naked as jaybirds. "Sleep well?"

"I did," she said, avoiding his gaze.

"I just got a call about another poker game in town," he said into the silence that followed. "This afternoon."

She looked up then, obviously happier to be on more solid ground. It was one thing to talk about the case and another to talk about the chemistry that arced between them like heat lightning. "Do you need a stake in the game?"

"I have money, Blaze."

She nodded as if realizing she'd stepped over a

line and quickly changed the subject. "What smells so good?"

"Besides me?" he joked and quickly added, "Pancakes and bacon. Again."

She laughed. "I could eat them every day of the week."

"I know," he said and grinned at her.

"I'm starved."

He chuckled. "Sit down and I'll get you a plate. What do you have planned today?"

"I'm going to see about hiring someone to clean up the debris left from the barn fire, then visit my father again. I'm also going to talk to some of the people who visited him in jail. I'm hoping one of them can shed some light on where his head is right now."

"I can get someone to clean up the mess out here. I'll also check the buffalo. I've already fed the horses. So give me half the names. Let me help." She looked as if she might argue, but to his surprise, she handed over the list. He didn't mention that he also planned to see if he could find out who'd set the barn fire.

"I didn't tell you what I found out from Rita yesterday. Frank owed Hutch money. She didn't admit it was gambling money, but it seems pretty clear. When Hutch came in the house, he ran me off. They're both upset about the money my father gave Allie. I suspect they'll be hitting her up for what Frank owed them. Knowing her, she'll probably pay them off."

Her cell phone rang and she quickly picked up as he slid a plate full of pancakes and bacon in front of her. "Hello?"

He watched her face as he brought his own plate over to the table and sat down. She was listening. Then she was hanging up without saying a word.

"What was that?" he asked.

She looked at him. "An anonymous caller who wanted me to know that Allie Anson is pregnant with my father's child." Her phone was still in her hand. She glanced down at it. "Looks like I have a text from Clarkston. I forgot he wanted me to go with him to talk to Allie. He'll be here soon."

BLAZE RODE WITH Clarkston over to Allie's house. She'd been inside the house as a kid a few times since her mother and Allie had been best friends. She'd found their talks boring and had spent most of her time outside with the animals. Frank would often catch her and chase her back to the house. By then, her mother was usually ready to leave anyway.

She remembered Frank as being an angry man with dark hair that stood up on end and even darker eyes. Her mother never said anything bad about him—Bethany McClintock never said anything bad about anyone—but Blaze had known that her mother could hardly stand the man and had felt sorry for Allie.

Now as they pulled up in the yard, Blaze wondered what her mother would think of the latest... situation. Her husband in jail for murder. Her best friend pregnant with her husband's baby.

As they climbed out of the car, she saw Allie step out the front door. She had one hand placed protectively over her stomach, the other shielding her eyes from the sun. The day was cold and clear, the sun glimmering off the light sprinkling of new snow.

"Mrs. Anson," the attorney said in greeting.

"Please, call me Allie. Everyone does." Her gaze shifted from him to Blaze. She smiled. "Please, come in."

The house was small and old, but neat and clean. Allie had made coffee and rhubarb muffins. She offered them a seat at the square oak table and joined them once she'd poured the mugs of coffee. "The muffins are made from rhubarb I froze last spring," she said, clearly nervous. She straightened the table runner under the plate of muffins before she put her hands around her mug as if to still them.

"Tell me about your husband," Clarkston said.

Allie took a breath and let it out before she spoke. "He was a very practical man. He wasted nothing and prided himself on living off the land." She smiled but couldn't hold it. "He was also a very hard man, unforgiving."

"Did you know he had a daughter?" the attorney asked.

Blaze swung her gaze to him in surprise.

"Sandra Westlake," Clarkston said.

Blaze couldn't have been more shocked. "The daughter of Pastor Wilber and Emma Jean Westlake?" She'd attended the church as a girl and knew the Westlakes. Sandra was five years older than Blaze so they hadn't attended school together. Tall with blond hair, Sandra had always seemed...aloof.

Nice enough at church, but Blaze had heard that she kept to herself, making few friends.

Clarkston didn't answer or look at her. His gaze was on Allie. Blaze turned back to the woman and saw that she wasn't the least bit surprised.

Allie swallowed before she spoke. "Yes, I know about Sandra."

Blaze felt as if she'd fallen into a rabbit hole. How had she not known about this? Sandra was two years away from forty. That would mean that Frank had gotten someone pregnant when they were both teenagers. Since Allie was Frank's first and only wife... "Who was her birth mother?"

"That I don't know," Allie said. "Frank took that information to his grave. The baby girl was left on the church steps shortly after being born with a note saying that the father of the baby was Frank Anson. The Westlakes kept that a secret and raised the girl as their own."

"How long have you known this?" Blaze demanded of Allie.

Allie looked away, a blush coloring her cheeks. "Not long. I confronted Frank about it after he went over to the Westlakes' and made a scene. At first he lied, then he admitted that he'd had a...dalliance when he was a teenager. The young woman became pregnant. He had no intention of marrying her and told her to get rid of the baby. He felt he'd been... tricked."

Blaze blinked. Had it been anyone but Frank Anson, she would have had a hard time believing a man could be that cold and uncaring. "Does Sandra know?"

Allie met her gaze. "She does now."

She stared aghast at the woman her father had apparently fallen in love with. *"You told her?"*

"No, of course not," Allie cried. "Frank…" She let out an exasperated breath. "One night after he'd been in town and had been drinking, he stopped by the Westlake house. I heard that the pastor and his wife were very upset and that Sandra was devastated since apparently she hadn't known that Frank was her father."

"Who wouldn't be?" Blaze said under her breath.

"When was this?" the attorney asked.

"A few weeks ago," Allie said and took a sip of her coffee.

The room fell silent.

"Given how upset the Westlake family was, especially Sandra, would you say one of them might be capable of killing your husband?" Clarkston asked.

Allie said nothing.

Blaze thought she couldn't be more shocked by any of this. "You can't think the pastor or his wife…" Her words died off as she thought of Sandra, who had Frank's blood and a mystery woman's running through her veins.

As Blaze made her way into Clarkston's car, Allie said, "You really should try the muffins. They were Frank's favorites."

On the drive back to the ranch, Blaze still felt shaken. "How did you—"

"Your father told me," he said, his eyes on the road.

She silently cursed her father. So why hadn't *her* father given her this information? "If I was Allie, I would have killed him myself." No wonder her father had been afraid that Allie had shot Frank. She knew that Allie had wanted children and felt Frank had lied to her about his desire to have them, as well.

Now the woman was pregnant in her forties with her first? Would they have more? Blaze was still trying to get her head around the fact that she was going to have a baby brother or sister. She hadn't even considered Allie and her father might have more.

She could see the turn ahead for the McClintock Ranch. "I can't imagine how devastating it must have been for Sandra to find out Frank Anson was her father and the circumstances of her birth and adoption."

"I'm sure it must have been quite upsetting for her parents, as well. I doubt it was something they ever wanted their daughter to know. Worse, your father said he went there demanding money to keep his mouth shut about it."

Blaze shot the attorney a look. "You think one of them shot Frank."

"I never jump to conclusions," Clarkston said as he turned into the ranch. "But it is always good to have other suspects."

"There might be someone else who wanted Frank dead," she said as they started down the road. She could see the ranch house in the distance and the burned-out shell of the small barn. Smoke rose from the fireplace chimney in the house, giving her a start for a moment. Jake had made a fire. "Allie told me that Frank had been acting strangely the last few months." Now that she knew about Sandra learning the truth, she wondered if the change in him had something to do with that. "She thought he might have been gambling because sometimes he came home happy with money and other times not so happy and broke. Jake is looking into it."

Clarkston pulled up in front of the ranch house. "I guess I don't have to tell the two of you to be careful."

"No," she agreed. But that didn't mean she didn't worry about Jake. He was playing poker with the men this afternoon. One of them could be a killer and if Jake got too close to the truth… She shivered as she opened her door to get out. Through the front window, she could see Jake watching her as she walked toward the house.

That aching feeling deep inside her deepened under his gaze. All the man had to do was look at her and her pulse took off. How much longer could she hold him at arm's length here on the ranch, just the two of them? Being within touching distance of each other and not being able to reach for him was killing her.

As CLARKSTON DROVE OFF, she stood for a moment listening to the wind in the bare limbs of the nearby cottonwood trees. The eerie sound did little to calm the growing sense of worry building in her.

After talking to Allie, she was even more convinced that her father had nothing to do with Frank's murder. She wasn't all that sure about Allie herself, though. She'd seen the hatred in the woman's eyes when she'd talked about her deceased husband.

Inside the house, she filled Jake in before he left to do some investigating on his own prior to his poker game. "Be careful," she called after him as he started to leave.

He stopped in the doorway and turned to look back at her. Something in his eyes made her heart leap. "You be careful, too. If you need me…" With that, he left.

She was too antsy to stick around the house. Not long after he left, she headed for her pickup. She needed to talk to the Westlakes. On the drive, she debated whom she should talk to first. Sandra? Or the pastor and his wife? Or just the pastor?

Reaching town, she was driving down the main street when she saw a woman bundled up in a long coat and wearing large dark glasses. She pulled over and parked. Getting out, she called, "Tawny?" She ran after her. "Tawny?"

Before her former friend finally stopped, Blaze was beginning to think she'd been mistaken. But as Tawny turned, it was clear she was the last person the woman had hoped to run into today.

"Didn't you hear me calling your name?"

"I must have been lost in thought," Tawny said. "I was on my way to the drugstore."

"I'm glad I saw you. Have a cup of coffee with me.

I need to ask you something." Before the woman could come up with a reason to decline, Blaze took her arm and steered her toward the small local coffee shop. This time of day, the place was practically empty.

"Tell me what you'd like and I'll get it," she said.

Tawny asked for plain black before moving to a table in a far dark corner.

When Blaze came back with the coffees, she noticed that her former best friend was still wearing her coat and sunglasses. She put down the coffees and studied Tawny for a moment before she reached over and pulled down her sunglasses to expose a bruised black eye.

"It isn't what you think," Tawny cried and pulled her glasses back up.

Blaze sat down and took a sip of her coffee. "You never asked me why I broke up with LJ."

"Don't start, okay? I love him."

"I'm betting the eye isn't the only bruise on your body. Tawny, I know the man. I know how he gets when things aren't going his way." She sighed. "Please think long and hard before you go through with the marriage. He isn't going to change, but I'm betting that you think you're the woman to do it." Her laugh held no humor. "A man who takes his anger out on a woman like that is no man."

"You sound like a domestic abuse ad."

"At least you know that it's abuse," Blaze said. "That's only one reason I asked you to join me for coffee. I wanted to apologize for the other day. I've been so upset over my father... So, tell me what's been going on since I've been gone. I heard Sandra Westlake got married."

Tawny looked relieved that the lecture was over. She picked up her coffee and took a drink. "She's married to Lonny Dean. He manages the stockyard."

Blaze said, "She always seemed…"

"Standoffish?" Tawny nodded in agreement. "I always thought she thought she was better than the rest of us because she was a preacher's daughter." She took another sip of her coffee and seemed to relax.

Blaze watched her, looking for any sign that Tawny knew about Sandra's biological father. "They have any kids?"

Tawny shook her head. "Other than church, the only thing Sandra does is quilt. There's a small group of them who get together in the church basement occasionally. I guess they are a bunch of old women. There is a group closer to Sandra's age, but I heard they make her uncomfortable because they drink wine." Tawny laughed, although it seemed to hurt her. She hugged her ribs, making Blaze suspect they were bruised if not broken. "The younger group probably talks about sex and makes suggestive jokes about the opposite sex. Sandra's not that much older than us but she's always been reserved. What a prude."

To cover what she really wanted, Blaze asked about other people in town that the two of them had known even though she had little interest. By the time they'd finished their coffee and stood to leave, she almost felt as if it had been like it used to be when they were good friends.

As they walked to the door, Tawny said, "You don't have to say anything, okay?"

Blaze smiled and touched her friend's shoulder. "It was good to see you."

Tears filled Tawny's eyes. "You, too."

She watched her walk away, hoping she'd gotten through to her. LJ had only been rough with her once, but once had been plenty enough. She'd broken up with him, and even when he'd come begging for her forgiveness and promising he'd never lay a hand on her again, she'd known it was a lie. Men like LJ didn't change. For Tawny's sake, she hoped the woman would realize that before it was too late.

CHAPTER FOURTEEN

BLAZE FOUND PASTOR WILBER WESTLAKE in his office at the back of the church. He was writing in longhand on a yellow tablet, stopping, scratching out words, then adding others.

He looked up at her knock on his open door. "Hello, Pastor." It seemed to take him a moment to recognize her. It had been years since she and her mother had attended this church. "Blaze McClintock. Come in. I was so sorry to hear about your father." He pushed aside whatever he'd been working on as he rose and motioned to the empty chair in front of his desk. "I suppose you heard that I visited him."

She took the chair he offered her. "I heard. I was surprised. I didn't think he was one of your flock."

The pastor chuckled as he sat down again. "No, but I can only hope, can't I?"

"So your visit to him was about saving his soul?"

He leaned back in his chair, studying her for a moment. "Why do I get the feeling that there is something else you want to discuss with me?"

"When I first came back, I thought my father was probably guilty. It's no secret about him and Allie Anson. But after a few days in town, I'm convinced he didn't do it. Which makes me wonder who else had reason to want Frank Anson dead."

Pastor Westlake nodded as he got up to close his office door. He waited until he took his seat again before he spoke. "Is there some reason you're asking me about this?"

"Is there some reason you felt the need to close your office door? Pastor, I know about Sandra." She watched him swallow, his Adam's apple bobbing up and down for a moment.

"And because of that you think I had reason to harm Frank?"

"I think you had a very good reason since as I understand it, Frank was the one who told your daughter."

Leaning back again, he stared up at the ceiling for a moment before he sighed and said, "I didn't kill Frank."

"I'm sorry, I can see that this is upsetting you, but I have to ask. How did your wife take the news?"

He looked surprised. "You think Emma Jean...?" This time he laughed. "You know my wife. Do you really think—"

"I think my father wanted to plead guilty to protect someone. At first I thought it was Allie Anson. But after hearing about your visit to him and learning what I have, now I'm wondering if it was your daughter he's protecting."

The pastor froze for a moment as color rushed to his cheeks. "I need you to stay away from Sandra."

"I understand that you're protective of her."

"I don't think you do understand." He rose to his feet as he leaned toward her, his hands planted on the top of his desk. "She's been through enough," his voice broke. "I'm going to have to ask you to leave."

JAKE TOOK IN the men gathered around the table. He'd had a lot to think about on his way into town for the poker game. Blaze had filled him in on what she'd learned at Allie's. The suspect list was getting longer by the minute. Now he considered who at this table might have wanted Frank Anson dead.

He'd spent his life assessing his environment for danger. The men at the table looked like a bunch of local ranchers. All except one. Deputy LJ Fraser leaned back in his chair as he clocked Jake coming into the room. His expression was one of surprise, then amusement. "Well, look what the cat dragged in."

"Knock it off, LJ," hardware store owner Herb Perkins told him.

"I don't mine taking his money," the deputy blustered. "Just make sure he doesn't deal off the bottom of the deck."

"That would be your trick," Herb said before rising to introduce him to the other men at the table. Jake put the names with the men. Bob Christianson of Christianson Cattle Company, Sonny Dix from the local grocery, Dale Allan from the ranch supply store, Hutch Durham, whom Frank owed money, and Deputy LJ Fraser.

He nodded to each man around the table. "Jake Horn." All the men but Hutch met his gaze. Hutch fidgeted in his chair, saying impatiently, "Can we get started now?" as if he had somewhere to be later.

"How's Blaze?" LJ asked from his seat across the table.

"You want to chew the fat or play poker?" Jake asked, meeting with Hutch's approval. Herb whipped out a new deck of cards, letting the man next to him open them, and the games began.

Jake's plan was to lose just enough money that they invited him back. The worst thing he could do was fleece these men, especially LJ. So he played smart, winning a little, losing more.

The whole time, LJ watched him as if he really did expect him to deal off the bottom of the deck. At one point, he had a full house, aces and jacks. He knew he could take the pot. It was a big one.

When everyone but LJ folded, Jake had to fight a burning desire to take his money. He stayed in just long enough to make LJ sweat and then he folded.

As the deputy reached for Jake's cards, curious to see what he'd had, Jake shoved them deep into the discarded pile. No one but LJ seemed to notice what he'd done. He could feel the deputy studying him with suspicion. Jake knew he would have to be more careful next time. If there *was* a next time.

Hutch won a little money and seemed to relax as the evening progressed.

When the game finally broke up, it was late. He'd sized up the men at the table by the way they played poker and had a pretty good idea who to question about Frank.

Several of the men were headed for First Street Bar across the alley, but Hutch declined, saying he had to get home. Jake held back to talk to Bob Christianson, a shy rancher who'd played conservatively all night.

"What happens if you lose more than you can afford in this group?" Jake asked.

Bob shot him a look. "They won't let you do that."

"They let Frank Anson."

The rancher stared at his boots and sighed. "Everyone in this group knows why you're in town." He slowly raised his gaze. "I have nothing against Monte McClintock. I don't even care that he raises bison. But people are upset over Frank's death. You need to be careful asking about Frank."

"*Careful* is my middle name."

Bob shook his head. "Son, I saw the way you play poker. For whatever reason, you could have taken that last pot and you didn't. I don't know what you're up to—"

"I want to find out who killed Frank. I don't believe it was Monte. I'm guessing that Frank was a poor poker player."

Bob seemed to hesitate. The others had gone out into the alley. Jake could hear them discussing the bar, the weather, their good and bad hands tonight. The man slowly zipped up his down coat before looking at Jake again. "Frank lost more than he won and couldn't pay up."

"Who'd he lose to the most besides Hutch?"

Bob seemed surprised that Jake already knew

that. He sighed and rubbed the back of his neck, hesitating again.

Jake could hear the others outside breaking up, some going home, some headed for the bar. Time was running out. Herb would be anxious to lock up.

"I'm sure you've already figured out who the weakest player is." LJ Fraser, the sheriff's son. He'd paid a little visit to LJ's place outside town. It had been easy enough to take a peek into his barn. As expected, he found the Appaloosa horse he'd seen the day of the bison stampede.

"You have a nice night," Bob said and turned and walked out.

Jake followed, thanking Herb as he started toward for his pickup.

"If you'd like to come back tomorrow," Herb called after him, "same time. Same place."

"Same group?" he asked.

"Pretty much."

Jake gave him a nod and continued to his pickup. He wouldn't mind playing Deputy LJ Fraser again. The man was dangerous because he was reckless. Hutch lacked skill whereas LJ was overconfident to a fault.

He could see either of them getting angry and shooting Frank. But what would they have gained by doing that? They still wouldn't have gotten their money. So why do it? There had to be more to Frank's murder.

ALLIE HEARD THE sound of a vehicle and moved to the door, where she kept Frank's old shotgun loaded and ready. She recognized the pickup that pulled in. She'd been expecting him, knowing he would come in darkness.

As she watched Hutch Durham climb out of his truck and look around, she picked up the shotgun and opened the door.

At the sound, he turned, his eyes narrowing. "Not very neighborly, *Mrs*. Anson."

"What do you want, Hutch?" She held the shotgun across her chest, but her finger rested on the trigger. Frank had told her enough about Hutch that she had good reason to be leery of the man. Since then, she'd learned that her husband's trips to town had definitely been so he could gamble. Hutch's wife had let her know that Frank had reneged on the poker money he owed. Hutch was no doubt here to collect. "I already told your wife I would pay what Frank owed you once I had the note my husband signed."

Hutch scratched his grizzled chin. "Well, that's the thing. I'm going to need interest on that money compounded daily."

"You sound like a loan shark."

The man grinned and took a step toward her.

"I wouldn't come any closer if I were you," she said, shifting the barrel so it was pointed at his chest.

Hutch looked around again before settling an intent gaze on her. "You all alone out here, Allie?" He knew she was. Frank only hired occasional help, and that was when he was desperate. That was why Everett had been here the day Frank died. Most of the time it was just the two of them. "Dangerous, a woman alone this far out with neighbors nowhere near enough should you have to call for help."

He took another step toward her.

"I hope you don't think I won't shoot you."

"Maybe I just want some of what you've been giving away to McClintock," Hutch said, baring his stained teeth in a sneer.

She swung the shotgun off to the side and fired, swinging it just as quickly back to him. "It's a double barrel. This next one is for you."

He jumped back, anger contorting his face. "This isn't over. I'll get my money and some satisfaction, as well. You won't always have that shotgun in your hands."

She heard the threat, her trigger finger itching to end this now right here in Frank's front yard. He'd brought this on her. Even dead he was making her life a living hell.

"You come back, Hutch, and I'll kill you."

He smirked. "I guess we'll see about that."

JAKE HAD HOPED to find Blaze watching another Christmas movie. He had a craving for her and popcorn. At least he could fulfill one of those cravings.

But instead of being curled up in front of the television, he found her opening what he quickly realized wasn't her first beer of the night.

"So, did you win?" she asked and handed him a beer.

He took it, trying to evaluate her mood. Not good, that much he could see. Something had her worked up. "I won and lost enough. I've been invited back tomorrow night."

She shook her head. "Why bother? I know who killed Frank. The person my father is protecting."

He listened as she told him about her visit to Pastor Westlake's office. "It's a theory," he said when she finished.

"You have a better one?"

"Not yet. But I'm not giving up." She didn't look convinced. He worried that his coming to town was a mistake. Maybe he was making things worse for Blaze. He said as much.

She looked over at him, her gaze softening. "I told you. I'm glad you're here. I'll admit I wasn't at first. Because of our past. I didn't want to be reminded."

"And now?"

She chuckled and took a long drink of her beer. "I can't believe any of this is happening."

"At least your father has come to his senses and is pleading not guilty."

"As if he can get a fair trial in this town."

"A trial is months off—if it comes to that. In the meantime, we'll get to the truth. Isn't that what we do?"

She nodded as she finished her beer and was getting up to get another when he grabbed her arm and pulled her toward him. She stumbled and fell into his lap, her arms going around his neck. Her full breasts brushed against him, stirring his desire instantly. She smiled, her blue eyes wide and inviting. The woman knew how much he wanted her.

He drew her closer, even as his mind argued that this wasn't the time. She was half-drunk and he was... Just the scent of her made him hard. He grasped the back of her neck. "Are you through fighting it?" He saw the answer in her eyes. Her defenses were down, her desire so strong that she could no longer hide it from him. She wanted him desperately. As desperately as he wanted her?

He dragged her to him. His mouth took hers in a blistering kiss as his free hand cupped her breast. His thumb caressed her pebble-hard nipple. She made a sound low in her throat and grabbed the front of his shirt in her two hands. As she jerked it open, the snaps sang as they came apart. He felt her warm palms on his bare chest and groaned against her lips.

But as her hand slid down to his crotch, he lifted her off him and stood, holding her at arm's length. "I can't do this."

BLAZE STARED AT HIM. "I beg your pardon?"

"Not like this."

His kiss had stolen her breath and her resolve. She had felt the pounding of his heart as she'd looped her arms around his neck and let herself enjoy the feel of him after days of pushing him away. More than anything she wanted to lose her naked self in him. She needed this. Needed him.

She reached for him but he stepped back. She frowned in confusion and met his gaze.

"I want more," he said simply.

"So do I. Thought that's what we were just about to do."

He shook his head. "I want you, Blaze. All of you."

She took a step toward him, caught the collar of his open shirt in one hand and pressed her palm to his warm, hard chest. He caught her hands in his and shook his head.

Her gaze went to his crouch. "Jake, it's clear that you want me as much as I want you."

"I'm not talking about sex. I'm talking about *love*. Commitment, Blaze. Forever. Till death."

She jerked her hands free and glared at him. "Forever? You can't really believe that anyone can make such a commitment and actually keep it."

"It's not unheard-of, Blaze. But without a commitment..."

She took a step back from him, shaking her head. She felt dizzy, the beer she'd drunk making her queasy. She'd wanted this so desperately. She'd wanted him. She swallowed back the disappointment. "You ask too much."

"Probably, but I won't settle for less. Not this time."

Her stomach knotted as she looked at him. She needed him in her bed. As her gaze met his again, he must have seen the torment in her eyes.

"Blaze—"

"You can't kiss me like that and then..."

He reached for her but she sidestepped him. "You

broke my heart. Now you want me to trust you? To commit forever to you?"

"You *do* trust me. You might have felt hurt but only because you told yourself a story that wasn't true. You knew I didn't love that woman. You knew I wasn't sleeping with her. You were scared. Admit it."

She glared at him. "How do you know what I felt?"

"Because I know you. Surely you can't doubt that. Not after everything we've been through, everything we've meant to each other."

"I don't believe in love-ever-after." She let out a laugh that broke with emotion. "Look at my father and mother. Now there's a love story for you."

"That's just fear talking. It's scary surrendering to another person, letting them see into your heart. Into your soul."

"I…" She couldn't finish. And yet she couldn't move. She looked at him, knowing how weak she seemed with tears filling her eyes. Her heart felt as if it would break all over again.

He slowly began to snap his shirt closed. "I love you. And I know you love me. But maybe not enough." He met her gaze. "Good night, Blaze." With that, he turned and walked out.

She picked up the closest thing at hand, her empty beer bottle. She hurled it. The bottle hit the door as he closed it behind him. The glass shattered and sprinkled to the floor. Her heart shattered with it as she let out a howl of pain.

CHAPTER FIFTEEN

THE NEXT MORNING Blaze came into the kitchen to find no pancakes and bacon cooking on the stove. No Jake. She glanced out the window and saw that his pickup was gone. Gone for good?

The thought squeezed her heart like a fist even as she told herself it was probably for the best. She decided to stop by the local café for breakfast, then go see her father. On the way, she replayed what had happened—and didn't happen—last night.

She couldn't help being disappointed and angry with Jake. What man in his right mind would pass up a physical relationship with no strings? Only Jake Horn. She thought of his kiss and groaned in agony. The man knew how she felt about him. Why did he have to take this ridiculous stand? It wasn't like he'd promised marriage.

By the time she'd reached town, she was fuming. After parking in front of the café, she entered to find the place just starting to empty out following the early-morning rush.

"Take a seat," an elderly waitress told her.

She'd just sat down in a booth, facing the windows looking out on the main drag, when the waitress put down a menu and a glass of ice water in front of her. "Coffee?" She looked up at the woman, saw her name tag and only got off a nod before Luella produced a cup and filled it from the pot in her other hand. "Think you know what you want?"

Blaze opened the menu. She could have been in any café across Montana since it offered the same thing. "I'll have a short stack with bacon," she said, handing back the menu, and the woman was off to the kitchen to place her order.

Sipping the coffee, she tried to clear her mind of everything but the reason she'd come back here. Through the front window she saw that it had begun to snow. Huge flakes whirled through the air in a mesmerizing fashion. She heard a couple talking excitedly about a white Christmas as they left.

She hadn't thought about Christmas. The days at the ranch had all run together since she'd been here. Most years, she did little decorating since she was usually on a job somewhere and the day would pass with hardly any notice. She tried not to think about last Christmas. She and Jake had been together.

Christmas was still weeks away. She figured they would be finished here. If Jake hadn't already left. It wasn't like she needed his help, she told herself.

"A short stack and bacon." Luella plopped the plates down. "Get you anything else?"

"As a matter of fact," Blaze said and looked around the café. "It isn't busy right now. Can I ask you why you visited Montgomery McClintock in jail?"

Luella leaned back a little as she looked at her. "You're the daughter. Blair."

"Blaze."

The woman nodded sagely. "Right. I guess you should ask your father about it."

"I plan to. But in the meantime, why don't you tell me? Unless it's a secret."

Luella laughed. "Oh, honey, you can't think that I'm hitting on your father." She shook her head. "He got a message to me. Seems he hates the slop the jail was feeding him from that place a few doors down. I promised to see that he got what he likes. Wish it was something more...sinister."

With that, the waitress left her to her pancakes and bacon.

JAKE HAD WOKEN before daylight after a restless night filled with bad dreams. He'd showered, dressed and left the ranch, not in the mood to see Blaze this morning. Once in town, he stopped by the sheriff's office to see Monte.

"Where's Blaze?" the prisoner asked as he entered the room to find only Jake.

"I thought we should talk without her," Jake told him.

Monte stood just inside the door as if bracing himself for what was to come.

"I'm in love with your daughter."

The words seemed to take the man off guard. "This is what you want to talk to me about?" He looked relieved and amused.

"I want to ask you for her hand."

"Seriously?" Monte shook his head as he walked around to take a chair. "That's a bit old-fashioned."

"*I'm* old-fashioned."

"Really?"

"You seem surprised," Jake said.

"It's just that I know my daughter. So she's agreed to this?"

"No," he said. "She's fighting it."

Monte laughed again. "I hate to even ask. How do you plan to get her to the post, then?"

"I'm working on it. I want to marry her, raise a family, settle down."

"We are talking about Blaze, right?"

"She is more conventional than she likes to admit," he said.

"I'd have to take your word for that." Monte seemed to consider him seriously. "How do you intend to support her?"

"I make good enough money as a private investigator. I also own a small ranch, run a few hundred head of cattle. I'll make sure she's taken care of, you don't have to worry about that."

"You are aware that I'm leaving Blaze the ranch."

"That doesn't have anything to do with me," Jake said. "I don't want or need your ranch."

"I see. But if you married Blaze and she wanted to stay on the ranch?"

"If that's what made her happy, I'd be there for her."

"Then I give you my blessing," Monte said, smiling. "Good luck." He started to rise.

"One more thing," Jake said. "Who killed Frank?"

The older man sat back down. "Haven't we already had this conversation?"

"You haven't been honest with your daughter. She's planning to talk to the Westlakes. Sandra and her mother and probably Sandra's husband, Lonny Dean."

Monte swore. "I don't want her doing that. She's just going to stir up things best left alone."

"Things are already stirred up, if you haven't noticed. You're in jail looking at spending the rest of your life behind bars. Your girlfriend is pregnant. I know about Sandra's father. What I don't know is if you're protecting the Westlake family."

"If you know about Sandra's…biological father, then you know why I don't want that family any more upset than they have been because of Frank."

"Blaze thinks you wanted to plead guilty to protect Sandra, which means you think she's capable of murdering her…biological father."

Monte groaned and raked a hand through his graying hair. "I don't know who killed Frank. Just that there were other people who despised him even more than I did, okay? I don't want to see them suffer because of his death."

"That is very noble. I suspect ultimately, you're trying to protect Allie and your unborn child since she was married to Frank. That is quite the sacrifice just to keep Allie from being upset about her husband's love child."

The door opened and LJ stuck his head in. "Time to go, Monte." His gaze slid over Jake. "Time's up, Horn."

Monte got to his feet. "I'm not as noble as you think I am." With that, he let LJ take him from the room.

"You, too," the deputy said to Jake. "You need to go. Now."

Following breakfast, Blaze swung by the Westlake house after making sure that the pastor's vehicle was parked down at the church. His wife answered the door in a dress, low heels and a gingham apron surrounded by the scent of homemade cinnamon rolls. Blaze had forgotten Emma Jean's famous rolls. She used to bring them to church potlucks. Her mouth watered at the memory of how delicious they were—even though she was still full from breakfast.

"Mrs. Westlake—"

"Blaze, how wonderful. And please, call me Emma Jean. Come in, come in. I have cinnamon rolls in the oven. You're just in time." She waved her back toward the kitchen.

Blaze followed the short, rather plump woman through the neat living room to the bright, airy kitchen. She couldn't help but think about Sandra being raised in this house. She felt a stab of jealousy and wondered if she was totally off track. How could anyone kill after being raised here?

Emma Jean had gone to the oven to check the cinnamon rolls. Blaze breathed in the amazing scent and took the stool at the counter that the woman offered. "Coffee?" she asked after peeking into the oven.

"No, thanks, I just had some."

"Oh my," the woman said, hands clasped over her heart. "You look just like your mother. Oh, I do so miss her. Have you heard from her?"

Blaze shook her head, taken aback. She forgot sometimes that she resembled her mother enough that anyone who knew her would comment. Then again, she hadn't been around anyone who knew her for a very long time.

"I adored your mother. So, how are you? Did I hear that you're a private investigator? Oh my. What an exciting profession."

She had to smile. "It's really not that exciting most of the time. I once was on a stakeout where the most interesting thing that happened was watching a caterpillar cross the road."

Emma Jean laughed but quickly sobered. "Wilber told me that you stopped by his office."

"Did he also tell you what we talked about?"

The older woman smiled. She had a dimple in her left cheek and sparkling blue eyes that twinkled in the kitchen light. "We have few secrets."

"I'm trying to find out who killed Frank Anson," Blaze said.

Emma Jean nodded. "He was an awful man. I doubt he'll be missed all that much. I suspect you're planning to talk to my daughter."

She nodded. "And her husband."

"Yes. Well, I hate to have Sandra upset, so all I ask is that you do it gently since I can see there is no changing your mind. Imagine how you would feel if you found out that Frank was your father, after in a drunken rage he tried to blackmail your family before blurting out the truth."

"I'm sorry. This was a few weeks ago?"

The woman nodded. Blaze noticed that Emma Jean's hands had grabbed handfuls of her apron hem and balled the fabric in her fists. "Apparently he needed money, felt desperate and didn't care if it destroyed his own daughter's life."

"I'm sure Sandra was upset."

"Upset?" She scoffed at that. "Maybe my husband didn't tell you, but Sandra is pregnant with her first child. She's had several miscarriages. We were so afraid that she might lose this one." As if realizing what she'd been doing, Emma Jean released her hold on her apron and stretched out her fingers. Even her voice sounded more relaxed. "Right now the baby is fine. But you can understand why I need you to be careful when you speak with her. I can't stop you from doing that. If you really must." The timer went off on the cinnamon rolls. "I remember how much you used to love my rolls. You must stay and have one."

"I can't, really. I'm stuffed from breakfast," Blaze said as she got to her feet.

"Then you must take two home. I understand you

have a young man staying with you out at the ranch." Word had definitely traveled to even this house.

"That is very nice of you," Blaze said as she watched the woman cut into the pan of warm cinnamon rolls and place two large ones, dripping with brown sugar and butter, in a plastic container. Blaze started to stop the woman from using one of her containers, but Emma Jean cut her off.

"Don't worry about getting my dish back right away." She left the lid cracked so the hot rolls could cool and handed it to her. "I'm sure we'll be seeing each other again. Wilber has a wonderful service planned this Sunday."

JAKE WENT STRAIGHT to the bar from the jail. It was still early, but several regulars were already perched on stools with their elbows on the bar, sipping coffee and watching the news on the television on the wall.

Bar owner Ron Pierce was about Jake's age, tall and muscular with the body of a bouncer. But he flashed Jake a smile as he came down the bar. "What can I get you?"

"I could use a Bloody Mary."

Ron laughed. "You have come to the right place." The bartender went back down the bar and began to make his drink.

Jake looked around, curious how a man his age had come into bar ownership. From what he was able to find out, Ron had come up with a fairly large down payment and was now paying down the mortgage at a surprising rate. But there couldn't be that much business in a town this size.

So he suspected Ron had a business on the side. What that had to do with the man visiting Monte in jail, Jake had no idea. Not unless Monte had gotten into the drug business along with buffalo.

Ron put down a bar napkin, then set the drink in front of him. A pepper, an olive and a slice of lime were skewered onto a toothpick and floating on top. "Holler when you need another."

He'd thought about asking the man point-blank why he'd visited Monte in jail. But following his instincts, he bit the pepper off the toothpick and smiled to himself. He liked spicy and this pepper was a doozy. He took a sip of his drink and saw Ron get a text on his phone.

Excusing himself, the bar owner went back into his office. The regulars took no notice, but Jake watched in the mirror over the bar as the man came out with a small package wrapped in brown paper. Ron headed down the hallway past the sign for the restrooms toward the back door.

Jake took another drink, then pretended to head for the men's room. Hurrying down the hall, he reached the end just moments after Ron had exited into the alley. He pushed open the door just wide enough to watch through the crack as the bar owner walked up to the driver's-side window of the car idling in the alley.

The window came down. He handed off the package. Allie Anson handed him a white envelope thick with what Jake would bet was cash. He quickly turned and ducked into the men's restroom only seconds before he heard Ron come back inside.

Jake stepped to the sink, washed his hands and was reaching for a paper towel when he heard the door open a few inches and then close. He listened to Ron's footfalls disappear down the hall before he came back out to take his spot on the barstool. He sipped his Bloody Mary as the bar owner went into his office, coming out empty-handed, and returned to the bar.

"Is your drink all right?" Ron asked as he came down the bar to stop in front of him. The bar owner had heard him in the hallway. That was why he'd peeked into the men's room. He was afraid he'd been followed.

"Rough night last night," Jake said. "I thought maybe the hair of the dog would help..." He picked up his glass and finished the last of his drink. "Not sure another one is going to cure me, though, but thanks." He pulled out his wallet, tossed a few bills on the bar and smiled at the man as he slid off his stool.

Ron seemed to relax a little as he scooped up the money. "Hope your day gets better."

"I'm sure it will," Jake said as he left.

BLAZE FELT OFF balance as she left Emma Jean's house carrying the warm cinnamon rolls. She put the container on the passenger seat but didn't start the engine. She'd planned to pay Lonny Dean, Sandra's husband, a visit. But finding out that she was pregnant and there was a chance she could lose her child…

"Maybe I don't have the stomach for this anymore," she said to herself as she reached to start the engine. Also, the smell of the cinnamon rolls was killing her. Before she could shift into Drive, a pickup came roaring up and pulled in front of her, blocking her retreat.

Shane Garrison jumped out, leaving his truck running, and came toward her. She'd parked in front of another car, which was directly behind her. Unless Shane moved his pickup, she wasn't going anywhere.

She put down her driver's-side window, wondering what this was about. She just hoped that his son Ty was all right. She'd called the hospital the day after she'd gone to visit and was told that the boy had been released.

"Shane," she said as the rancher bent down to look into her window. "Is Ty all right?"

He looked confused for a moment. "My son? He's fine. Well, as fine as he can be with a broken arm and a lot of bruises." He waved that off. "I saw you sitting here and…" He looked away for a moment.

"I want to thank you again for the other night. The barn fire."

"I'm a volunteer fireman. I would have done it for any fire, any rancher."

She wondered if he would get to whatever it was he wanted to talk about but said nothing as she waited.

"This is probably not the place to discuss this. Like I said, I saw you…"

He finally looked at her again. "I figure you'll be selling your place, you know, with your father in jail and all. A bunch of us were thinking that we might be able to raise enough money, at least for a down payment. I just hoped that you'd give us a chance."

"Don't you think this is a little premature? My father hasn't been convicted of anything." She saw him pull back and look embarrassed. "But, Shane, I promise you, if it comes to that and I do put the ranch up for sale, I would definitely consider your offer."

That seemed to relieve him.

"Thanks," the rancher said and took a step back, looking ill at ease. He walked to his truck, climbed in and took off in a cloud of diesel exhaust.

It bothered her that Shane already had her father convicted and off to prison. Not if she could help it, she thought as she pulled out onto the street and headed for the jail.

CHAPTER SIXTEEN

JAKE GOT THE call as he was leaving the bar. He thought it would be Blaze, but saw that it was Herb Perkins.

"We've moved the private poker game up," Herb said without preamble. "I'm closing early so the game will start at four."

"I'll be there," he said. "Anyone I know playing?"

"A couple of new guys I'm not sure you've met."

Jake nodded as he disconnected, having heard something in Herb's voice. All his instincts told him he was being suckered in and Herb knew it. As he slid behind the wheel, his cell rang again. This time it was Blaze.

"I just tried to see my father," she said, sounding irritated. "But he already had a visitor. Allie." He wasn't surprised and told her what he'd seen while at Ron Pierce's bar.

"Drugs?" Blaze asked, sounding confused.

"That was my first thought, but I'm thinking more like a passport."

"But Allie already has her passport."

"But your father doesn't, especially in another name," Jake said.

"What are you talking about?"

"Just a theory I have. I'll explain later. By the way, you remember that I have another poker game this afternoon."

"That's right." Did she sound disappointed? He could only hope.

He didn't mention that he thought he would be walking into a trap. "Tell me how your morning went." He listened as she told him about Luella's reason for visiting her father and then about Emma Jean and finally Shane Garrison's offer.

"I have a headache and the smell of these cinnamon rolls is killing me. I think I might head home and eat one of them. I might save you the other one. Or I might not."

Jake chuckled. "They're all yours. Enjoy." He knew she would save him one.

"You don't know what you're missing. But maybe that's good or you would never forgive me for eating them both."

He could tell that a lot more than the cinnamon rolls was bothering her. "Are you okay?"

"A little discouraged. I feel as if I'm spinning my wheels."

"Don't. I think we're making progress."

She chuckled at that. "You're just trying to make me feel better."

"Is that so bad?"

"I'm going to swing by the bank and talk to Martin Shores but I'm pretty sure I know why he visited my father," she said. "But this whole thing with the passports makes me wonder."

"Find out what you can about your father's money. I suspect he's had it moved to a foreign account."

A few beats of silence before she said, "You think my father and Allie are planning to change their names, skip the country and what, exactly? Do I have to remind you that my father is in jail and facing a life sentence in prison?"

Across the street, Jake saw Deputy LJ Fraser talking to a man he recognized. "Listen, I have to go, but we'll talk about this later, okay?" He disconnected as he watched LJ and Herb Perkins arguing in front of the hardware store before disappearing inside.

MARTIN SHORES HAD a large office with a window and a receptionist outside his door at his bank. From his window, he could see not just the competing bank across the street, but Abram Curtis's office. According to local scuttlebutt, both men were now president of their respective banks, the two of them had been in competition since they were boys.

Martin looked up as Blaze stepped into his office. He smiled and quickly got to his feet.

"Miss McClintock, please come in." He motioned to a chair in front of his desk. The moment she was seated, he asked, "What can I do for you?"

"Are you aware that I have my father's power of attorney?" She saw his skepticism and reached into her purse to pull out the copy she'd had made. She slid it across the desk. "I want to know what is going on with my father's finances."

Martin leaned back in his chair. He was a large man with broad shoulders, gray hair cut military short and small hazel eyes. He wore an expensive suit, just as he wore his position. In Saddle Butte, Martin Shores was somebody.

"Your father warned me that you might be coming in," the man said.

"Interesting way to put it," Blaze said.

With a sigh, Martin sat forward, pulling his computer to him. He tapped on the keys for a moment and then looked up at her. "If you're concerned about your financial future should your father go to prison—"

"I take care of my own financial future," she said, feeling her hackles rise. "I'm not asking for myself. I want to know—"

The bank president continued as if she hadn't spoken. "Monte has made provisions for you including a reservoir of funds so you can keep running the ranch, should you so decide."

She waited not exactly patiently as he outlined the provisions her father had made for her to take over the ranch and run it. Was that really what Monte thought she would do if he went to prison? Was he that sure he was going to be behind bars for the rest of his life?

"Can we please cut to the chase?" she finally asked, interrupting the man. "Did my father send the bulk of his money to a foreign bank?"

Martin looked up and blinked. She saw the answer even on his professional poker face. She swore an oath under her breath. One minute it appeared that her father had accepted spending the rest of his life in prison. The next he'd made arrangements apparently to skip the country with Allie?

"You really should discuss your father's business with him directly or speak with his lawyer regarding his will," Martin said, closing his laptop and sitting back again.

She got to her feet. "I'll do that. In the meantime, I want a complete report of his finances. Please don't leave anything out." She saw the man's resistance. "Should I have attorney Clarkston Evans stop by to discuss it with you?"

The bank president was smart enough to know that she would sue him for the information if she had to. He nodded. "Shall I send it to the ranch?"

"Yes. Today." He started to argue, but she cut him off. "Please make the time." She leaned toward him, placing her palms on his large desk. "Has my father been a good customer over the years? I would think you'd want that same kind of relationship with me should my father go to prison and I decide to stick around. But there is another bank in town, isn't there? I wonder how the president of the bank over there would like my father's and my business."

"You're a lot like your father," Martin said.

"I'm going to take that as a compliment." Although it was clear that was definitely not the way he meant it.

She knew she wasn't up to facing her father right now. She felt too upset with him and feared he hadn't told her the truth about anything. Starting her SUV, she drove over to Thomas Franklin's office. It was on a side street near a residential area. Thomas had been her father's lawyer from as far back as she could remember. His name was still on the building, so she was hoping she might catch him as she pushed open the door and stepped inside.

The receptionist wasn't a day under eighty. A tiny woman with two spots of red rouge on her cheeks, she led Blaze back to Thomas's office. The elderly man behind the desk was gray and weathered, but his gaze was bright and alert.

"I wondered when I'd be seeing you," he said and motioned her into a chair as he told his secretary to pull Montgomery McClintock's file.

Blaze settled into the chair, glad she wasn't going to have to put up a fight here, as well.

"Would you like something to drink?" the attorney asked.

"No, thank you. I'm fine."

Thomas made small talk until the secretary brought in the file and left, closing the door behind her. Opening the file, he said, "I could read this to you and bore you to tears." He looked up. "What exactly is it you want to know?"

"I know he's made provisions for me to run the ranch. Martin Shores told me that. I'm assuming that you know Allie Anson is pregnant with his child." Thomas nodded. "He's made provisions for the child and Allie, as well." Another nod. "Is he planning to be with them?"

The attorney seemed surprised by the question. "If you're asking me whether or not he will go to prison—"

"I think he's planning to skip the country with Allie."

Thomas leaned back, studying her openly. "His will covers a lot. But as far as his plans for himself and his future…"

Blaze wondered what she'd hoped to accomplish here. She didn't know her father's mind any more than she had earlier and said as much.

"If I had to guess, I'd say your father was covering his bets no matter what happens," Thomas said and closed the folder.

Blaze thanked him and left. She couldn't wait to get back to the ranch. It was the one place now where she could get away for a while. But as she started toward her pickup, she saw Deputy LJ Fraser leaning against it. He had a toothpick sticking out one side of his grin.

From past experience, she knew from the look on his face that this wouldn't go well.

ALLIE LISTENED TO her landline ring again and again. She stared at the wall phone in the kitchen. It was the same one that had been there for years, according to Frank. She tried to drown out the ring, the same way she tried to drown out Frank's voice in the back of her mind. Years of listening to him say "Well, it was good enough for my mother" still rang in her ears.

When she couldn't take it any longer, she picked up the receiver, already knowing what she would hear. Heavy breathing before Hutch Durham's angry voice warning her that he was coming for her and she would pay, pay in ways she couldn't even imagine.

She slammed down the phone only to have it start ringing again. This time she answered but didn't listen. She disconnected and then took it off the hook. The receiver dangled from its cord, banging against the kitchen wall for a moment before it settled. Pulling out her cell phone, she called the phone company and asked that they send someone out to disconnect the landline.

"We have your order right here," a woman told her. "You're on our list."

"I'm getting crank calls. I really need the line disconnected." She hated that she sounded close to tears.

"Have you reported them?"

"Yes, but nothing's been done about it." The phone began to beep, sounding the alarm that it was off the hook.

"I'll see what I can do. In the meantime, you can just unplug it."

She had tried to disconnect the phone from the kitchen wall. Unfortunately, every time the kitchen had been painted over the years, the phone had gotten permanently sealed to the Sheetrock.

Allie hugged herself as she thanked the woman

and disconnected. She didn't want the landline. But at the same time, she feared if Hutch couldn't call, he'd come back out to the ranch. She glanced toward the back door. Now she kept the doors locked even in daylight.

But she wasn't sure how much more of this she could take.

"Pay Hutch off," Montgomery had advised her. "And if he comes out to the ranch again, call the sheriff."

She'd already called Bud and been told that there was nothing he could do unless she wanted to have him arrested for trespassing. She knew that would only make things worse since it probably wouldn't keep him in a jail for a night.

She hadn't wanted to worry Montgomery. He had enough to worry about as it was. "I'll take care of it," she'd assured him. That day she'd bought herself a baseball bat to keep by the back door. She had a shotgun by the front door and a loaded pistol in her purse. She didn't know what more she could do.

She could hear the incessant beeping of the phone telling her it was off the hook. Stepping to the back door, she picked up the baseball bat and swung it hard at the base of the phone.

The side of the case shattered, but the beeping didn't stop. She swung again. A large chunk of the plastic flew off. Another swing, another piece of plastic crumbled, this one connected to the cord. The receiver skidded across the floor, coming to rest in the doorway.

The beeping stopped. She stared at the receiver and began to laugh. All she'd had to do was unplug the receiver from the wall phone. It, too, had been painted over for so many years, she hadn't realized she could have pulled the plug a long time ago. Her laughter turned to tears as she leaned on the bat like a cane. She wondered if Frank was watching all of this from hell. That buoyed her.

Lifting the bat again, she sent the remaining piece of phone flying from the wall. "That was for your mother," she said as she replaced the bat by the back door and began to clean up the kitchen.

"IS THERE A PROBLEM, Deputy?" Blaze asked. The last thing she needed right now was a confrontation with her old high school boyfriend.

"I don't like the way you parked," LJ said, clearly looking for a fight.

Having known him so well, she could have predicted this simply by his grin. "Why, I'm so sorry, Officer. Let me move it." She started to step toward the driver's-side door, but he blocked her way.

"Not so fast. I'm going to have to write you a ticket."

"Write away," she said taking a step back. "Shall I go shopping while you do that? Or call my attorney?" She started to pull out her cell phone, but LJ knocked it out of her hand. It hit the ground and slid a few yards away.

She'd had about all she was going to take of him as he closed the distance between them. He grabbed her arm, looking around to make sure no one was watching. Because it was so close to the residential area, there wasn't anyone on the sidewalk.

"You think you can come back here and start giving my fiancée advice on me?" he demanded, getting into her face. "I guess you've forgotten what happens when you make me mad."

"No more than Tawny has forgotten what it's like being engaged to an immature bully," she said, returning his glare even as he tightened his hold on her arm enough to make her eyes water from the pain. "You going to beat me up on the street, Deputy? Because before you knocked my phone to the ground, I called the sheriff. I have your father on speed dial."

LJ's grip loosened as he looked from her to her phone lying in the skiff of snow covering the ground. He shoved her, slamming her against the pickup, as he started to reach for her cell phone.

But Jake got there first. He seemed to appear out of nowhere, catching them both by surprise. Jake snatched up the phone from the snow, handed it to her as he got in the deputy's face. "You ever lay a finger on her again and she will be the last woman you touch."

LJ started to say something about how he was an officer of the law, but Jake was ushering Blaze into the passenger side of her pickup. He pushed past LJ to climb behind the wheel. As if in a daze, she handed him her keys wordlessly.

As Jake pulled away, leaving the deputy muttering to himself and shooting daggers at them, she finally found her voice. "Where did you come from?"

Jake glanced over at her, looking surprised. "I've been keeping an eye on you since we got here. Sorry I didn't get to you sooner. Did he hurt you?"

She rubbed her arm. "No," she lied, half-afraid of what Jake might do to the deputy. She didn't need him in jail in addition to her father. "I thought you have a poker game."

"I do. Were you headed home?" She nodded. "Good, I'd appreciate it if you would stay there while I'm at the game. It could run late. If you change your mind, give me a call. Does your cell phone still work?"

She checked it. "The phone's fine."

He pulled up beside his pickup parked along the main drag and, shutting off the engine, looked over at her again. "How about you? Are you all right?"

"Fine. I could have handled him, you know."

Jake smiled. "I know."

"But thanks." She returned his smile.

"Anytime."

JAKE TOOK IN the other poker players seated at the table. He'd felt the tension in the air the moment he'd walked in. The first red flag was seeing that Herb Perkins wasn't at the table. But Hutch Durham was, along with Deputy LJ Fraser and three men he'd never met before.

Kirk, Bubba and Lou were big boys who looked as if they'd all played football, and not that many years ago. What they didn't play well was poker. Jake caught on right away when they appeared to not mind losing. He played along, taking their money with relish—including Hutch's and especially LJ's, even though he knew it would cost him in the end.

He wasn't stupid. He knew what was coming. As the afternoon wore on into night, Durham cashed in almost broke. When he left, the atmosphere quickly changed.

After several others ran out of money, including LJ and the man called Bubba, Jake picked up his winnings. He made a show of taking all the bills, rolling them into a ball and putting them into the right-hand side of his coat pocket. He could feel all eyes on him as he got up and went into the bathroom.

Once he closed the door and locked it, he looked around for what he needed. He found a discarded cardboard tissue holder, tore it down to size and then wrapped the small bills around it, covering it with a larger one, before sticking it back into his jacket pocket.

The rest of his winnings he hid in his boots before he flushed and came back out. He'd known they would jump him the moment they all stepped outside. What he hadn't expected was to see the deputy waiting patiently out in the cold.

He realized with a laugh that he should have, though, given their earlier confrontation. Of course LJ would demand satisfaction especially after losing all his money tonight.

Jake put the hurt on several of them, but as tough and trained as he was, he couldn't take on four men, especially when three of them were much younger.

They kicked the crap out of him. When Herb Perkins appeared at the back door, having come to lock up, they took the money from his coat pocket and ran, leaving him lying in the falling snow bleeding as they took off down the alley.

CHAPTER SEVENTEEN

"WHAT HAPPENED TO YOU?" Blaze cried when she saw Jake. She'd seen him drive up and had stepped out to watch him get out of his pickup. She'd had a bad feeling all night. Once she'd seen him holding his side as he limped toward her, she knew that her premonition had come true. "You're hurt!"

"I'm fine. Just a little dustup after the poker game."

"Dustup?" She drew him into the living room and into the light. Tears rushed to her eyes when she saw how badly he'd been beaten.

"Four guys jumped me." He shrugged but she saw him grimace in pain. He put a hand over his ribs. "They were a little rough, but I got in a few licks. A couple of them will be limping for a while. Your old boyfriend's nose won't ever be straight again." He laughed but she could tell it hurt him to do so. "He should have a black eye tomorrow."

"I'm taking you to the emergency room."

"No, you're not. I've had worse, trust me. I'm fine."

"Jake—"

"Please. I was hoping you wouldn't see me like this. Why aren't you watching one of your holiday movies?"

"I was worried about you and with good reason. Here, if you won't let me take you to the hospital, then sit down. I'll get the first-aid kit." She returned a few minutes later to see that he had leaned back against the chair where she'd left him. To her surprise, he was grinning.

She shook her head in both disgust and a reluctant respect for the man. "I'm guessing that you won a lot of money tonight."

His grin broadened, making his cut lip bleed. "I did. I fleeced them all."

"To what end?" she demanded as she began to clean up his wounds. "You had to know they were going to do this—and take back all the money you'd won." He nodded, still grinning. "What?"

"Pull off my boots, will you?"

She quit what she was doing to pull off one boot, then the other. As she did, money fluttered out onto the floor. She looked at it and then at him, shaking her head in wonder. "Why are you missing a sock?"

"I made a show of putting the roll of bills into my coat pocket, then I stopped at the bathroom before I left the building. I rolled the small ones around an empty cardboard toilet paper holder. Then I pulled off a boot, took off my sock and put all the change into it and tied it in a knot before hiding the large bills in my boots." He chuckled. "I suspected they would jump me. I'd been expecting three young cowboys wanting to kick my butt and rob me. Four made it a little too challenging."

She went back to cleaning his wounds. "You almost sound as if you enjoyed it."

"Sometimes you have to take your enjoyment where you find it."

Blaze met his gaze and let out a snort. "Seriously, you could have been killed."

He grabbed her hand, his fingers sliding up her wrist. His thumb made a circular motion against the tender skin there. She felt a current race along her veins even before he met her gaze and held it. "I wasn't."

She couldn't bear the thought that next time... "I don't want you looking into Frank Anson's death anymore. Next time—"

"You're worried about me?" He sounded surprised and amused.

She pulled her hand away and felt a sense of loss with him no longer touching her. "That's the best I can do," she said as she started to put the first-aid kit away. He grabbed her hand again to stop her.

"Admit it. You care about me. Come on, Blaze. It's just you and me here. Be honest."

She studied him for a long moment. "I don't like seeing you hurt."

"Is that all?"

"Jake—"

He looked down at her hand in his. "Why is it so hard for you to admit how you feel about me? I've told you repeatedly that I love you."

"You and I..." She didn't know how to finish. The passion had always been there. If anything it was stronger than she remembered it. "We're like oil and water. It would never work. I'm too headstrong and you're too…" She shook her head and started to pull away again, but he was on his feet, reaching out to draw her back.

"There's something we need to get straight," he said, his big hands cupping her shoulders. "I love how independent you are and I'm fine with letting you take the lead on just about everything. But," he said as he drew her closer and lowered his voice. The timbre of it echoed in the hollow of her chest, making goose bumps ripple across her skin. "Don't think for a minute that I won't rein you in to save your life. I might seem too easygoing to you, but, Blaze, I'm still a man. There are still times when I will run the show." He moved a hand to the back of her neck and pulled her to him, dropping his mouth to hers.

She put up a struggle but only long enough to assuage her pride. He backed her against the wall and, reaching down, lifted her skirt to trail his fingerprints up her thigh to her panties. She let out a gasp as he reached under the warm silk to touch her most intimate spot, making her shudder as her knees went weak.

She threw her head back to give him access to her throat as he nibbled his way down to the rise of her breasts, thumbing one button after another to reach an aching nipple. As his fingers moved under her skirt, he dropped his mouth to the hardened tip of her breast and sucked hard. She let out a cry of pure pleasure and pressed herself against him, desperately needing the release he promised.

Feeling him grimace in pain as she jarred his injured ribs, she was reminded that he was badly beaten. "Can you do this?" she asked.

He chuckled as he released her hard nipple from his mouth and raised his head. "I could make love to you on my deathbed. Never doubt that." He let go of her and stepped back. "My injuries aren't why we aren't making love tonight," he said as he walked back over to where he'd left his boots and began to pull them on.

Blaze had trouble catching her breath. Her body ached with need for him. She felt tears burn her eyes, tears of aching pain and anger. "Then what was that about a few moments ago?"

Jake met her gaze, his expression sad. "A moment of weakness. I do have them." He shook his head with obvious regret. "Hell, woman, can't you tell that I want you desperately?"

"Then stop pushing me away!"

"I could say the same to you. You want me but only to fill one need you have. I want all of you. You're either in all the way. Or you're not." He finished pulling on his boots, clearly the effort painful for him. "And do me a favor, don't throw anything at me this time as I leave. I'm not moving as quickly as I was the other night."

She opened her mouth, trying to find the words that would stop him as she desperately wanted to call him back. Telling herself that all she had to do was tell the truth. She *did* love him. He opened the door and, hesitating, looked back at her.

"Just say the words, Blaze. Three little simple words."

Her heart pounded. She wanted him as badly as her next breath. But what he wanted was more than a commitment. He wanted her to surrender to him, heart and soul. Opening herself up to Jake like that, exposing everything about herself to him… She closed her lips and watched him walk out. It wasn't until he'd closed the door that she burst into angry, frustrated, stubborn tears.

FIRST THING THE next morning, Sheriff Bud Fraser swore and threw the ballistics report down on this desk. He'd had the tests run three times—each with the same results. The gun Montgomery McClintock had been holding when found standing over Frank Anson's dead body wasn't the murder weapon. How was that even possible?

He'd been so sure. He'd thought he'd had him dead to rights. This should have been a slam dunk, especially since the man hadn't even tried to defend himself. Even when Blaze had brought in that fancy lawyer, Bud hadn't worried. He'd been so sure that Monte wouldn't get away with murder again.

Just the thought of Bethany McClintock made his chest ache. He swore that Monte had gotten away with killing his wife and now he was about to get away with Frank's murder, as well.

Picking up the ballistics report, he balled it up in

his hand and threw it into the trash. Not that it would do any good. The report would have been sent to the prosecutor. He was waiting for an angry visit from Dave. Worse, he knew what this meant. He didn't have enough evidence to hold Monte.

None of the other weapons taken from Monte's house were the murder weapon, either. He'd even gotten a warrant to have Frank's guns confiscated just in case Monte had used one of the man's own guns to kill him.

But the murder weapon hadn't been found.

Furthermore, Monte couldn't have fired the shot. The coroner said that given the lack of deformities with the slug found in the body, the .30 bullet had traveled some distance. Which meant that Frank wasn't shot by the man standing over him.

A .30 caliber bullet could have come from a lot of commonly used hunting rifles, much like the .300 savage he had at home that had belonged to his father. Monte owned several rifles that the bullet could have been fired from. Unfortunately, they weren't a ballistics match.

Which meant he was no closer to finding Frank's murderer than he had been the day he'd arrested Monte. Now he had several deputies out searching for shell casings on the road overlooking both the McClintock Ranch and the Anson place. The new theory was that the shot could have been fired from the county road.

A hard knock at his door was followed by the door swinging open as the prosecutor burst in.

"Have you seen this?" Dave demanded, waving the ballistics report in the air. Bud didn't have to see the paper to know what it was. "What were you thinking?"

He felt heat rush to his face. "You find a man standing over a dead body with a gun in his hand, and what are you going to think happened?"

"Maybe if you asked a few questions—"

"Monte refused to say anything. He just dropped his gun and stood there as he was handcuffed and taken in. Hell, how much more guilty could he have looked?"

"Quite a bit more had he actually shot the man," the prosecutor snapped. "If he'd actually committed the crime. If he was actually guilty." Dave stepped into the middle of the room, the ballistics report crushed in his hand.

From behind him in the doorway, attorney Clarkston Evans cleared his throat, making them turn. "So it appears that the pistol my client had on him wasn't the murder weapon. Nor were any of the other guns confiscated from his house. Am I correct?" The sheriff grunted. "So there is no evidence that my client shot Mr. Anson, correct?" He didn't wait for an answer. "I ask that my client be released at once."

Bud started to argue but the prosecutor cut him off. "Release the man. Now."

Bud stared down at his boots for a moment as he chewed at his cheek. "There's paperwork that needs to be filled out first. I can't see how he can be released before morning."

Dave glared at him. "Release him. Today."

Bud swore under his breath as the prosecutor turned to the attorney. "I'll give my apologies to Monte when I see him."

Clarkston nodded. "I'll go wait for my client to be released." He started to leave but turned back. "He'll need everything taken from his home to be returned in the condition it was in when taken, also."

"I'll see to it," Dave said and shot Bud a warning look. "Make it happen."

BLAZE COULDN'T BELIEVE it when she got the call from Clarkston just before noon. She'd spent the morning going over the papers Martin Shores had messengered to her early this morning. Also she'd wanted to make sure that Jake was all right. As angry as she'd been with him last night, she was worried that he was hurt much more than he'd wanted her to know.

She hadn't seen him all morning, but was determined not to make a point of checking on him, even though if she didn't see him soon, she was going out to the bunkhouse.

"They're letting him go?" She looked across the living room to where Jake had just come in the door. She grimaced at the sight of his battered handsome face and felt her own face warm at the memory of the two of them last night. Relief flooded her as she met his eyes. He was all right, moving a little awk-

wardly, but he would live, just as he said. He was watching her with interest.

"The ballistics test results cleared him," the criminal attorney was saying. "None of his weapons matched the one that killed Frank Anson."

She let out a breath. Just like that it was over? "You don't think they'll arrest him again?"

"I can't see why they would. The victim was shot with a rifle. Your father wasn't in possession of a rifle of that caliber at the time he was arrested, nor did any of his weapons match the slug taken from Mr. Anson's body. There is no other evidence against him."

"So it's really over." She met Jake's eyes and expected to see more surprise there. She still couldn't believe it. It seemed too good to be true. She'd believed that they would have to find Frank's killer to exonerate Monte.

"Your father is being released now."

"I'll drive in to pick him up."

"That won't be necessary," the lawyer said. "I'll give him a ride to the ranch. We can complete our transactions and then I plan to leave."

"Thank you." She disconnected and looked at Jake. She saw that he'd overheard enough to know what was going on. "The ballistics test results… They can't tie the shooting to him. The bullet came from a rifle and not one of my father's."

"So as it turned out, Monte would have been released even without the lawyer," Jake said.

"Didn't hurt to have Clarkston, trust me." Blaze

shook her head. "Look how they dragged their feet on releasing the results of the ballistics tests. He's been pushing for that report. They had to realize there was nothing more they could do to hold Monte. They must be quaking in their boots, worried that Monte will sue them for false arrest and imprisonment."

"I doubt that's what he has on his mind," Jake said.

She looked at him, realizing that she had no idea what her father might be thinking. "I guess there is nothing standing in his and Allie's way now. I just find it hard to believe that it's over." Also hard to believe that her father was about to have another child.

"Because it's not over," Jake said. "Frank Anson's killer is still out there."

She cocked her head at him, eyeing him closely. "What are you saying?"

"That I'm not finished."

"Jake—"

"Maybe this is something you don't know about me, but I finish what I start."

Blaze sighed, pretty sure he wasn't talking about Frank Anson anymore. "Not always," she said, remembering last night.

He smiled at that.

She didn't like the idea of him continuing to search for Frank's killer. Look what had happened last night. "I think you just like taking chances."

He grinned, though it seemed to hurt him. "Nothing wrong with taking a gamble if the stakes are high enough and winning means you get what you want more than anything."

She shook her head and walked into the kitchen, knowing that he wanted her to gamble on him. She didn't feel that lucky. "I still can't believe it," she said as she came out of the kitchen with two beers to celebrate. Maybe they would break out champagne later.

She handed Jake a beer. "WT was right. The sheriff *had* rushed to judgment, the animosity between them making Bud determined that Monte was guilty." She'd believed the same thing, she reminded herself as she curled up in a chair.

Now, as she took a sip of her cold beer, she felt weak with relief. She hadn't wanted to believe that her father could kill and yet... "The ballistics report saved him. No wonder it has taken so long. I'm sure the sheriff kept running the test, convinced Monte did it."

"Well, your father is free," Jake said as he took a seat. "I wonder what he'll do now, though."

She hadn't considered that. She'd just assumed he'd do what he had been doing for years, running the ranch, buffalo and all. She'd forgotten that things weren't the same now. "Allie's pregnancy. I suppose they'll get married."

"Nothing standing in their way. But will they stay here, though?"

She looked around the ranch house. When she'd come back, she'd wanted it to have changed. Now she couldn't conceive of this place not being the Mc-Clintock Ranch.

"I can't believe he'd sell out and leave," she said. "Where would he go? What would he do?" She remembered the papers she'd been studying just that morning and what Jake had said yesterday about passports. "You really believe that he'll skip the country now that he's been exonerated?"

"He hasn't been exonerated. They just don't have enough evidence to hold him," Jake said. "Do you really think the sheriff won't stop coming after him?"

She should have realized that. There would still be people who thought her father was guilty of the crime. And Jake was right. Bud would keep looking for something against her father. "I would imagine Monte could make enough money by selling the ranch that he could do whatever he wanted. If Allie's selling hers, too, I would think they'd be financially set."

Blaze looked around, suddenly feeling oddly nostalgic about the place. What had changed since she'd arrived? Some locals had tried to run her off after stampeding the buffalo. Some other fools had burned down one of the barns. It wasn't as if she'd had any ties to Saddle Butte or the ranch in years.

Even when she'd refused to come back to the ranch, she'd always known it would be here. Now that it might not be, she felt a sense of loss.

"You're right, I can't see any reason my father would want to stay here," she said after a moment.

"He's alienated most everyone. And with Frank's murder hanging over both of them…"

At the sound of a vehicle, they turned to see the attorney's rental car pull up. She rose, feeling anxious about seeing her father. Did he have a plan to leave the country with Allie as Jake suspected?

"I need to settle up with the lawyer," she said, glad that she had something to keep her busy as she headed for the door. It was over. That meant there was nothing keeping her here. Nothing keeping Jake here, either, but he was determined to stay until he found out who killed Frank.

She felt surprised by the rush of mixed emotions she felt. How could she leave until it was really over? But how could she stay?

THE SHERIFF SLAMMED his fist against his desk. Monte had walked right out of jail and there wasn't a damn thing Bud could do about it. He'd had him and now he had to let him go. Worse, his job hung in the balance because of the arrest. He knew he should go home, but he couldn't face an empty house right now.

He was actually glad when he heard LJ come in saying, "I figured I'd find you here. I heard. A hell of a deal."

Worse than his son knew. He turned as LJ slumped into a chair across from the desk. "What the hell happened to you?" he demanded, seeing his son's black eye, cut lip and bruised and skinned knuckles.

"Got into a fight last night. Nothing to worry about."

Bud added worrying about LJ to his long list and said as much.

His son waved it off. "Wait until you see Jake Horn."

The sheriff groaned. He'd told his son to stay clear of the McClintock Ranch and Blaze and her boyfriend. LJ just didn't listen sometimes. He wanted to yell at him, for all the good it would do. "Isn't it your day off? Shouldn't you be with your fiancée?"

LJ groaned. "We had a little disagreement. She's staying with her mom for a few days. I don't want to talk about it."

Bud swore under his breath. LJ was going to blow it with Tawny just as he had with the others. Maybe if his mother had stuck around to help raise him…

"You have to accept the fact that Monte might not have killed Frank," LJ said, changing the subject as he stretched out his long legs.

"Then who the hell did?" Bud asked as he got to his feet to pace the floor. It was all he'd been doing since getting the ballistics reports—cussing, fuming and pacing.

His son shrugged. "I'd put my money on Frank's wife. Everyone in town knew what was going on out there."

Except he couldn't put Monte in prison for adultery. "I still can't believe that none of his weapons matched the bullet Doc dug out of Frank. He had to have gotten rid of the weapon."

"Can't see how. Everett heard the shots, rode right over the hill to find him standing there. Anyway, didn't the coroner say the bullet was probably from a rifle? Where's he going to hide a rifle out there in the middle of the prairie?"

Bud glared at the back of his son's head. He'd heard all this from the prosecutor. He didn't need to hear it again from his son, who didn't seem to have the sense God gave him and was now making sense.

"I supposed someone could have shot him from the road," LJ was saying. "Have to be a pretty good shot, though. Kind of like shooting a deer. Could have laid the rifle over the hood of his vehicle."

He glanced at him. That was exactly what it appeared had happened. LJ worried him. He kept waiting for him to grow up. Maybe by the time he was forty. If he lived that long. If he stayed out of jail that long. "What was Monte doing that he was so close by when Frank was shot? That's what I'd like to know," Bud said.

His son rubbed the back of his neck. "You need to forget about Monte and find Frank's killer if you hope to get Dave and the county commissioners off your back."

This, as true as it was, wasn't something he wanted to hear, either. He didn't have any idea of who might have reason to kill Frank Anson other than Monte McClintock. He'd been so sure. He didn't need anyone to tell him that he'd been hoping it was Monte. That he'd been waiting for the day when he could lock him up. He hadn't been able to get justice for Bethany but at least he could have kept Monte from getting away with it again.

If only the ballistics on that bullet had matched the pistol in the man's hand.

He cursed as he paced. "It's bullshit," he said. "The man got away with murder once. Is it any wonder I thought he'd try to do it again?"

"Wait, who'd he kill?" LJ asked, that lazy look clearing off his face.

Bud stopped pacing. He was sure he'd mentioned his suspicion to his son before. "I know damned well he killed his wife."

"Seriously?" LJ said, sitting up.

"She leaves presumably in the middle of the night and is never heard from again?" Bud shook his head. "No way is she alive. After all this time she would have turned up. Damn fine-looking woman, too. Sweet, not like her daughter, who might have gotten her mother's looks, but she's her old man through and through."

"If he killed her, what did he do with her body?" LJ asked, interested now.

Bud had given it thought over the years. "His daughter was sixteen at the time and living in the house. I would assume he would have had to bury Bethany on the property."

LJ scratched his neck in obvious thought. "He's got a lot of acreage. Can't imagine her body would ever be found. But what about her car? What did he do with that?"

"That's a damn good question. Supposedly she packed her bags and left in it. You're right, he would have had to get rid of her car. Couldn't go far or he would have been seen driving it."

LJ was sitting on the edge of his seat now, excited. "If we could find her car then we'd have him."

"It hasn't turned up in sixteen years," Bud said. "So if it is still around, it's hidden well. Or he found a way to get rid of it where it would never be found. Every rancher has a backhoe. It could be anywhere, even buried behind his barn for all we know."

"Has anyone ever looked for it?" LJ asked.

Bud stared at him. "Not that I know of. Everyone seems to have accepted Monte's story that she packed up and left to start a new life. Maybe got herself a new name, even a new man."

"And was never heard from again? I find that hard to believe. I remember when Blaze and I were dating, she said her mother had promised to come back for her once she got settled."

Bud had stopped pacing. He'd had to let Monte walk on the Anson killing, but if he could get him on Bethany's... There might just be a way to get justice after all. He slapped his son on the back as he walked past to his desk, took his chair and leaned back to consider what it might take to find the car. "Get me a topographical map of the area around the McClintock Ranch."

CHAPTER EIGHTEEN

As CLARKSTON EVANS climbed out of the rental car in front of the ranch house, Jake watched for Monte to get out of the passenger side. He wondered what was going through the rancher's mind. Had he known this was how it would all shake out? What was the attempt to plead guilty all about, then?

Jake couldn't help feeling suspicious of Monte's motivations. If he hadn't wanted Blaze involved, then he wouldn't have given her his power of attorney. He had to know that she wouldn't let him plead guilty to something he didn't do. Just as he had to know she'd hire the best criminal attorney she could find.

Even if Monte had known he would get off, they still had no idea who had killed Frank. Blaze's theory that her father had been covering for someone had seemed the most credible. If Monte thought Allie had killed Frank then he would have tried to protect the woman who was carrying his child.

But Allie had an alibi. She'd been seen in town that morning. But Jake knew that she could have easily returned and fired the shot from the road and then left again to return only when the sheriff was arresting Monte. He didn't believe she was guilty of her husband's murder, though. Then again, he'd been surprised before.

He watched Blaze hug her father. Jake had stayed inside, hanging back to let her have the reunion without him. What would happen now that Monte was free? Blaze had seemed upset when he'd told her that her father might sell the ranch and leave with Allie. Clearly she'd assumed the ranch would always be here should she ever want to return. The thought gave him hope that the woman might someday consider settling down.

He watched Blaze and her father talk for a moment before Monte headed for his pickup. Was that disappointment he saw on her face? Or worry? As Blaze came into the house with Clarkston, he could see that she was now all business as she went to her father's office to cut the lawyer a check.

Jake followed her. "Where's your father off to?"

"He's going over to see Allie," she said without looking up from what she was doing. He watched her make out the check. As she rose, she avoided his gaze. She didn't want him to see that anything was wrong, he thought. Didn't she realize that he knew her inside and out?

Back in the living room, the lawyer shook their hands, said if they needed any more help to call and left.

Blaze stood, watching him go. "I suppose I should call WT."

"Or we could talk," Jake suggested.

She avoided his gaze as she pulled out her cell

phone. "It's Blaze," he heard her say into the phone as she walked back down the hall away from him.

WHEN LJ RETURNED to his office with the map, Bud took a piece of string. Estimating a fifty-mile radius, he drew a circle around the McClintock Ranch.

"You think that's where we'll find the car?" LJ asked, studying the area within the circle.

"I figure he couldn't have gone far or he would have been seen driving her car, so yes, that's what I suspect," Bud said. Now that he was looking at the area, though, he realized how difficult it was going to be since to the south were the Missouri Breaks, miles and miles of deep ravines, stands of dense pines, ponds, not to mention the muddy Missouri River itself. He said as much to his son.

"Then there are the old buildings on those abandoned homesteads." It was no wonder her car had never been found, he thought as he looked at the map and felt discouraged.

"No way could we search all that," LJ agreed. "Unless we did it from the air."

Bud looked up at his son. Yes, sometimes LJ amazed him. "From the air. The sheriff's department does have a plane and I doubt anyone ever looked for the car."

His son's eyes lit. "You know what it means if we find it."

He nodded solemnly. "It means I'm right and Bethany McClintock is dead and Monte will be behind bars again soon." Then it would be just a matter of keeping him there.

JAKE COULD HEAR Blaze on the phone with the judge, but not what she was saying. He realized that she thought it was all over. It wouldn't be over until Frank's killer was caught, he told himself. It had nothing to do with him wanting to stay until he finished what he'd started—not just with this case but with Blaze.

For all he knew the woman might leave now. Hell, she might be gone when he returned. He had to take that chance, he told himself. He started for his pickup when he realized that she would think he'd packed up and left.

Back in the living room, he left her a note telling her where he had gone and why. He stuck it on the refrigerator since she was still on the phone. He was sure that WT had a lot of questions. He wasn't the only one.

Once behind the wheel, he headed for town. He was moving slow this morning. Nothing was broken but his ribs were definitely bruised along with a lot of other parts of him. He glanced in the rearview mirror. His cut lip had started to bleed again and he had one hell of a black eye. He couldn't help but smile, wondering what LJ looked like today, not to mention some of the others.

This morning while he'd let his body recuperate, he'd done some research on his phone. Local boy Lonny Dean had dated Sandra Westlake throughout high school and college. They'd married after graduation and moved back to Saddle Butte. Sandra helped out at the church and Lonny managed the stockyard.

He found Lonny in the stockyard office. A small-framed man with brown eyes and brown thinning hair, Lonny looked up, startled to see Jake standing in his office doorway. He pushed his paperwork aside and got to his feet. Frowning, he asked, "Can I help you?"

"I'm Jake Horn—"

"I know who you are. What do you want?"

"I need to ask you a few questions. About Frank."

Lonny motioned for him to close the door even though the place appeared to be empty except for the two of them. "I have nothing to say on this subject."

"You must have been angry when Frank told your wife—"

"Look, it's apparent that someone has already beaten you up," Lonny interrupted. "I abhor violence, but if you continue butting in where you have no business and upset my wife—"

"I'm just trying to find out who killed Frank Anson," Jake said, holding up his hands.

"Well, you're looking in the wrong place."

"Abhorring violence or not, you must have been upset when Frank told your wife that he was her biological father."

Lonny looked at the floor, his jaw working. "I was very upset, yes. But not enough to kill him, if that is what you're suggesting."

"What about your wife?"

"Clearly, you've never met Sandra and if I have my way, you never will." The man took a step around his desk toward him. "Sandra is the sweetest, gentlest person you could ever meet. She won't even kill a spider. She scoops them up and takes them outside." The man's voice broke. "She wouldn't kill anyone. Not ever."

Jake could have argued that even the most sweet and gentle person could be pushed into violence, but he held his tongue. "Do you know who Sandra's birth mother is?"

Lonny blinked as if that was the last thing he'd expected Jake to ask. "I have no idea. But surely, you can't think—"

"Someone killed Frank."

"Monte McClintock."

Jake shook his head. "He was released from jail hours ago. None of Monte's guns were the murder weapon. Frank was believed shot with a rifle from the road. Monte was standing only yards away when Frank was shot. He didn't do it."

Lonny looked even more upset. A streak of red climbed his neck. He reached up to loosen the collar of his shirt. He looked more worried than Jake thought he should since the man and his wife were innocent. "I was so sure…"

"Yes, apparently so was the sheriff. Do you own a rifle, Lonny?"

"No. I wouldn't have guns in my house."

That surprised him. "But it wouldn't be hard for you to get your hands on a hunting rifle in this town."

"I told you. I didn't kill Frank."

"I would imagine your father-in-law was quite upset with Frank, as well," Jake said.

The man groaned. "Pastor Westlake?" He laughed. "You can't be serious?"

Jake was studying him. "Who is Sandra's biological mother?"

"I don't know. Even if I knew—"

"Oh, I think you know. It's a small town. She had to hate Frank more than any of the rest of you. And why would Frank tell your wife that he was her father without telling her who her birth mother had been? I just want to talk to the woman. Or I can ask your wife."

Lonny's face turned scarlet as his hands balled into fists. Jake no longer believed that the man couldn't kill or that he wouldn't use a gun when it suited his purposes. He glanced toward his desk as if looking for something he could use as a weapon before taking a threatening step toward Jake. "I forbid you to speak to my wife."

Holding up his hands again, Jake took a step back. He didn't want to fight this man. Not that he couldn't take him. He didn't want to fight anyone at least for a few days until he was healed up from his last fight. "The birth mother's name. Let's start there. The last thing I want to do is upset your wife, okay?"

THE SHERIFF FELT better after he'd taken the map and, sending his son home telling him to make up with his fiancée, headed for his own house. He told himself that Bethany McClintock's car was out there. That it could be found. That somehow he would do it.

But even as he thought it, he realized how long it might take. That was if he didn't run into trouble for using the sheriff's department plane. There was another problem, as well. He'd gotten an anonymous call at his office from someone who claimed that Allie Anson was pregnant with Monte's child.

He hadn't been surprised. But he wondered what Monte and Allie would do now that the rancher was out of jail. He'd heard that Allie had already checked with a Realtor about selling Frank's ranch. That, too, wasn't a surprise. But with Monte out of the jail, would they stay? Or put both ranches up for sale.

Worst-case scenario, they might decide to leave the state. Maybe even the country. If that happened, he'd play hell getting Monte back into custody unless he could find Bethany's car. Once they started looking for the vehicle, word would get out. If Monte McClintock were as guilty as he suspected, the man would run. Bud realized he would have to move fast.

Almost home, he took a quick right. He knew it was a long shot, but there was one judge in town who might give him the warrant he needed. While Bethany's car could be anywhere, he suspected her body was closer to home. If he could get a warrant to search the ranch property, maybe bring in some cadaver dogs…

He pulled up in front of the house, got out and hurried to the door. He found Judge Alfred Green watching television and, after apologizing for stopping by so late, got right to it.

"Let me get this straight," the judge said after Bud had pled his case. "You already had the man in jail. You had a warrant to take all of McClintock's firearms and came up empty."

Bud knew what was coming and rubbed a hand over his face. "None of the weapons matched the slug taken from Frank Anson's body," he said even though he was sure that Alfred had already heard. News traveled fast in this county, especially bad news. "But I'm convinced he killed his wife."

"I see. And now you want another warrant to go on a fishing exhibition after arresting the wrong man. On top of that, you have no evidence at all that, number one—" the judge ticked them off on his fingers "—Bethany McClintock is even dead. Two, that she is buried on the McClintock property. And three, that a crime was even committed."

"I know it in my gut."

The judge grunted.

Bud picked his Stetson off his knee, where he'd been balancing it, and lumbered to his feet. "Sorry to have bothered you, Judge." He started for the door.

"Evidence, Sheriff. Bring me some evidence and I'd be happy to help you put that son of a bitch behind bars."

Bud stopped to look back at the man in surprise. "You believe me?"

"That he killed his wife? I've never been a betting man, but I'd wager McClintock is guilty as hell of something. Did he kill his wife?" Alfred shrugged. "Evidence, Bud." With that, the judge went back to watching the news.

BLAZE FINISHED HER phone call with WT and came back to the living room to find Jake gone. She felt her heart drop before she saw the note he'd left her on the front of the refrigerator. Pulling it off, she read his neat left-handed script and swore.

What was he doing? It was over. He was doing what he said he was going to do. The man wouldn't quit until he'd found Frank Anson's killer.

Shaking her head, she told herself she wasn't sticking around. Her father was out of jail. Clarkston didn't think any more charges would be coming. That meant her job here was done. Monte and Allie would probably be getting married. She doubted it would be a big wedding, and she wasn't even sure she'd be back for it.

She had to admit, she'd been a little hurt when her father had left so quickly earlier. She'd hoped that they could put the past behind them. Even the thought surprised her since she hadn't admitted that she wanted to until this moment. She wanted to mend things between them. Once she did that, she could leave here no matter what happened next.

Blaze understood that he was anxious to get to the woman who was carrying his child. His other child. She felt a stab of jealousy. This child would have a mother and a father.

Feeling at loose ends, she was glad when her cell

phone rang. She thought it would be Jake. She hated the way things were between them. But those burned bridges weren't that easy to repair. And now he was still trying to find Frank's killer. Wasn't it enough that he'd gotten beaten up last night? Was he trying to get himself killed?

She checked her phone and saw with disappointment that it wasn't Jake. Her pulse did a little bump, though, when she saw the name on the screen. Sandra Dean, the pastor's daughter?

"Hello?" she said into the phone, wondering why the woman would be calling her.

"I thought we should meet," Sandra said without preamble. She was soft-spoken, sounding very calm. Too calm?

"Maybe you haven't heard, but my father has been released from jail. I'm no longer looking into Frank's murder."

"Are you familiar with the River View?"

The restaurant was at the local golf course. It still amazed Blaze that a tiny Western town without even a stoplight had a golf course.

"Is thirty minutes too soon for you?" Sandra asked as if Blaze had agreed to the meeting.

She had to admit, she was curious why the woman was so insistent. "Thirty minutes is no problem. I drive fast."

CHAPTER NINETEEN

JAKE RECOGNIZED THE name at once. He stared at Lonny Dean for a moment before he repeated the name. "Luella Brown is Sandra's mother?" The waitress at the local café who'd visited Monte in jail and told Blaze it was because he'd asked her to bring him some decent food? Or had the woman lied about her reasons for visiting him in jail?

"Why can't you leave this alone?" Lonny demanded. His face had turned scarlet, his knuckles white as he gripped his hands in fists.

"Because a man is dead."

"A man who deserved to die," Lonny spit. "I'm sure you know what he did to my wife. Do you care about that?"

"I'm sorry she had to find out the way she did," Jake said. "Did you or your wife contact Luella after you learned the truth?"

Lonny moved back to his desk, pulled out his chair and dropped into it. Jake watched him try to control his anger. "No, we didn't contact her. It was already traumatic enough for Sandra to find out who her parents were. Not that we have anything against Luella."

"Except for the fact that she left Sandra on the church doorstep right after she was born," Jake said.

"Clearly, she was desperate and as it was, it was a blessing for Sandra. Wilber and Emma Jean are the kind of parents we all wish we'd had." Lonny seemed to realize what he'd said. "Not that mine weren't fine." He raked a hand through his thinning hair and looked distraught. "All this is so upsetting. You must understand that. Finding out what your true genetic makeup really is when you're pregnant."

Jake wondered if Sandra had been more upset than her husband. "So Luella has never tried to contact you?"

The man shook his head. "We thought it was best to just let everything calm down."

"And then Frank was murdered." Jake didn't know how much he believed of what the man had told him. Maybe they hadn't reached out to Luella. Maybe they never would. "Thank you for the information." He started to leave when Lonny rose again and grabbed his arm to stop him. His grip was iron-like. This was not a gentle man.

"You won't bother Sandra, promise me."

Jake pried the man's fingers from his arm. "I can't do that. But I don't want to cause her any more stress than she's already gone through."

Anger made the man's next words come out with spittle. "You'll be sorry if you go near my wife."

"That sounds like a threat, Lonny. It makes me wonder if you threatened Frank, as well. For a non-violent man, you seem dangerous to me."

THE RIVER VIEW was a small restaurant overlooking the river and the golf course. With it being winter, the course was covered with snow. Steam rose up from the river and into the cold, blue, wintery day.

Sandra was waiting for her at a table by the window. The place was empty except for the bartender and what sounded like the cook banging around back in the kitchen. Blaze figured Sandra had some pull to get them a table this early. She hadn't even had breakfast, so she could use a good meal—if that was what Sandra had in mind.

Her first impression of the woman was of elegance. Sandra was tall and blonde with a regal air about her. She was dressed like a woman of privilege and good upbringing. While Blaze was wearing jeans and a winter sweater, Sandra wore a wool dress and knee-high boots. A colorful scarf graced her slim neck. The blue in the scarf matched her eyes perfectly and Blaze suspected the woman knew it.

Sandra extended one manicured hand. A thin gold bracelet tinkled faintly from her wrist as Blaze took her firm hand.

"Lunch was a nice idea," Blaze said, wondering what the woman was really up to. She hated that she was always suspicious, but it did come with the job.

"Please join me," Sandra said motioning to the chair opposite her.

Shrugging out of her winter coat, Blaze took a seat. A waitress appeared at once and took her coat. She ordered coffee with cream and sugar. Sandra said she'd take the same, only black, before she opened her menu.

By the time the waitress returned with their coffees, they were both ready to order. Sandra opted for a salad, no surprise there.

"I'll take the burger and fries," Blaze said, not to be intimidated. "Make it a cheeseburger, loaded." She handed off the menu and added, "I'm starved. I didn't have breakfast."

Her companion said nothing, picking up her cup and sipping her coffee.

"I'm curious why you wanted to see me," Blaze said after stirring cream and sugar into hers.

"I thought I would beat you to it so we could meet at my convenience and on my…"

"Turf, so to speak?"

The woman nodded with a faint unamused smile. "I don't want you to misconstrue why I invited you here."

"For lunch." She smiled but got no reaction from the woman, so she added, "I'm assuming it was to try to convince me that you didn't kill your father."

"If you're referring to Frank Anson, he isn't my father. He was merely a sperm donor, so to speak," Sandra said.

"Okay, but I'm sure it must have been a shock to find out that Frank Anson was your…biological father."

The woman looked as she was going to correct her again, but either gave up or thought better of it.

"It was a shock. I'll admit it. I'd always wondered who my biological parents were."

"You never asked?"

She shook her head. "You know my parents. It was clear to me that they would have told me if they had wanted me to know."

Blaze studied her, looking for cracks in her perfectly made-up exterior. Had this woman never gone through rebellious teenage years when she might have demanded to know the truth? "I'm surprised you weren't curious."

Sandra shrugged slightly. "I had won the jackpot, so to speak, by getting the adoptive parents I had."

"You must have been furious at Frank for trying to blackmail your seemingly perfect parents."

Sandra tilted her head and gave her a triumphant smile. "I don't have extremes of emotion such as fury. So if you're hoping that I became unhinged and killed the man, you're sadly mistaken. I'm sorry to ruin your theory."

Her manner was calm as she spoke. Blaze also thought that it wouldn't take much to misconstrue her tone as someone who was talking down to her. She said as much to the woman.

Just then, Sandra's cell phone, lying next to her coffee cup, pinged. She looked down at the text she'd just received and picked up the phone. "It's my husband. Apparently he's upset because your boyfriend paid him a visit." She pocketed the phone. "I'd answer it, but he'd be worried that I was meeting with you."

"Then I suggest you not tell him."

Sandra gave her a weak, sympathetic smile. "We don't keep secrets."

"No? You didn't tell him beforehand that you were going to ask me to lunch."

All sweetness had left the woman's face. "Because if I had, he would be bursting in here right now to save me from you."

The waitress appeared with their food. Blaze wasn't going to let this woman ruin her appetite. She dumped ketchup on her burger and took a bite. It was delicious, and the french fries were hot and crispy on the outside and soft inside. Sandra picked at her salad.

"So you're pregnant," Blaze said between mouthfuls.

"Yes." Sandra's hand went to her stomach. It reminded Blaze of when Allie had done the same thing. It gave her a strange feeling, almost a longing to belong to a club she'd never given a thought to before.

She ate in silence for a while. "When are you due?"

"June."

"Boy? Girl?"

"Boy."

Blaze put down her half-eaten burger and pushed her plate away. "Are you curious at all as to who killed Frank?"

Sandra lifted her chin slightly. "Not at all."

"So you aren't worried that it was your husband, who, according to you, would have been bursting in here right now if he'd known about this...lunch."

For the first time, color stained the woman's cheeks. Was that a crack in the woman's impeccable veneer?

"It was more of a figure of speech."

"I highly doubt that."

Sandra put down her fork, no longer pretending to eat her salad. "You don't know me, and you certainly don't know Lonny."

"Do you?"

The woman tossed down her napkin and signaled for the bill.

"You seem scared to me," Blaze said as she watched Sandra's right eye twitch. "For your sake and your child's, I hope you have nothing to fear."

Sandra quickly paid the bill.

"Thank you for lunch," Blaze said as they both rose to leave. "If you ever need to talk to someone…"

The woman shot her a look as if to say Blaze would be the last person on earth that she would call. Then Sandra flounced out, grabbing her coat from the waitress as she left.

JAKE STOPPED BY the local café only to find out that Luella had left for the day. On his phone, he'd found out what he could about her. The newspaper had done a story on her. Her father had advised her to get a good job and keep it. She'd gone to work at the café at fifteen and had been there ever since. From her Facebook page, he gathered that she'd been married and divorced twice. She had been living with a man until recently.

He drove by her address to see that her older-model sedan was parked next to a small house that needed a good coat of paint. Pulling out his cell phone, he called Blaze.

"Where are you?"

"I was just leaving the River View. Why?"

He filled her in on what he'd learned and listened as she told him about Sandra's call and their lunch. "Do you believe she didn't know?"

"I'm not sure. She's one cold fish and it sounds like her husband is a hothead."

"That was my impression, too," Jake said. "He seemed under a lot of stress. But I can understand wanting to protect the person you love."

"And now there's the baby. It's a boy, by the way."

"I've pulled over down the street from Luella's. I thought we might want to do this together." He read off the woman's address.

"I'm on my way."

It didn't take her long. Once he saw her rig pull in next to the curb in front of Luella's, he swung around and went back. "How was lunch?" he asked as she got out of her pickup. Food was a subject they'd never argued over since they both loved to eat.

"You should try the burgers and fries at the River View." She kissed her fingers, making him laugh.

"You smell like fries," he said as they walked up the broken sidewalk to Luella's front door. "I like it."

She grinned over at him as if, like him, she felt it was nice to be on the same page—at least on some things.

Luella answered on the third knock. She came to the door still dressed in her waitress uniform, but she'd kicked off her white nursing shoes. She looked from him to Blaze and back for a moment. "If this is about Monte…"

"It's about Frank and your daughter," Jake said.

The older woman seemed to take his words like a gust of wind. She swayed a little before stepping aside to let them in.

The house was neat and clean and would have looked lived-in twenty years ago. Now it appeared dilapidated and as tired as Luella appeared. In her midfifties, she'd been working on her feet for more than forty years.

"I don't believe we've met," Jake said and introduced himself. "You've already met Blaze."

Luella nodded and motioned for them to sit. She lowered herself into a ragged recliner. He and Blaze sat down on the blanket covering the couch. He felt a broken spring and had to shift over a little.

The older woman didn't say anything for a few moments. She reached a hand up to brush back a lock of hair, looking embarrassed. Letting out a hoarse little laugh, she said, "You're probably wondering what I ever saw in Frank. This might surprise you, but back in the day, he was quite cute and charming. He had a way with women. He was actually very funny at times." She shook her head as if even she couldn't believe it.

"You've watched Sandra grow up," Blaze said.

The woman nodded vacantly. "You never approached her or her family with the truth?"

"Why would I do that? I gave her up so she could have a good life, and she has." Luella pursed her lips and rocked a little in the recliner.

"Did the Westlakes know about you?" Jake asked.

"You'd have to ask them. I certainly never said anything."

"Sandra said she didn't know about either you or Frank before the night he tried to blackmail the pastor," Blaze said.

Something flickered in Luella's old eyes. "Frank could be a bastard. I'm so sorry he did that. I was happy watching Sandra from a distance." She smiled. "She would come into the café sometimes. She always left me a large tip, so I thought maybe she knew." The woman shrugged. "She never said anything."

"You know she's pregnant," Blaze said and the woman nodded, those eyes filling with tears.

"You must have been upset when Frank told Sandra the truth."

Luella wiped at her tears, her gaze filling with a fire that hadn't been there moments before. "What do you want me to say? That I could have killed him for doing that? Damn him to hell. Don't look so surprised. It wasn't the first time I wanted to kill him. I was fifteen and pregnant when he dumped me. My mother had kicked me out. My father's only advice was to get a job. I had no money, nowhere to go. If Patsy down at the café hadn't taken pity on me…"

"You own a gun, Luella?" Jake asked.

The woman laughed, exposing missing teeth. "You can search my house, if you like. If I had a gun, I would have pawned it years ago. Or one of my no-account husbands or boyfriends would have."

"What kind of relationship did you have with Frank?" he asked.

Luella looked at him askance. "*Relationship?* Weren't you just listening? I hadn't talked to that man in almost forty years."

"Surely he came into the café," Blaze said.

"That cheap bastard?" The woman scoffed. "He avoided me and I avoided him."

"You must have been furious when he brought home a young wife," Jake said.

"Allie?" Luella shook her head. "That poor woman. All I felt for her was pity. Everyone did. Frank had become someone no one liked. Probably from living all those years with that awful mother of his. I wasn't surprised someone shot him."

Jake looked over at Blaze and saw that she, too, was inclined to believe the woman. "So if you had to pick someone, who would you say wanted him dead the most?"

Luella chuckled and then seemed to give that some thought.

He named off the suspects. With each she shook her head. "What about Sandra's husband, Lonny Dean?" He caught her reaction and the quick way she tried to hide it.

"I'm not that wild about him, but if Sandra likes him…"

"You think he's capable of murder?" Blaze asked.

She shook her head. "I don't take him for a shooter. That is how Frank died, right? Someone shot him? At least that's what I heard."

"Then who?" Jake prodded.

"There's another possibility," the woman said slowly, looking away. He could tell that she was deciding whether or not to tell them. With a sigh, she said, "I've kept this secret long enough. I wasn't the only one Frank got in a family way back then. Like I said, he was a charmer." She seemed lost in the past for a moment before her gaze came back to them. "The difference is the other woman was engaged to someone else at the time. Her fiancé apparently has always thought the child was his."

"Who was the other woman?" Blaze asked.

"Lorna Cutter."

Jake frowned and looked over at Blaze to see if the name meant anything to her.

"Lorna Cutter?" she asked as if trying to place the name.

"Well, that was her name before she married Bud Fraser."

Blaze let out a gasp. "Are you telling me that LJ is Frank's son?" Her gaze shot to Jake before returning to Luella. "Are you sure about this?"

"It's the best-kept secret in Saddle Butte," Luella said. "Because Frank wasn't about to tell. Bud's father, the sheriff back then, would have killed him.

And Lorna wasn't saying a word. But I knew. I'd known that Frank was cheating on me. I just didn't know he'd gotten her pregnant not long after he did me. Lorna had been holding off poor Bud until after that fancy wedding she was planning. Told everyone that she'd gotten pregnant on their honeymoon to Yellowstone Park. No big surprise when the baby came early. So if you're looking for someone who just might have hated Frank more than me, don't overlook your former boyfriend LJ Fraser and his clueless daddy."

"Wait, are you saying that LJ knows?" Blaze asked.

"It crossed my mind when I heard that Frank had been shot," Luella said slowly. "If Frank was desperate enough to try to blackmail the Westlakes, the damned fool might have gone to the sheriff or his son."

BLAZE FELT SHAKEN as she left Luella's. "I'll meet you back at the ranch?" Jake nodded, his expression unreadable. "You aren't going to—"

"Confront the sheriff or his son?" He shook his head. "But this definitely adds a new dimension to Frank's murder."

As she drove out of town, she couldn't shake the feeling that Luella might have just given them the connection they needed. It would explain why the sheriff had been so determined to send her father to prison for Frank's murder. But was he covering for himself or his son?

She thought about LJ. He'd been older, wilder, just her type back then. It hadn't hurt that he'd been a star athlete at their small high school, playing both football and basketball. He'd had some natural ability that his coaches said could have sent him far. But he'd opted to stay in Saddle Butte, where he was a big fish in a small pond.

LJ was violent enough to kill, she had no doubt about that. But if he'd killed Frank, it would have been an impulsive thing. Seeing Frank from the road, she could imagine LJ pulling out his rifle, the one that always hung on the rack in the back window of his pickup, and firing. LJ was a pretty decent shot if you believed his Facebook posts with dead animals.

Then again, there was his father. Bud always had a chip on his shoulder when it came to anyone who inherited land. With Monte being one of the largest landowners in the county, he'd especially been a target of that wrath. She'd overheard him one time at the coffee shop saying he could have made something of himself if his daddy left him a few thousand acres.

But his bias against those who were born into land wouldn't have been why he'd want Frank Anson dead. If Luella was telling the truth, which Blaze suspected she was, then LJ was Frank's son—not Bud's. That would be reason enough for Bud to take out the man—especially if he'd heard about Frank going to the Westlakes and feared Frank might tell LJ out of spite. Because Frank would have known that Bud and his son didn't have any money. He might also have been worried about trying to blackmail a sheriff.

As she pulled into the ranch yard, Jake parked next to her. They exited their rigs and hurried into the ranch house out of the cold.

"If what she told us is true…" Blaze said as she took off her coat and hung it up in the closet by the door.

"LJ is Frank's son. We just don't know if Frank went to the sheriff or LJ after his plan to blackmail the Westlakes failed."

"Or if Bud had just heard what Frank did and wasn't about to let the man shoot off his mouth to the rest of the town. I can see Bud killing him."

"I'd put my money on LJ," Jake said, rubbing his swollen jaw. "That man has a lot of pent-up anger."

"You didn't tell me he was one of the men who attacked you after the poker game." Jake said nothing. "What are we going to do?"

He started to answer when she saw him cock his head. "Do you hear that?"

She listened. "That buzzing sound?"

JAKE STEPPED OUT to see a plane flying low over the ranch. He recognized the logo on the side. It was a sheriff's department single-engine one. He watched it barely clear the barn and then follow the fence line toward the Little Rockies.

"I wonder what that's about," Blaze said, appearing beside him. Jake shook his head. Whatever it was, he doubted it was good.

"Maybe the sheriff just wanted to let your dad know that he's still around."

"Still, it seems odd," she said as she hugged herself against the cold before going back inside.

Jake watched the plane bank in the clear, icy blue winter sky and head back their way, flying even lower over the pasture. He had a bad feeling in his gut. What were they looking for from the air?

Another sound caught his attention as Monte drove up in his pickup. Allie sat on the passenger side. Jake waved, then headed for the bunkhouse to give the three of them time alone.

At the bunkhouse, though, he turned to look back. Monte had stopped on his way to the house. He was watching the plane making another pass over the ranch. His expression was dark and foreboding, making that bad feeling in Jake's gut worsen before Monte ushered Allie inside.

BLAZE WENT INSIDE to see Allie looking pale. Her father didn't look all that chipper, either. The sheriff's plan to harass them seemed to be working. Bud wanted to drive her father and Allie away. She feared Jake might be right and the two might leave the country.

"I'm sorry," Allie said. "Would you mind if I lie down for a few minutes?"

Monte stepped to her, taking her hand in his. "Are you all right?" The concern in his voice pricked at Blaze's jealousy.

"I'm just a little tired," Allie said quickly. "It's nothing. Stop being such a worrywart. Stay here and visit with your daughter. I'll be fine after just a short nap."

Blaze watched the woman go down the hall to her father's room and disappear inside. She turned to her father. "She's right. We haven't had a minute together since you got out."

Monte turned to her. "I'm sorry about that. I've been worried about Allie and the pregnancy. But I've also been worried about you. Now that I'm out, there is no reason for you to stay here." His words hurt. He seemed to realize it and quickly stepped to her to place his big hands on her shoulders. "It isn't that I don't love your being here. I've missed you so much. I never thought anything could get you back here."

She hated to admit that if WT hadn't called and asked her to come, she wouldn't have. "I need to be honest with you. Do you mind if we sit down?"

He nodded and took a chair. She sat across from him. "I need to know what happened with you and my mother."

Her father suddenly looked ten years older. "I blame myself. I knew your mother wanted to leave Saddle Butte. She was raised on a ranch outside town. Her father was a ranch manager. She wanted to do something more with her life than be the wife of a rancher. But you know me. I'd set my sights on her and I wasn't about to let her get away."

He sighed and looked toward the window.

She could hear the buzz of the sheriff's department plane. Did her father look worried? "I always thought she was happy."

"She was," he said, turning back to her. "She was upset at first when she realized she was pregnant, but once you were born…" He smiled. "Just the sight of you made her light up. After that, she seemed content. I thought everything would be all right."

"So what happened?"

"As you grew up, she became restless. She talked about how she wanted more for you. That she wasn't going to let you settle on the likes of LJ Fraser. She'd seen him flirting with you. She told me that she was leaving and taking you. We argued. I didn't want to lose you. But it was clear that nothing could change her mind."

"But she didn't take me."

"That was my fault. I agreed that she could leave. I would give her money and a divorce so she could start a new life somewhere else. But I didn't want her uprooting you until she was settled somewhere. She agreed, then she packed up and left even though it was late. I begged her to wait until morning, but I could tell that leaving you was so hard that she couldn't face you in the morning."

"So she left. And you never heard from her again?"

He shook his head. "She was supposed to call the next morning. I knew you'd want to talk to her. I wanted your mother to be the one to explain all this to you because damned if I understood it."

"Maybe she chickened out."

Her father shook his head. "Blaze, there is no way your mother wouldn't have come back for you.

She would have moved heaven and earth if that's what it took."

"Then why didn't she?"

"I don't know what happened. Just that there is only one explanation. Someone stopped her." He shook his head. "She has to be dead."

"How long have you known that?" she demanded.

"In my heart, almost sixteen years. When we didn't hear from her the next day…" He met her gaze, his eyes so much like her own. "I was the one who wouldn't let her take you that night. I promised that we could make arrangements as soon as she was settled, but she'd insisted that she couldn't wait that long. She would call the next day. She would have called. If she could have."

"Did you notify the sheriff?"

He looked away. "I was young and foolish and there was my stubborn pride, but when I didn't hear from her after a couple of weeks, I did notify the sheriff. There was no sign of her. It's been that way for sixteen years."

BUD KNEW HIS expectations were too high. What were the chances that they would find the car the first day they flew the area? Monte had been out of jail now for twenty-four hours. The clock felt as if it was ticking. Bud couldn't explain why he felt so anxious. As far as he knew, Monte hadn't tried to leave the area, let alone the country. So why did he have the feeling that the man was planning to run?

As LJ came through his office door, Bud looked

up expectantly. "Did you find anything?" He asked the question even though he could see the answer on his son's face.

"We flew that entire grid just as you wanted," his son said as he slumped into a chair, looking exhausted. LJ often looked that way even on his day off when he did little more than eat, drink, sleep and watch hunting shows on television. "Nothing from the air. We can fly it again…"

Bud didn't see the point unless… "Maybe we need to expand the area."

"There are a lot of old abandoned buildings out there, not to mention deep ravines down in the Breaks," his son said.

"Those will have to be searched on foot," Bud said, more to himself than LJ.

"We don't have the manpower," his son said as if he needed to be reminded of that. Nor would it be considered the best use of what manpower they had, Bud reminded himself.

LJ pushed to his feet. "You want us to fly it again tomorrow?"

Bud couldn't hide his disappointment. He'd known it was a long shot, but he'd hoped… "Let me think about it."

After his son left, he was just getting ready to lock up his office, when the prosecutor stepped in. One look at Dave and Bud knew he'd gotten wind of what was going on.

"I just got a call from one of the ranch wives down south," the prosecutor said. "Something about the sheriff's department plane flying around her house? What's going on, Bud? Or do you want me to guess. The woman has a place not all that far from the McClintock Ranch. If you're harassing them from the air—"

Bud went around his desk and dropped into his chair. "I'm not harassing Monte."

"Then what is going on? Because we're lucky we haven't been sued for false arrest. Yet."

"The man wanted to plead guilty. If they hadn't brought in that lawyer and the judge and just let him…"

Dave stepped up to the desk. "Bud, so help me, what are you doing?"

He'd known this might happen when word got out. "I have my boy flying over the area looking for something."

"Something?" Dave sounded disbelieving.

"Bethany McClintock's car."

The prosecutor took a step back as if Bud had punched him. *"Are you kidding me?* You decided to do that now? After sixteen years?"

"I've always believed that he killed her," Bud argued. "I'll admit that's why I jumped so quickly when he was found standing over Frank Anson with a loaded gun in his hand. I knew he'd killed before."

Dave groaned. "I don't know what burr you have under your saddle when it comes to Monte McClintock, but you're costing this county a lot of money. If you value your job, I suggest you back off. You have got to quit making rash decisions like this based on…nothing but your personal animosity toward the man." With that, the prosecutor turned and left.

Bud swore, feeling as if someone had just kicked his favorite dog. He wanted Monte because the man was a killer. He was convinced of it. So he'd been wrong about Frank, but he wasn't about Bethany.

He started to rise, when his cell phone rang. He glanced at it. Unnamed caller. He almost didn't pick up. "Hello?" Silence. He started to disconnect when a low, hoarse voice said, "I know what you're looking for."

Bud felt a chill rattle up his spine. "I beg your pardon?"

"I know where it is," the voice said. He couldn't tell if it was male or female, young or old, and he figured that was the way the caller wanted it.

"I can tell you where to find it, but it's going to cost you five hundred dollars."

The sheriff let out a laugh even as he felt a stab of disappointment. The caller had seen the plane, knew that they were looking for something and thought he or she would cash in. "Right. Nice try. Why don't you tell me what I'm looking for?"

"Bethany McClintock's car."

CHAPTER TWENTY

BUD DIDN'T RECOGNIZE the voice, but he did the background noise. Whoever it was had called from outside one of the local bars. He could hear the gambling machines dinging over a country song on the jukebox.

"You do realize that you're talking to the sheriff, right?"

"You want the car or not? You're never going to find it from the air."

"How is it that you know where it is?"

"How badly do you want the information? This is a onetime offer. If it's worth five hundred bucks to you… Otherwise, I'm going to hang up."

"Fine. Let's meet and I'll—"

"I think not. Put the five one-hundred-dollar bills into a small plain white envelope and seal it. On Sunday morning, write *For New Roof* on it and drop the envelope in Reverend Westlake's collection plate. I'll call you Sunday night with the information."

"Wait a minute. How do I know—" But he realized the person had already hung up. Bud wanted to find the man and arrest him. Better yet, find him and get the truth out of him.

He told himself it was just some fool in town thinking he'd found a way to make a few bucks off someone's misery. In this case, Bud's own. But the caller had known that they were searching for— Bethany McClintock's car. Unless his loudmouthed son had told someone…

All that night he tried to talk himself out of doing such a fool thing. He'd be better-off to take five hundred dollars out of his bank account and throw it into the wind. Either way, the money would be gone, and he'd be left feeling like a jerk.

But the next morning, he found himself headed for the bank.

BLAZE FELT JAKE pulling away from her. Yesterday when they returned to the ranch, he'd disappeared into the bunkhouse. Later she'd heard him leave in his pickup. She'd been visiting with her father and Allie while her father packed.

"We're going down to Billings," Monte had told her. "We feel the need to get away for a few days."

She must have looked concerned because he'd tried to reassure her, giving her his cell phone number and saying they would be staying probably at the Northern Hotel, if she needed him.

"I didn't ask you what your plans were now," her father had said when he'd come out of his bedroom with his packed suitcase. "I would imagine you'll be leaving."

"Not yet," she'd said. "Jake and I are still looking

into Frank's murder." She'd noticed that Allie had been especially quiet all this time.

"Is that wise?" Allie had asked as if surprised. "I thought once your father was free…"

"Allie's right," he had said, looking just as concerned. "I think it's best if you let it go. You're welcome to stay on the ranch as long as you like, but I'd rather you let the sheriff handle it from here on out."

She'd stared at him in surprise. "The sheriff? The same one who threw you in jail without any real evidence?"

Her father had looked as if he wanted to say more on the subject, but had merely given her a shake of his head and said, "Suit yourself. I know you will anyway." And he and Allie had left.

She'd watched them go, noticing that Jake hadn't returned. She'd just hoped he hadn't gone back for more poker and another possible beating. Restless, she'd tried to watch a movie, but had been too distracted.

After a hot shower, she'd finally gone to bed. Sometime later she'd heard Jake return and, after a while, had finally fallen asleep.

But when she'd gotten up in the morning, she found his pickup gone. Standing in the kitchen, she thought of the pancakes and bacon he'd made her those mornings and yearned for that time together back.

Deciding to go into town for breakfast, she drove in, only to realize that she was short on cash. She swung by the bank, saw the long line at the drive-up window and parked. As she entered the building, she saw the sheriff at the first teller's window. She thought about waiting in a longer line to avoid him, but she was hungry and went to stand in the shorter line behind him.

The sheriff was dressed in his uniform. He shifted from foot to foot as if anxious to get to work. When it was finally his turn, Blaze stood behind him waiting. She listened to the teller count out five hundred dollars, which the sheriff quickly pocketed in a way that made her suspicious. Was he also involved in these high-stakes poker games Jake had told her about?

"You're just throwing your money away," Blaze joked as he started past her toward the exit.

Bud seemed startled. She merely grinned and stepped up to the teller's window he'd vacated to take care of her own business. When she was finished, she saw the sheriff getting into his patrol SUV across the street.

He glanced in her direction for a moment before ducking his head and sliding behind the wheel.

BUD HAD BARELY gotten settled behind his desk when he looked up to find Jake Horn standing in the doorway. His hand went to his pocket, where he'd stuffed the crisp bills, five hundred dollars' worth, taken from his personal savings account.

The sight of the man reminded him of what Blaze McClintock had said to him as he was leaving the bank. Was it possible the two of them were in on this together? She'd seen him take the five hundred dollars out of his savings account. Was it coincidence that she just happened to be there this morning?

He told himself he was being paranoid as Jake stepped in and closed the door behind him. Tell that to his pounding heart. If he was right, they weren't waiting until Sunday service at the church.

"Can I help you?" Bud asked, thinking he wouldn't mind throwing them both in jail.

"I've come into some information that I thought I should mention to you."

He felt impatient and out of sorts.

"Spit it out. I'm busy."

"It's about your ex-wife, Lorna."

That got Bud's attention. He froze for a moment, staring at Horn. "What about her?" He knew she'd remarried some rancher in North Dakota. LJ had more contact with her than he did.

"I'm told she was pregnant when she married you."

He felt all the air rush from his lungs as his heart took off like a wild stallion in the wind. When he found his voice, it came out high and thin. "That's a damn lie," he said, shoving to his feet.

Jake Horn said nothing for a moment. "You know that LJ is Frank's son. Did Frank tell you? Or did you know long before you married Lorna?"

Bud braced himself on the desk. Had he been younger, he would have launched himself at the smug man.

"All it would take is a DNA test to prove it," Jake

continued. "Frank's body is still at the morgue. Wouldn't take much."

"You need to get out of my office." The words came out hard like bullets. But they seemed to bounce off Jake Horn as if he was bulletproof. Bulletproof just like Monte McClintock.

"That gives you one hell of a motive for murder, wouldn't you say? It could also explain why you were so anxious to send Monte to prison. I wonder what the prosecutor would make of it."

Bud pointed a quaking finger at him. "You… you…" He felt as if a piano had suddenly been dropped onto his chest. Gasping, he leaned forward over the desk. His vision blurred. He couldn't catch his breath and the pain in his chest…

He heard Jake on the phone calling 911. The next thing he knew he was on the floor staring up at the ceiling. He couldn't die now. Not until he found Bethany's car. Not until he got her the justice she deserved.

"THE DOCTOR THOUGHT it was nothing more than an anxiety attack," Jake told Blaze when he found her at the local café. He had slid into the booth, clearly surprising her. When she'd asked where he'd been, he'd told her and then ordered ham and eggs with a side of pancakes. A young waitress said she would bring their orders out together. There was no sign of Luella.

"Do you think Bud already knew?" Blaze asked after the waitress left.

Jake shrugged. "Hard to tell. He was so upset. I thought for sure he'd had a heart attack."

Their orders came and they dug in, falling into a companionable silence for a while.

"Have you been avoiding me?" Blaze asked after finishing off half her breakfast.

He looked up in surprise. "Is that what you think? Sorry, I've just had a lot on my mind."

"My father wants me to quit looking into Frank's murder and leave," she said. "I talked to WT. He'd thought I *had* already left."

Jake put down his fork and leaned forward. "What do you want to do?"

"I don't know. You were gone a long time last night. I thought you might have returned to the poker game."

He shook his head, chuckling as he picked up his fork again. "I haven't healed up completely from the last one. No, I went into town to get something to eat and then just drove around for a while, did a little stakeout here and there."

She laughed and lowered her voice. "Whom did you stake out?"

"Lonny and Sandra Dean's house."

"Really? Why?"

Jake shrugged. "Just a feeling. Lonny didn't get home until late. At eight, he was staggering as he got out of his car. He tried to kick the neighbor's cat as he headed for his front door."

"What was the cat doing?"

"Probably using his flowerbed as a toilet, but he

seemed so…angry. Too angry. Once he got inside, he and Sandra had an argument and he ended up watching television alone from the couch."

"Did you stake out anyone else?" she asked. He could tell that she was enjoying this.

"Everything was fine at Luella's and at the Westlake house." He saw that she was waiting, wanting more. "Okay, I did check on Tawny. She's still at her mother's house. LJ's pickup was parked off the alley behind the hardware store so I'm assuming he was at the poker game."

"Maybe Tawny's come to her senses." She frowned. "I just had a weird thought. LJ and Frank must have played poker together. Do you think LJ knew?"

Jake shrugged. "I doubt Bud told him."

"That's assuming Bud knew before you told him today."

"He had to know. According to Luella, Lorna refused to have sex with him until they were married. Bud can certainly count to nine. If he didn't know, he suspected."

"The thing is, we don't know that it's even true. Luella might not have her facts straight." He saw that she didn't believe that any more than he did.

Blaze picked up her coffee cup but didn't take a drink. He could see that she was deep in thought and wasn't surprised that she was thinking the same thing he was. "Frank was apparently desperate for money to pay his poker debt from what we've learned. Hutch was putting pressure on him. Seems like he might have hit the deputy up for it."

"And when LJ tried to brush him off, Frank told him that he was his father and, in Frank's twisted way of thinking, he would feel that LJ owed him."

Blaze met his gaze. "I've seen how protective LJ is of his father. He would have killed Frank rather than let the man hurt Bud. Or tell anyone else, something Frank might have been threatening to do."

"Especially if Frank was threatening to go to Bud with his story?"

She nodded. "LJ idolizes Bud. He would have done anything to protect him—and his reputation. Jake, if LJ finds out that you told Bud, that we know the truth…"

"I think your father's right," he said as he reached for his wallet to pay for their breakfast. "I think it's time you let this go."

"Wait. Time *I* let this go?" She shook her head. "I'm not quitting and I'm certainly not leaving you here alone."

He smiled across the table at her. "Is that all it is? Just worry about me? Or am I growing on you?"

She groaned. "You're so full of yourself." But she said it without rancor. "Maybe you are growing on me some," she said, smiling at him.

"Then I'm making progress. So it's worth it."

CHAPTER TWENTY-ONE

BUD COULDN'T WAIT to get out of the hospital. A panic attack? He'd never heard of such a thing. Maybe in lesser men. But certainly not him. "It felt like a heart attack."

"You know what a heart attack feels like?" the doctor asked him, clearly bristling to be called on his diagnosis. "Panic attacks are short bursts of intense fear often marked by increased heart rate, brief chest pain or shortness of breath."

"*Brief*, my ass."

"Usually lasting less that thirty minutes."

Bud growled under his breath. "That was one long thirty minutes."

"Should it happen again, just knowing what it is will help you calm down so it doesn't last as long," the doctor said.

"Well, if it's no big deal, then sign me out of here," Bud groused.

The doctor considered for a moment, sighed and then wrote on his chart. "Be sure to stop at administration to give them your insurance information."

Bud cursed under his breath. He wondered what this was going to cost him out of pocket. Whatever it was, it was too much. A panic attack?

He thought of Jake Horn's visit to his office and his heart began to pound. *Calm down.* He couldn't afford another minute in this hospital. *Calm down.* How the hell had Jake Horn found out? Frank must have blabbed all over the place. That son of a—

"Dad!" LJ came running into the hospital room as Bud finished dressing. "I heard you'd been brought in here." His son was breathing hard and was flushed, about to have a panic attack of his own.

"I'm fine," he quickly assured LJ, touched by his son's concern. "It was just a false alarm."

"What happened? I heard at the station that they thought you were having a heart attack."

"Like I said, false alarm. My heart is fine. Nothing to worry about." He watched LJ rake a hand through his hair, still looking wild-eyed.

"I understand Jake Horn was with you? If he's the reason you had…whatever you had…"

Bud chuckled. "Jake Horn? Not likely. I didn't give him a second thought. It's my need to find that damned car. It keeps me up at night."

LJ nodded but didn't look all that convinced. "We'll find the car. I'll find it, if it's the last thing I do. I promise."

He hated for his son to make a promise like that but wasn't about to argue the point. "Let's get out of here," Bud said. "I hate this place."

BLAZE WAS LEAVING the café, chuckling about something Jake had said, when her cell phone rang. "It's Tawny," she told him.

"Take it. I'll meet you at home and we'll talk about what to do now."

Home. She was starting to think of the ranch as home instead of her small apartment that she kept in Jackson Hole, Wyoming. "Hello?"

"I need to see you," Tawny said. Blaze heard the tears in her voice. She guessed this was about LJ.

"Where are you?"

"At my mother's, but could we meet at the old mill?"

The old mill? "Is it even still standing?"

"Barely. I just thought we could talk there. I have some good memories from the time we used to hang out there." So did Blaze.

"I'm in town so I can be there in less than five minutes," she told her.

"Thanks."

Disconnecting, she walked to her SUV. As she started to get in, she saw LJ drive past. He didn't see her as he sped by and headed out of town, definitely going over the speed limit.

The old mill had once manufactured carpets back in Saddle Butte's short heyday. From as far back as Blaze could remember, the large old building had been empty. She remembered it as the perfect place to hang out and drink beer. Driving north, she hadn't gone far when she turned off onto a dirt road that circled behind what was left of the building. The front had caved in, probably in the winter of 2011, when Saddle Butte had reported more snow than ever in its history.

But the back of the building was still standing. Tawny had parked next to the huge gaping hole that had once been the loading dock area.

Blaze parked and got out, joining Tawny in her older-model sedan. The heater was on, the air inside scented with onion rings from the only fast-food place in town, Jerry's In and Out, and Tawny's perfume, the same scent she wore in high school.

The familiarity of it made her feel nostalgic. She glanced into the dark of the old mill, remembering better times. At least more innocent times. "We used to have fun out here."

As she turned, she was shocked to see her old friend was holding a gun on her. "What the—"

"It's not loaded," Tawny said.

"Then why are you…" She grabbed the barrel, pointing it away from her as she took it from the woman. Tawny was digging in her coat pocket. Cartridges for the .22 spilled out into her hand.

"I need you to show me how to use it," the woman said.

Blaze stared at her. "Where did you get this?"

"It's an old one my mother kept in a drawer by her bed."

She removed the clip and saw with relief that it was empty and so was the chamber. "Tawny, what is this about?"

"LJ. He's scaring me. Something's going on with him. He's so angry all the time. I have to be able to protect myself from him."

"Why is he angry?" She suspected it probably had

to do with her father being released from jail and his father's need to catch Frank's killer now more than ever.

"I don't know. But now… Did you hear about his father? Bud had to be taken to the hospital after Jake visited him. LJ's furious and blames Jake."

Blaze recalled the expression on LJ's face as he sped through town toward the outskirts, headed south. In the same direction as McClintock Ranch. She set the pistol on the floorboard at her feet and pulled out her phone to call Jake.

JAKE WAS HEADED back to the ranch feeling pretty good. His stomach was full, he'd just had breakfast with the woman he loved and he really did think he and Blaze were getting closer. Maybe there was hope yet.

But he worried that they might be getting too close to the truth about Frank's murder. It felt more dangerous. Blaze wouldn't leave unless he did. Maybe they should let this go, let the sheriff try to find the killer. Unless the sheriff *was* the killer.

Jake couldn't help rebelling at the idea of letting the person who killed Frank get away with it. Even as much as Frank was apparently hated, Jake still believed in justice because of WT. The judge had changed his life. Jake couldn't let this go. But how would he get Blaze to leave?

The road to the ranch was dirt with some gravel, narrow and winding. In some shady places, the ground was covered from the last snowfall. He realized that

he'd been so deep in thought that he hadn't been paying attention. The back of the pickup lost traction for
a moment. He touched the brakes, got the truck under
control again and slowed down.

He'd just come into a straight part when he looked
back and saw a pickup roaring up the road behind
him. Whoever it was, they were driving fast and
furious, actually kicking up snow along with dirt
and rocks.

As the truck behind him hit the straight stretch,
he got a good look at it. LJ Fraser. Jake swore under
his breath. He knew it was just a matter of time
before the man heard who'd been with the sheriff
when he'd had his attack. Jake wasn't responsible.
Fortunately, it hadn't been heart failure, just a panic
attack. Not that it would change how LJ felt about
it. The deputy would blame him.

The truck was gaining on him fast. Jake thought
about trying to outrun the man but knew that was
suicide on this road, especially since there was ice
in places under the snow and even where the snow
had blown off, leaving dirt and rocks.

He was deciding where he wanted to have this
out with the deputy when his cell phone rang. Blaze.
She'd be worried if he didn't answer it. He started to
when LJ crashed into the back of his pickup. The jar-
ring thud knocked the cell phone of his hand. It fell
to the opposite floorboard as he grabbed the wheel
and fought to keep his pickup on the road as LJ's
front bumper smashed into him again.

Had the man lost his mind? Quite possibly. Jake

hit the gas just to put a little distance between them as he decided how best to handle this. His cell phone kept ringing from the floorboard as he roared down the road, looking for a place to end this before LJ ended it for him.

"JAKE'S NOT ANSWERING." Blaze couldn't help being worried. He'd been headed back to the ranch and LJ had taken off in that direction. Maybe there was nothing to worry about. But she couldn't shake the feeling that Jake was in trouble.

"I have to go," she said and started to open her door.

Tawny grabbed her arm and burst into tears. "You can't. You have to help me. You have to show me how to shoot the gun."

"A gun isn't the answer, especially when you haven't ever shot one. Get yourself some bear spray. Keep it handy so you can pepper spray anyone who tries to hurt you. Even better, stay away from LJ until all of this is over, at least."

Tawny let go of her arm. "I thought he was the one."

Blaze shook her head. "I went out with him because he felt dangerous. He *is* dangerous and at that time of my life, I thought I wanted that. You have to decide what you want. Trust me, he will continue to hurt you and ultimately might accidentally kill you. Is that the kind of husband you really want?"

Tawny wiped at her tears. "But when he's nice, when he's sorry, he's so sweet."

Blaze groaned. "Until the next time he comes home drunk and mad. Your decision, but I have to go." She threw open the door and stepped out. The gun still lay on the floorboard where she'd dropped it. She grabbed it up along with some of the cartridges and put them into the clip before loading the gun. "This is the safety, see? When it's off like this, it's loaded and all you have to do is pull the trigger. Go into the mill and practice shooting it."

Tawny nodded, eyes wide. "You think I'm going to need it."

Her stomach roiled at the thought. "Get some pepper spray, but as a last resort…" She flipped the safety back on and dropped the gun on the passenger seat before closing the door and running to her pickup.

THE CRAZY BASTARD, Jake thought as he saw LJ coming for him again. The man's pickup was fishtailing all over the road. LJ looked as if he might lose control at any moment. Ahead Jake saw a nasty curve that dropped down on the other side into a swell and rose at an angle. If he could make it without losing control himself…

He kept his foot on the gas. His phone had quit ringing, but was now ringing again. He didn't need to check it to know it had to be Blaze. He barely heard it over the roar of his engine as he raced up the hill and dropped. He felt his stomach rise and come falling down along with the pickup under it.

For a moment he saw nothing in his rearview, but

then LJ topped the hill. The man was going so fast that all four wheels came off the ground as the truck flew up and out.

Jake hit the bottom of the hill hard. The back of the truck fishtailed. He pulled it out by giving it even more gas. The tires finally caught and he shot up the other side. He was almost to the top when he looked back.

LJ's pickup had landed badly, almost sideways in the road. The man had overcorrected and shot across the other side. Jake could see the tracks in the snow at the edge of the road. Some of the snow still hung in the air. LJ had jerked the wheel back, but because of the incline of the hill, he'd probably done it too hard, too fast.

At that speed and those conditions, the truck did the only thing it could. It rolled. What Jake saw in the mirror was the pickup tumbling down the hill to come to a snow-boiling stop upside down at the bottom.

He threw on his brakes, parking at the rise of the hill. He turned on his flashers, hoping no one else was coming up the road right now, then grabbed his phone up from the floorboard where it had fallen and called 911 before he took off down the hill. Steam was rising from the wrecked pickup's engine as he approached. The road down the hill was slick and he had to take it slow to keep from falling on his ass.

When the 911 operator answered, he told her there had been an accident. As he reached the pickup, he called out LJ's name. The only sound was the truck's engine, still running. He moved around to the driver's side, glad to see that at least the fool had been wearing his seat belt.

LJ's head was thrown back. Blood ran down the side of his face, but when Jake checked his pulse, he noticed the man was still breathing. He turned off the engine and relayed the information to the 911 operator. Then he disconnected and called Blaze as he used his gloves to stanch the bleeding on LJ's head until the ambulance arrived.

"I GAVE HER the loaded gun before I knew about this latest incident with LJ," Blaze said, throwing down her coat on the couch and joining it. They'd been kept at the sheriff's department giving their statements while the sheriff was down at the hospital with his son. There'd been no word on LJ's condition. Now she regretted telling Jake about meeting Tawny out at the old mill.

"Still, you loaded Tawny's gun? Does she even know how to shoot it?" Jake demanded as he stalked around the living room at the ranch. He'd been worked up long before she'd told him about her trip out to the old mill.

"She does now. I told her to practice. Jake," she cried plaintively. "She is terrified of LJ and obviously with good reason. I told her to get pepper spray, but if you could have seen her... Then, after what happened with you..."

He raked a hand through his hair. She noticed how tired he looked. All of this had been a strain on him, too. Not to mention the beating he'd taken. Now this thing with LJ. "I'm sorry I got you into this."

Jake shook his head and stopping pacing. "You didn't get me into it. Anyway, there is no other place I want to be than with you. I'm just frustrated. People are trying to kill us—"

"The gun wasn't loaded and she wasn't going to shoot me even if it had been."

"It's gotten more dangerous and we aren't any closer to finding Frank's murderer."

"We should both quit and clear out of here."

He turned to look at her for a moment before he pulled out his phone. She listened to him calling the hospital for an update on LJ.

"Stable," he said as he got off the phone and sighed. "Stupid fool could have killed himself. He was so out of control…" Jake pocketed his phone and dropped into a chair across from her. For a moment he stared down at his boots before lifting his head to meet her gaze. "I have a bad feeling about this that I can't shake. Let's leave. Your father's out of jail. Bud will eventually find Frank's killer or not. It's not our problem."

Even as he said it, Blaze knew that until the killer was caught, the suspicion would hang over her father and Allie. He was the one who said they couldn't leave because of that.

He must have seen what she was thinking, because he swore and got to his feet again. "I'm going to take a hot shower. Will you be all right?"

She nodded and started to tell him that he could

use her shower but he was out the door, his long legs carrying him across the yard to the bunkhouse.

BUD COULDN'T BELIEVE what he was being told. "You're sure Jake Horn didn't have something to do with this?"

The deputy shook his head. "The evidence is pretty clear. LJ smashed into the back of Horn's pickup numerous times before he lost control and rolled down into that gully. Horn's statement substantiates it. Says LJ came after him at a high rate of speed."

Bud rubbed a hand over his face before waving the deputy off.

"Sheriff?" He turned to see the doctor headed his way. His heart lodged in his throat, his pulse a deafening thrum. For a moment he thought he'd have another panic attack and end up on the floor again.

"My son? How is my son?"

"He is very lucky. He has a minor concussion and some lacerations."

Bud let out the breath he'd been holding. "Unconscious?"

"He's conscious," the doctor said. "We're going to keep a close eye on him. I'd suggest you go on home."

He nodded, feeling the weight of the world on his shoulders. He couldn't remember ever being this tired. Why had LJ done such a fool thing? But he knew. LJ had gone after Horn because he'd heard about Bud's collapse. Of course he blamed Jake Horn and, being LJ, he'd decided to go after him.

Bud groaned inwardly as he climbed into his patrol SUV and sat for a moment looking out at the cold winter afternoon. So many people he knew left this time of year for Arizona. Sunshine and cacti. Lorna had always wanted to go. Told him he could take up golf. Golf! He shook his head.

Maybe it would have saved their marriage, though, if he had retired and gone to Arizona in the winter. But he knew that it wasn't winter and Montana that had caused the problem between them. From the time LJ was born, he'd watched his wife looking at her son as if waiting for the truth to come out. Every time LJ got into a fight at school. Every time the boy threw a tantrum. Every time their son behaved badly. He'd watched Lorna pull away from LJ and finally Bud as well, as if distancing herself from the truth.

He sighed and started his patrol SUV. He didn't give a damn about other people's truths. LJ was his son. Right now, he wanted to wring the young man's fool neck. But as he drove away from the hospital, he didn't see any way to keep it from LJ. Too many people knew. Too many people like Jake Horn and Blaze McClintock, who wanted to make something of it. He worried what it would do to LJ when he found out the truth. Maybe he already had.

Wasn't that what scared him? Horn had practically accused him of murdering Frank. He rubbed the back of his neck as he drove down the main drag of Saddle Butte. How long before LJ was accused of the same thing? Especially if they found out that LJ no longer had his favorite rifle, a .30-06. The same type of rifle that had killed Frank.

LJ had sworn that he'd forgotten to lock his truck and someone had stolen the rifle. But when Bud had wanted to write a report so LJ could turn the loss in to insurance, his son had said he felt bad enough about it and just wanted to forget it.

The next day LJ bought a new rifle, a .30-06, just like his old one. Except the new one didn't have his name carved into the stock, a little something extra Bud had done when he'd given the boy the rifle on his fifteenth birthday.

CHAPTER TWENTY-TWO

WHEN JAKE DIDN'T come back, Blaze went over to the bunkhouse to check on him. She found him sprawled facedown on his bed, wearing nothing but a towel. She'd gotten everything out of the refrigerator to make quesadillas and thought he might be hungry.

"Jake?" She touched his bare shoulder. He made a sleepy sound but didn't stir. She stared down at his broad back. Her fingers ached to run down the hollow between those broad shoulders to the edge of the towel.

It would have been so easy to climb in next to him. The thought of him taking her in his arms made her feel weak with something more than need for this man. She took hold of the towel covering his behind. It felt damp. She gently tugged on it and it came loose. Hanging it over the bed frame, she pulled one of the old quilts over him. She stood for a moment, listening to him sleep before she headed back to the house.

On the way across the yard, her cell phone rang. It was Emma Jean Westlake. "I just wanted to be sure you were coming to tomorrow morning's service at the church. Your father and Allie have agreed to attend. Bring your friend… Jake Horn, isn't that his name?"

Blaze was too surprised to hear that her father and Allie were coming back from Billings to attend church tomorrow to say more than "Yes."

"Wonderful. See you then." And the line went dead.

It had been years since she'd been in that church. She'd quit going after her mother left. She didn't want to psychoanalyze her reasons. She'd lost a lot of hope after her mother left. It had changed everything. It had especially changed her father.

She thought of what Allie had said. Had she had reason to worry that Monte would take his own life? Blaze found that hard to believe, but if true, her father had been putting on a good front for her while all the time suffering badly. The only person he'd shared it with had been the woman on the ranch next door.

BUD KNEW THERE was only one way he could keep his five hundred dollars safe and at the same time, make sure that he got what his anonymous caller had promised him.

Last night, once back at home, he'd called one of his deputies. He hated this kind of underhanded bullshit, but he also couldn't afford to lose five hundred dollars right now. One of the ushers at church was behind in his alimony and child support. The man's ex had been bugging Bud for several months to help her get her money since she knew that they both went to the same church.

Gambling that Earl Harper hadn't been his anonymous caller, Bud had told his deputy, "Pick up Earl.
Maybe a night in jail is what he needs to cough up
some money for his ex and the kids."

"You're seriously going to lock him up?" the deputy had said in surprise.

"Just overnight. See if he takes paying his child
support more seriously after a night in jail. I'll spring
him after church."

He'd then called Pastor Westlake to tell him that
Earl couldn't make Sunday services and volunteered
to be an usher. This morning, he'd prepared the envelope, put the five hundred dollars into it and sealed
it. He had the envelope in his pocket, folded in half,
as he entered the church.

To his shock, he saw his son sitting at the back of
the church. "What are you doing here?" he demanded
in a hushed tone.

LJ laughed. "You've been trying to get me to
come back to church since I was twelve. Now I'm
here. I thought you'd be glad. I thought maybe I
needed it."

Bud couldn't argue that. But why today of all
days? "I thought you weren't getting out of the hospital until tomorrow."

"I told the doc that I needed to be in church. I
thought you'd be happy to see me."

"I am, son. I am." He patted his son's shoulder
and took a seat, the money feeling as if it was burning a hole in his pocket all through the first part of
the service. He was relieved when it was finally time

to pass the collection plate. As he started down the aisle, he pulled out the envelope and placed it on the plate, then handed it to the first person on the far side of the church.

Bud never took his eyes off the plate as it was passed down the row, then to the next row before it came back. He watched parishioners drop something in and pass it. A few merely passed it.

When the plate reached him, he noticed that the envelope was still in there. What would he do if no one took it? How would he explain taking it back out? He felt blood rushing to his head. Now was not the time to have another panic attack. This had been one of the stupidest things he'd ever done.

When the tray came back after it had gone down another two rows, he almost pulled out his envelope but realized someone might see him and think he was stealing. He cursed himself and watched the collection plate go down another two rows and then another two and another two until it came back to him.

Bud realized he was sweating. He wiped at his upper lip, wishing he'd never agreed to this as the plate made its way toward him. This had been a fool's errand.

The plate was slowly making its way to him. A man in the last row added a few dollars and handed it off to LJ, who dug out a dollar and dropped it in before passing it on to the next few people in the row.

When the last man handed Bud the collection plate, he almost dropped it. His envelope was gone. He stared down at it, then at the rows of individuals seated in the last two pews as the organ music swelled and Pastor Westlake finished speaking to one of the men at the end of the row and took his place at the pulpit. He knew all the men and women in those rows. Which one of them was his caller? Which one of them was now five hundred dollars richer?

Everyone looked toward the front of the church as Pastor Westlake began to speak. The next thing Bud knew, the whole congregation was on its feet. Music swelled. He felt someone tap him on his shoulder and sleepwalked along with the other ushers back to the office, where they would leave the money collected today. His hands were shaking. His envelope with his money was gone. He thought he might throw up.

He left the head usher to take care of the offerings and headed to drop into a space on the back row of the church. He needed to sit down.

But as he slid into the pew, he saw Blaze McClintock sitting in the opposite back row. She glanced at him, then back at the pastor. He felt his pulse throb in his temple. What was *she* doing here? He looked around for her boyfriend but didn't see him anywhere. Blaze had come to church alone? That was when he saw the woman next to her. Allie Anson. Allie was holding Montgomery McClintock's hand.

He realized with a start was that the rumors were apparently true. Allie Anson was pregnant and definitely showing. It struck him as odd that they would attend church today since it had been a very long time since he'd seen Monte here.

And they were in one of the last rows, the rows

where his money had disappeared. He tried to calm himself. His anonymous caller could be anyone. He tried to remember everyone he'd seen but he'd been so shocked to see the money gone...

Blaze glanced at him again. She almost looked concerned. He felt light-headed, but was determined not to have another attack. Worse, he'd been had and was now five hundred dollars poorer. The only good news was that LJ was out of the hospital and...

But as he looked past Blaze to her father and his...girlfriend, he thought what a trick of fate it would be if Monte were his anonymous caller. He wiped his face, his hand coming away wet with perspiration. He knew he was being ridiculous. Why would Monte tell him where he'd hidden Bethany's car unless...unless he wanted to be caught?

He wasn't thinking clearly. Monte hadn't been the caller. It made no sense. He'd just lost five hundred dollars for absolutely nothing but his own gullibility. Whoever had pocketed his envelope would be laughing his ass off tonight. Bud felt sick as he tried to concentrate on the sermon about forgiveness.

JAKE WAS WAITING outside the church when Blaze came out. "Up for lunch?"

Blaze realized she was starving, but when she looked to her father and Allie, both declined.

"You two go on," Monte said. "Allie's not feeling well. I think we'll go back to her place." His gaze met hers and held it for a moment. "Thank you for coming to church today," he said to her. "It's been a long time."

"Not since Mom was here," she said, and he nodded and smiled.

"Let's go to that burger joint on the edge of town," Jake suggested and Blaze quickly agreed. As she and Jake started toward his pickup, she remembered the container she needed to return to the pastor's wife. "Go on ahead. I'll meet you there," she said, opening the passenger side of her pickup to pull out the container. She'd washed it, but she liked to think it still smelled like cinnamon rolls.

"Tell her thank you," Jake said. "That was definitely the best cinnamon roll I've ever eaten." He grinned. "And thank you for saving me one. I'm not sure I could have been as strong as you and not eaten them both."

She laughed and headed back. Only a few stragglers were driving away. She saw the man who'd been with Sandra Dean in church earlier. She started to speak to him when she noticed what he was doing. He had something tucked against his side and was trying to get into LJ's pickup.

"Lonny?"

The man spun around, keeping whatever he had in his other hand tucked behind him. "Oh, it's you." He took a couple of steps back, opened the rear door of the sedan parked next to the pickup and tossed what looked like a rolled-up rug into the back, then slammed the door. "You startled me." He turned to face her. "I hope you aren't here harassing my in-laws."

"I was returning a container your mother-in-law lent me." He seemed angrier than he should have been. "Isn't that LJ's pickup?"

"I thought he'd left his lights on." He was lying and they both knew it. But why? Because of whatever he'd been trying to put in LJ's truck?

"LJ's inside visiting with the pastor, something about turning over a new leaf, if you need to talk to him." She'd believe it when she saw it.

Lonny nodded. "Well, I'm sure he won't be that long that his battery will run all the way down. I need to get home to Sandra."

"How is she feeling?"

"Fine. The doctor wants her to stay in bed for most of the rest of her pregnancy, though." He took another step back and opened his car door.

She couldn't help being curious. She took a few steps toward the sedan. She got only a glimpse of the back seat. She'd been right about the package he'd been carrying being something wrapped in a rug.

The contents had slipped out of the rug in his hurry to throw it into the back seat of his car. She saw the barrel of a rifle. Had he taken it from LJ's pickup or was he putting it back?

"I thought you didn't like guns," she said as Lonny followed her gaze to the back seat of his car.

"It's none of your business, but I've been keeping it for LJ. I was just going to return it." He grabbed her arm roughly. "You really need to butt out of everyone's business."

"Lonny!" Emma Jean called from the front of the church. "I'm so glad you haven't left. Sandra's on the phone."

He let go of Blaze's arm. "Tell her I'm on my way home." With that, he slid behind the wheel and took off, making the tires squeal.

She thanked Emma Jean as she returned the container but felt distracted over her encounter with Lonny. On the way to the burger place, she couldn't get it out of her mind.

"Are you all right?" Jake asked as she joined him in a booth.

She told him what had happened in the parking lot of the church.

"He said he'd been keeping the rifle for LJ? Any chance you could tell what caliber the rifle was?"

Blaze shook her head. "You think it might be the murder weapon?"

"Well, if it is, Lonny's getting rid of it right now."

"I suppose asking LJ about it—"

Jake chuckled. "Probably not a good idea under the circumstances. You said he was at church today?"

She nodded. "Turning over a new leaf. It seems my father is, as well. It's as if he is starting his life over, new soon-to-be wife, new baby…"

"Are you feeling left out?"

She laughed. "Strangely, no. I'm happy for him." She realized it was true. "But did you notice people looking at him after church? They believe he's guilty and that he got away with murder. The fact that he's with the dead man's wife doesn't help."

"I've been doing a little footwork this morning while you were seeking salvation," Jake joked.

The waitress at the local burger joint came up to their table to take their orders. They asked for cheeseburgers, fries and chocolate milkshakes. "So, what have you been up to?" she asked after the waitress left.

The place was fairly noisy for a Sunday after church. An elderly couple was seated in the booth next to them. From all the times she'd heard them repeating what they'd just said, Blaze was pretty much sure they were hard of hearing.

Still, Jake lowered his voice as he leaned over the table toward her. "I talked my way into the newspaper office and looked at some old papers that aren't available online."

She frowned. "What were you looking for?"

"Whoever killed Frank had to be a pretty good shot. It's about eight hundred yards from the road to where he was shot. The average person couldn't make an accurate shot from that far, even laying the rifle over the hood of their car."

"So it wasn't your average person. Or the person just got lucky."

He shook his head. "The person knew what he or she was doing. This is Montana. Boys—and girls— grow up shooting guns at tin cans, gophers, signs on fence posts. They even compete." He pulled out a folded copy from one of the newspaper articles he'd found and pushed it over for her to see.

She looked down to see LJ Fraser's smiling mug in a photo calling him the sharpshooter champion. He was holding a rifle in one hand and an award in the other. "LJ."

"But he wasn't the only one. Look who came in second."

Blaze scrolled down to see another name she recognized. Lonny Dean. And yet another. Wade Cameron. Followed in the older division by Bud Fraser and Hutch Durham.

"Did you know that LJ and Lonny were in the same class? I found photos of the two of them in a variety of sports. It's possible they were friends."

She stared at the article. "A whole list of suspects."

"Including two of your old boyfriends," he said with a grin.

"Wade doesn't live here anymore. He's married with a toddler and has twins on the way."

Jake nodded. "You don't need to defend him. I already crossed him off my list."

"I'm not defending him." She met Jake's gaze. "In case you're wondering, there isn't anything there anymore. If there ever was."

"Hmm." He looked deep into her eyes as if digging for the truth before he said, "I'm glad to hear that."

She studied the newspaper article for a moment before handing it back. "At least three people on that list have motive—LJ, Lonny and Hutch, not to mention the sheriff, who seems to want to put my father behind bars come hell or high water."

"Check out the winner in the women's shooting competition," Jake said, grinning as he pointed to the bottom of the article. "Rita Lee, now Rita Durham, Hutch's wife."

Their meals came and they ate, both seemingly lost in their own thoughts. Blaze was thinking about the list of suspects. What if Lonny had been telling the truth and he'd kept LJ's rifle for him, just as he'd said? If it was the murder weapon, then Lonny would get rid of it now.

She realized there was something else bothering her. The sheriff had been acting stranger than usual at church. She mentioned it to Jake.

"What was the sermon about?" he asked.

"Forgiveness."

Jake chuckled. "Maybe the topic hit too close to home."

BUD GOT THE call only minutes after he walked in his door. He felt his pulse jump as he looked down at his phone. Unknown caller. Could it be the same one who'd taken his five hundred bucks?

"Hello?"

For a moment there was only heavy breathing, then, "Do you know where the old Murray place is?" It was the same low, hoarse whisper.

"I do."

"Check the buildings, especially the ones farthest from the main road."

"Wait, how do you know where the car is?" More heavy breathing, then silence. For a moment he thought that the person had hung up. Bud couldn't help feeling suspicious and at the same time, relieved that he hadn't been completely cheated out of his money. Not that this couldn't be a runaround just to amuse the caller on the other end of the line.

But he knew the old Murray place. It was in the middle of nowhere. A perfect location to hide a car. An even better one for an ambush. "Why now? Why tell me now?"

"I didn't know anyone was looking for it until now." The line went dead.

Bud stood holding the phone, his heart a sledgehammer in his chest. The old Murray place. He grabbed his coat and keys. It was about ten miles from McClintock Ranch if you followed the main road south, but Bud knew of another road that could get you there faster if you opened a few gates and trespassed. Monte knew the area just as well or better. He could have ditched the car quickly and returned to the ranch without anyone being the wiser.

The old homestead had numerous buildings. The place had been sold off for grazing to a larger ranch, so Bud doubted that anyone had gone near the buildings in years. As he drove in, he saw no other tracks. His caller was either sending him on a wild-goose chase or the person hadn't been in here recently. Or he was walking into a trap.

He stopped by a bunch of old structures and got out. Taking his flashlight, he looked in one after another. Most were almost falling down, dark and musty inside. He heard a rustle in one and felt a shudder as something small and fast disappeared under an old mattress. In the barn, he found a lot of old farming equipment, rusted and cold looking, but no car.

Back in his patrol SUV, he drove on up what had at one time been a road. The weeds were high, the tracks almost obliterated by time. As he came over a rise, he saw more buildings down by a ravine. He felt a stab of memory. Something about this scene felt…familiar. As he drove, weeds and sagebrush scraping the bottom of his vehicle loudly, the snow getting deeper where it had drifted, he realized he'd been here before.

He stopped some yards from the buildings, parked and sat listening to the tick of the cooling engine. LJ had shot a big mule deer buck on a neighboring ranch some distance from here. He'd only wounded it and they'd had to track it.

Across the ravine, he recognized the hillside where they'd found it. LJ had been about sixteen, his first hunting season. Bud remembered leaving his son to gut the deer while he went back to get the truck.

A bad feeling settled in the pit of his stomach. It was also familiar, one that he'd pushed away since LJ was born. Frank Anson's genes ran through his son's body, bringing with it worry. Frank had been mean, cruel even. Look what he'd done to Lorna. And she wasn't the only one. He didn't want to believe that his son had inherited something…dark and danger-ous, especially when it came to women.

LJ had played down his fight with his fiancée. But Bud had heard that Tawny had a black eye and bruises. His son had been wild at sixteen—just like his biological father. He couldn't believe the path his thoughts had taken. Did he really think that LJ at that young age might have come across Bethany as she was leaving town and—

Shoving the thought away, he climbed out and started for the first building, telling himself Beth-any's car probably wasn't even here. And if it was, it didn't mean that LJ had put it here.

Snow crunched under his feet where the wind had glazed the surface, turning it to ice. He snapped on his flashlight and peered through some broken boards on the side wall. The light cut through the darkness. Empty. He started for the next build-ing. The snow had drifted here and was deeper and harder to walk through.

He was sweating by the time he busted his way through the snowdrifts to the part of the building that was still standing. He could feel the cold and wetness from the snow seeping through his pant legs. This was the last building on the property. If it wasn't here…

He pried open a side door, exerting even more en-ergy. A flurry of movement inside made him start. Here he was. He felt as if he was looking for ghosts and almost feared he might find one.

Turning on his flashlight, he shone it into the dark

musty expanse, just wanting to get this over with. He was cold and tired and was anxious to get back to his patrol SUV. The light swept across the open space. He started to turn off the flashlight when the beam caught on something dull and still shiny enough that he recognized it for what it was. A bumper.

His heart began to race even as he told himself it might not be Bethany McClintock's car. This part of the country was riddled with abandoned old vehicles. He pushed his way in, shivering from the cold, from a growing exhaustion, from excitement.

A half-dozen crows burst out in a flood of flapping wings, making him jump. They disappeared through an opening on the collapsed side of the building. He grabbed his chest and fought to still his thundering pulse. All around him was silence. Deathly cold silence.

His flashlight beam skimmed over the back of the vehicle and the license plate.

It was Bethany's car.

His legs felt weak from relief and dread as he made his way along the side of the car, ducking to keep from hitting his head on the side of the building that had caved in. Another bad winter and the roof would have collapsed and this car might have never been found.

At the dust-coated driver's-side window, he hesitated, afraid of what he would find. Using his gloved hand, he wiped at the glass. The driver's seat was empty.

He shone his flashlight beam across the front seat,

then the back, frowning in confusion when all he found was a flat tire resting in the back seat—and a suitcase. He'd been so sure he would find her body.

A chill moved through him as he glanced at the suitcase and then in the direction of the sedan's trunk. The driver's-side door groaned as he opened it. With his gloved hand, he pulled the lever that opened the trunk. As it yawned open, he moved toward it, already knowing what he would find.

Bethany McClintock's cramped metal grave.

CHAPTER TWENTY-THREE

BUD PULLED OUT his phone with trembling cold fingers and swore. No service. As he was pocketing his phone, he thought he heard a sound outside the building. He froze and listened. Only one person knew where he was—his caller.

That thought did nothing to calm his nerves. He picked up the heavy large flashlight from where he'd put it down to make the call. Placing it in his left hand, he unsnapped his revolver, telling himself that the noise was just the birds he'd heard earlier. But even as he tried to convince himself, he knew that the sound had been different.

He felt spooked, a feeling that left him off balance. He'd been at this lawman job for a long time. Nothing usually shook him. But then, finding what was left of Bethany in the trunk of her car would rattle anyone.

He pushed open the door along the side of the building. It groaned loudly. The afternoon sun hung low on the horizon, providing little warmth this time of year. It shone off the snow, almost blinding him.

Bud blinked and listened. He heard nothing but his own ragged breathing. He looked down and

saw only his footprints in the snow. The wind had
come up and now sung through the slits between the
weathered boards. What a desolate, cold spot for a
final resting place.

He thought of the young woman who'd enamored
him so and felt sick to his stomach. But Monte would
pay. Bud had never even considered that someone
else might have killed her and he certainly didn't
now. He finally had proof that Bethany McClintock
had never left the county.

Taking a deep breath, he began to trudge along
the edge of the building through his already-broken
tracks, just wanting to get to his patrol SUV and
radio this in. The wind buffeted him, making the
going through the deep, crusted snow even harder.
Maybe he was getting too old for this job.

Next to him, he heard the building creaking and
moaning in the gale. He assured himself that was all
he'd heard. He leaned against the worn wood as he
worked his way to the end of the building. He was
almost there when he heard a whisper of a sound. It
came from just around the corner.

He pulled his weapon and eased closer. As he
turned toward it, he saw a shadow fall over his face
only an instant before he fired. But he hadn't been
quick enough. He was struck in the face with something cold and hard that turned out the lights. He
didn't even feel himself falling.

ALLIE SNUGGLED AGAINST Montgomery on the couch
at her house. Her house. That was what it was now,

but she could feel Frank and his mother walking the halls. She couldn't wait to get it sold. But then what?

"Tell me what's bothering you?" he asked as he placed a hand over her swollen stomach.

She loved seeing his large, weathered hand there. She felt safe. Her baby felt safe. "I'm glad you had a chance to talk to Blaze."

He glanced over at her and laughed. "I should have known what you were up to."

"I was tired, but I felt the two of you needed to talk. Did it help?"

"I think so," he said after a moment. "I hope so. Blaze has been so angry with me for so long. But maybe now things will be better. I can only hope."

Allie nodded even though she couldn't shake the bad feeling she had.

"You haven't seen Hutch again out here, have you?"

"No. I reported him to the sheriff. I doubted Bud would do anything but maybe he talked to him." She shrugged. "I don't know how to say this. The one thing I never wanted to do was take you away from your ranch, but—"

Montgomery pulled her close with his arm around her and his other hand resting on her stomach. "We can't stay here." Tears filled her eyes. "I realized that a long time ago. It's one reason I gave Blaze my power of attorney after I contacted the judge who helped her. I want her to have the ranch. She probably doesn't want it, but I don't care. She can sell it, do whatever she wants with it. I want you, Allie. Wherever we are with our child, that will be my home."

"Are you sure?" she cried.

He smiled. "Positive. In fact, I think it's time we left. Blaze will understand. Don't even bother packing. We can buy whatever we need. I had wanted to come back for church today. I guess it was to say goodbye. But I'm ready to start a new life and there is nothing standing in our way." They'd made sure of that with the new passports in their new names just in case, she thought as they headed for the door.

She wondered if, like her, he'd sensed something bad headed their way, but she said nothing as they climbed into his pickup.

"To our new life," he said and smiled over at her as she buckled up.

BUD KNEW HE hadn't been out long. He woke lying against the warm boards of the building in a spot where the snow had melted away. And yet he woke shivering, his head beating like a bass drum. He blinked, pushing himself up on his elbows, and looked around for his gun. The last thing he remembered was hearing someone. He'd gotten off a shot…

He found his gun buried in the snow nearby. But there was no one on the ground anywhere. Had he missed?

The sun hadn't sunk much lower, but the wind had grown stronger. It howled around him, making him shiver even harder. He had to stand up and start moving. But when he tried to get to his feet, his head swam.

Leaning against the building, he managed to stand. He looked around for tracks in the snow. Footprints of the person who'd hit him. But all he saw were his own.

He tried to make sense of that. But his brain felt foggy. Laying his head back, he merely breathed for a few moments before he tried again to get to his feet.

As he worked his way up the wall, he heard a sound directly over him and shrank back as he looked up. It took him a moment to realize he was staring at what had hit him. A piece of solid iron hung down from the building and now swung in the wind, making that distinct sound that he'd heard.

Feeling even more like an old fool, Bud timed the iron's swing and pushed off the building. He stumbled through the snow to his patrol SUV, climbed in and locked the doors as he picked up the handset on his radio.

Even then, he waited a moment until he could catch his breath. In the rearview mirror, he could see the lump forming on his forehead. "Damned fool," he muttered and then made the call.

IT WAS TAWNY who called Blaze with the news.

"LJ just told me. I thought you'd want to know. The sheriff's been looking for your mother's car."

She thought of the plane that had flown over the ranch. *"My mother's car?"* Why would the sheriff think her car was on McClintock property unless—

"I heard an airplane, but why would the sheriff be looking for my mother's car?" She and Jake had both wondered what the sheriff had been looking for. They'd both thought it was a form of harassment. She still did. "My mother left here sixteen years ago. Her car—"

"Blaze, Bud found her car."

All the air rushed from her lungs. *"What?"* The word came out in a hoarse whisper. "That's impossible." If the sheriff had found her mother's car on the ranch, that would mean that she never left. "Where—"

"In an old abandoned building down in the Breaks."

She tried to wrap her head around what she was being told. "I don't understand." She was still having trouble catching her breath. Her pulse pounded so hard that she couldn't think. The consequences of what Tawny was saying were only starting to sink in.

"Your mother never left. Blaze…" The woman seemed to hesitate. "You were always suspicious of why your mother left to begin with and figured your father had something to do with it. Blaze, her body was in the trunk."

The words hit her in the face like a baseball bat. Her legs gave out under her and she sank to the floor. She heard Jake rush to her, asking what was wrong. She was afraid that if he touched her she would break down. Her hammering heart threatened to punch a hole in her chest.

Her mother's car had been found, her body in the

trunk. She'd never left. She'd been close by all these years. She hadn't gotten away. She felt the realization vibrate in her chest, an alarm in her head as she dropped her phone.

"Blaze," Jake said. "Tell me what's happened." He lifted her to her feet. This time she let him take her in his arms. She leaned into him, thankful for his strength. As she buried her face into his chest, she could hear the sound of sirens headed their way.

"WHAT'S HAPPENED?" Jake cried as he saw all the color drain from her face. One minute she'd been on the phone, the next on the floor.

"My mother's car," she said in a ragged breath. "Bud found it in an abandoned building down south. Tawny said they found her body in the trunk."

He stared at her, his heart breaking for her. Earlier she'd been so happy, he thought. She'd actually been making some progress in getting close to her father again. She'd confided in him yesterday that she felt at home on this ranch after so many years of avoiding it.

A bad feeling sent a stab of dread through him as he heard the sirens and looked up to see four sheriff's department rigs come roaring up.

He pulled out his phone and called Monte as the sheriff and his deputies began to pour out, headed for the house with guns drawn. "I called your father. There's no answer." He left a quick message on her father's cell phone and disconnected. Had Monte and Allie left the country? Had the man known when he'd seen the sheriff's plane searching the area what they were looking for and feared that if they found it—

The pounding on the front door pulled him back. "I'll answer it," he told Blaze as he helped her onto a nearby couch. "Let me handle it."

"They have to be mistaken. It can't be my mother's car." He doubted that was the kind of mistake the sheriff would make at this point. But when Blaze looked up at him, her blue eyes huge with shock, all he could do was nod.

He strode to the door, feeling helpless. If her mother's car had been located in the Breaks and they'd found a body in the trunk… His mind fought the obvious conclusion as he opened the door.

The sheriff thrust a handful of papers at him. "These are warrants to search the house and the premises, as well as a warrant for Montgomery Mc-Clintock's arrest. Please stand aside." Jake noticed the lump on the sheriff's forehead and wondered who'd put it there.

Bud pushed past him. "Where is your father? And don't lie."

"He isn't here," Blaze cried, but they paid her little mind as they all filed down the hallway, guns drawn.

"Sheriff's department!" they yelled, racing through the house.

When they came up empty, the sheriff told two of them to go to Allie Anson's house. He snatched the warrants back from Jake, taking the one for Monte's arrest and handing it to his two men. "I want that man in handcuffs within the hour."

The men left and only minutes later, Bud's radio squawked. "Tell me you have him."

"No sign of McClintock or Anson. But Hutch Durham is here."

"What?"

"He's drunk and tearing the place apart. I've never seen him like this. He keeps saying that Allie owes him and that he's going to collect or kill her."

The sheriff swore. "Arrest him and take him in. Is there any indication where McClintock might have gone?"

"Not that we could find. But it does appear that they left in a hurry."

BLAZE FELT NUMB. This wasn't happening. She watched the deputies going through the house and searching the barn and bunkhouse. She couldn't believe any of this. She stared down at the search warrant Jake had handed her as the deputies began to search the property.

"What are they looking for?" she'd asked Jake as he joined her on the couch and took her free hand in his. "If they have my mother's car and her...body."

"I have no idea. I heard him put a BOLO out on your father and Allie."

She looked over at him, feeling some of her strength come back as anger. "He's wrong. My father had nothing to do with this." She felt it heart-deep. She couldn't be wrong. She was just starting to get close to her father again. He couldn't have done this. "This is just part of Bud's vendetta against Monte."

When Jake said nothing, she felt the weight of the news. The ramifications punctured her heart like a knife. Her mother had never left. All these years, she'd been in some old building. Dead.

"The crazy thing is that I knew she was dead. I mean, she had to be. I kept thinking that she wouldn't leave me behind. She just wouldn't have." She met Jake's gaze. "I had to believe that."

He pulled her to him, cradling her head as she buried it against his chest. She listened to the steady beat of his heart, felt his strong arms around her. Her eyes filled with tears, but she couldn't cry. She was too shocked, too shaken, too scared.

She pulled back to look outside. The deputies were all standing around their vehicles. Whatever they'd been looking for, they hadn't found it. "They made it sound as if my father and Allie ran away. I don't understand why they came back for church. I thought they were trying to find a way that they could stay here and be part of this community." Still, Jake said nothing. He didn't have any more answers than she did.

She'd put the past behind her, believing what her father had told her was true. That her mother hadn't been happy, that she'd wanted and needed another life, that he'd never forgiven her for hurting Blaze by not sending for her daughter as she'd promised.

Blaze shook her head as she watched some of the deputies climb back into their cars and the sheriff headed back toward the front door of the ranch house.

She tried to swallow but her throat closed. Jake put his arm around her and pulled her closer. She was afraid his comforting gesture would only make her cry, so she pulled free and stood to let the sheriff in. But he didn't bother knocking. He stepped in, anger and disappointment in his expression.

"When you hear from your father, you tell him to come back and face what he's done," Bud said, his voice cracking with emotion. "He can't hide. If it's the last thing I do, I'll find him."

"You don't know that he's done anything," she said, surprised how calm she sounded. "He and Allie didn't run. They came home for church and then were going to take a few days to themselves." She could see that the sheriff didn't believe that any more than she did.

She remembered how worried her father had looked when he'd seen the sheriff's department plane flying so low over the ranch. He'd known that Bud wouldn't give up until he found something on Monte.

"What is it between you and my father?" she asked. The sheriff started to open his mouth, no doubt to say he was the law and Monte was a killer. "I know it's more than your need for justice."

Bud seemed to consider that for a moment. "I knew your mother. She was sweet and beautiful and she deserved better."

Blaze nodded in surprise. "You had a crush on her."

The sheriff scoffed. "It wasn't a crush. I would have done anything to make her happy. That's more than your father did."

She stared at him. He really believed that everything would have been different if her mother had married him. "Did you even ever ask her out?" She saw the answer on his reddened face. "She didn't know how you felt." A thought struck her. "But if you had the night she left, she might have laughed in your face."

"I see where you're going but I had nothing to do with your mother's death." He looked down at his boots for a moment before raising his head again, his eyes narrowed and moist. "And your mother wouldn't have laughed. She was a lady. She would have let me down easy. She was a class act."

His devotion to her mother surprised and worried her.

"Like I said, when you hear from your father—"

"We'll let you know," Jake said, joining her. "But I do have one question. After all this time, sixteen years, how is it that you suddenly found her car?"

For a moment, she thought Bud wouldn't answer. When he did, she couldn't believe his answer. "I got an anonymous call."

"Anonymous call?" she cried. "That's your story?"

"It's true." He had taken off his hat when he'd stepped in and now worked at the brim with his fingers. "Someone who'd seen an old car in a building but hadn't put two and two together." As if seeing how disbelieving they were, he let out a growl. "At least, that was the caller's story. Whoever it was, they were in church Sunday. That's right. They were there to take the money I left them in the collection plate. You were there, both of you, and your father and his girlfriend. So before you start giving me those disbelieving looks, maybe you should think about that." He turned and stormed out.

"YOU HEARD ALL THAT, right?" Blaze demanded after the sheriff left.

Jake nodded. "I have to admit it's a little hard to swallow. But I don't think he was involved in your mother's death."

"After sixteen years, he suddenly gets an anonymous phone call and finds her car? Seems a little coincidental, wouldn't you say? Especially since he thought he had Monte on Frank's murder. And right after that he finds the car and another reason to want to put him behind bars."

He rubbed his jaw for a moment. "Sounds like he paid the anonymous caller at church."

Blaze's eyes widened. "I saw him at the bank. He was acting odd. I was right behind him. He took out five hundred dollars in one-hundred-dollar bills and quickly pocketed them instead of putting them in his wallet. I thought he was involved in that poker group. I said something about him throwing his money away as he left. He looked so surprised… Now he's trying to make it seem like one of us was the caller?"

"Did you have any idea that your father was coming back just for the church service?" Jake asked her.

"You can't possibly think he—"

"I don't know what to think, truthfully. Just that it

doesn't look good for your dad." Tears filled her eyes. He pulled her to him. "He needs to come back and face this." She nodded against his shoulder before drawing back to meet his gaze. "You're worried that he did it."

Jake shook his head. He was thinking about the people he'd seen coming out of the church. One of them was the sheriff's anonymous caller? "I think there is more to all this. We'll know more once the report comes back on the car—" he didn't add the word *remains* "—from the crime lab. In the meantime, let's try not to jump to any conclusions."

"No, the sheriff is doing that."

"If you hear from Monte, try to talk him into coming back," Jake said, but he could tell from Blaze's expression, she hoped he kept going.

CHAPTER TWENTY-FOUR

JAKE FELT CONFLICTED as he disconnected from the call. He didn't want to leave Blaze alone. He'd heard earlier that a storm was blowing in. Rain turning to snow at midnight. Outside, the day had darkened from the low clouds. He glanced at the time, knowing he probably wouldn't get back until after dark. After the rain had begun.

"Tell me that wasn't my father," Blaze said.

"It was Herb Perkins from the hardware store."

She groaned. "You are not even considering another poker game."

Jake chuckled. "Don't worry. He asked if I could stop by. I think he feels bad about what happened. But he said he might have something for me."

"What does that mean?"

"Something about Frank's death."

"You should go," she said at once. He started to argue, but she cut him off. "I'm fine. This might be the break in the case that we've been looking for."

He still didn't want to leave her. She'd had a horrible shock. He doubted she'd even started to process it. "Come with me."

She shook her head. "I want to stay here in case

my father comes back. We don't know that they ran. They could be anywhere."

Blaze was clutching at straws, but he wasn't going to argue the point.

"Anyway," she said, "I want a hot bath and some time alone. All of this just came out of nowhere."

He nodded and pulled her to him to place a kiss on the top of her head. "Keep your phone handy. Call me if—"

"I'll call if I need you." She leaned back to smile at him. "I'm going to be okay, really."

He returned her smile. "I never doubted it. I won't be long."

BLAZE WATCHED JAKE drive away. The days were so short this time of year. It was already getting dark outside. The wind had come up and there were dark clouds scudding toward the ranch.

She stood at the window hugging herself as she thought of her mother and how much she'd hated winter in Montana. What had happened the night she'd left the ranch? Had she driven off, as her father had told her? Or was she already dead?

When she lost track of Jake's pickup's taillights, she shook off the thought that plagued her. Was Allie wrong? Were they both wrong? Was her father a killer?

She turned back to the empty living room, feeling shell-shocked. She tried her father's cell phone number again. It went straight to voice mail. She left a message for him to call, that it was urgent. Then, remembering her promise to Jake, she carried her phone down the hall toward her bathroom.

She'd known that Jake hadn't wanted to leave her alone, but she needed some time to herself. Maybe Herb Perkins did know something about Frank's murder. She had a sudden wish that she and Jake had left before this happened. She felt overwhelmed. It was bad enough hearing the news from Tawny. But then she had to watch the sheriff's department cars racing into the ranch yard, deputies pouring out as they began to search the house and property.

At the bathroom, she started to reach down to turn on the faucet to fill the tub when the lights went out. She froze. Earlier the wind had been blowing. Blowing hard enough to knock out the power? Losing electricity was common out here in the country. She wondered if her father still kept the candles in the bottom kitchen drawer? The thought of a hot bath in candlelight made her turn toward the door.

But she took only a step before she heard a familiar sound that made her freeze. Had someone just opened the back door? As she thought it, a gust of wind seemed to skitter across the floor. She shivered, listening, telling herself the wind had blown the back door open. Just like the wind had taken out the electricity? Except that she was sure she'd locked the back door, hadn't she? Maybe not, given her mental state.

Blaze realized she'd brought her cell phone into the bathroom with her. She could use the flashlight to find the candles—and close the back door. She felt around in the pitch-blackness for her phone, all the time listening to the howl of the wind outside. She'd laid the phone down when she was getting ready to prepare for her bath.

She froze again as she heard the creak of a floorboard in the hallway.

Had Jake come back? He would have come to the front door, which she was sure she'd locked. He wouldn't sneak up on her. She caught a whiff of men's aftershave. Nothing Jake would be caught dead wearing. Her pulse leaped as she heard another floorboard creak, this one closer. There was no denying it.

Someone was in the house and was carefully moving down the hallway.

JAKE HAD TIME to think on the way into Saddle Butte. He kept going back to what the sheriff had said about putting money in the collection plate for his anonymous caller. It had a ring of truth to it.

If Blaze was right, it had been five one-hundred-dollar bills. He remembered seeing an envelope folded in half. But how had the person picked up the money without being noticed?

He mulled that over as the lights of the small Western town came into view.

Herb Perkins was just closing up. He opened the front door to let Jake in and locked it behind him.

"Come with me," Herb said.

Jake felt the hair on the back of his neck rise. "If this is another ambush…"

The man stopped walking to turn to him. "I'm

sorry about that. I knew they planned to take your money, but I had no idea they planned to beat you up and steal it. I should have. I would have called the law when I found you in the alley—"

"But what would have been the point, right, since the sheriff's son was the instigator?" Herb looked embarrassed. "If it makes you feel better, they didn't get all the money—just a small part of it."

The man nodded. "I heard," he said with a wry smile. "You were expecting the ambush."

"I'm just not in the mood for another one."

"That isn't why I called you." Herb headed to the counter in the back. "I've been doing some thinking."

"It must be going around."

The man ignored that as he pulled out an old calendar. "I keep track of our poker games. I like to see how much I've won—and lost. I also keep track of the others who won and how much."

Jake frowned, waiting for the man to get to the point.

"I was looking over the last few months," Herb continued before glancing up from the calendar. "Frank Anson lost a lot of money. We shouldn't have given him any credit. He was desperate to win back what he lost, but he only dug himself into a deeper hole."

"I heard that. He owed Hutch Durham money."

"Not just Hutch, though Hutch was the most vocal." Herb shook his head. "Frank was desperate. He hit me up for a loan. I turned him down. He was furious. He said he'd already gone to the bank and had asked everyone else he knew. He left here, saying that I'd given him no choice. I had no idea what that meant, but it scared me. Then I heard that he'd gone to Pastor Westlake. They'd called the sheriff's office and LJ was off duty, but he told the dispatcher he would handle it."

"LJ told you all this?" Jake asked.

Herb nodded. "He said they were all there, the pastor, Emma Jean, Sandra and her husband, Lonny." The man seemed to hesitate. "LJ was leading Frank outside, trying to calm him down. He'd thought Lonny had left, but apparently he'd gone outside to cool off. LJ said he had to step between Lonny and Frank. Lonny was threatening to kill him."

"A lot of people seemed to want Frank dead. Are you saying you think Lonny killed him?"

Herb looked away for a moment. "Frank also owed LJ money. That night, LJ said Frank started walking back down to the bar, where he'd left his vehicle, and Lonny had started his car to let it warm up before he went in to get Sandra to go home. With both of them calmed down, LJ went into the house to make sure everyone was all right before he left.

"They talked to the pastor and Emma Jean about getting a restraining order on Frank. Sandra left with her husband. LJ said he handled everything, but when he came back out, his rifle was gone from his truck. He was convinced that Frank had doubled back and stolen it. He was royally pissed since he figured Frank would pawn it for peanuts and the man already owed LJ money."

It was quite the story. It sounded like something LJ had made up to explain what had happened to his rifle. "You have any idea what caliber the rifle was?"

"A .30-06," Herb said.

"LJ never got his rifle back?" Jake asked.

"Before he could confront Frank, the man was killed."

Killed with a bullet from a .30-06. "You told the sheriff about this?"

Herb frowned. "I'm sure LJ told him. Bud had given his son that rifle, had his name engraved on it. LJ was furious with Frank. I was worried that he might do something…stupid."

"Like go get his rifle back," Jake said.

Herb shrugged and looked guilty. "I'm not saying that LJ killed the man and got rid of his rifle. Hell, I don't know what I'm saying. I feel like I'm telling tales out of school, but I felt like I owed you after the other night."

"I appreciate that."

The man hurried around the counter to unlock the front door for him. Jake was anxious to get back to the ranch. Back to Blaze.

SOMEONE WAS MOVING carefully down the hallway.

Blaze froze with fear, afraid to move, afraid to breathe as she tried to convince herself that she was wrong. That she was jumping at shadows because of everything that had happened since she'd come back to Montana.

She had to breathe. She couldn't hold it any longer.

She also had to move. She tried once more to find her phone, feeling around blindly as her pulse thundered in her ears. Her fingertips hit the corner of the phone. It skidded across the vanity and fell between the basin and the tub, making a thudding sound.

Her heart lodged in her throat. Now whoever was out there knew exactly where she was!

She started to reach down to try to find it when another floorboard creaked. Closer. She didn't have time to make a call even if she could find her phone. No one could get to her fast enough anyway. She had to move! Now! She was on her own!

Her eyes had adjusted to the dark enough that the bathroom doorway was a lighter rectangle of shadow than the hallway. She burst through it, turning quickly toward the living room as she ran full out until she was almost to the front door.

Her mind whirled. Make a run for it? Or try to find a weapon to defend herself? Behind her, she heard startled movement. Whoever it was, he was no longer worried about sneaking in. He was coming after her!

She wouldn't be able to outrun him. She didn't have keys for her pickup. No phone. She had a better chance if she could find something to defend herself with. All of that raced through her mind in an instant before she stopped short of the front door and stepped into the living room.

Rain began to streak the front windows. From the darkness outside came the pelting of the rain as it slashed down, obliterating everything beyond the glass. Inside, she bumped into the end table. The lamp started to topple. She grabbed it, closing her fist around the base, and jerked the cord free of the outlet.

She heard him coming fast and swung the heavy lamp base. As it made contact, the man made an animal keening sound and grabbed for her. His fingers clamped down on the tail of her shirt. She heard the fabric tear as she jerked away and stumbled into the couch. Leaping over it, she came down hard on the other side. She let out a cry of pain as she put weight on her right ankle. If she could get to the island in the kitchen and find a weapon…

She was reaching out blind, hoping she wasn't turned around and headed in the wrong direction, when she limped into the edge of the kitchen island and quickly ducked behind it.

He let out a string of curses. It sounded as if he'd gotten tangled up in the lamp cord. He was breathing heavily as he kicked it away and began to work his way toward her through the blackness. She heard him collide with the couch. He was close now. Too close.

But it was his hoarse whispered words that turned her blood to ice.

"I'm going to kill you."

She didn't recognize the guttural winded voice. She didn't care who he was. She was fighting for her life, her mind on finding something to use as a weapon against him. She had no doubt that he had one. A knife? A gun? She remembered the cup she'd left on the counter and walked her fingers carefully across the granite until she bumped it. She snatched it up and threw it to the far corner of the living room.

The cup hit the wall, shattering. The noise was quickly drowned out by two quick booms of a gun as he fired into the corner where she'd thrown the cup. With the reports covering the sound she made, she opened the silverware drawer, reached in, grabbed a handful of silverware and froze. The gunshots had been deafening—just like the silence that followed it.

She threw a handful of silverware in the direction the shots had come from and quickly ducked down behind the island again. He let out a scream of pain and fired two more shots in her direction. Behind her, she heard the microwave door explode. Another shot pinged off the tile backsplash and sent tile shards spraying over her.

Now he knew she was in the kitchen. He would be coming for her. She heard him advance toward her and crash into the coffee table. She grabbed another handful of silverware, the butter knives this time, threw them and dropped down again, her heart racing. She knew she couldn't hold him off much longer. She had to find where her father now kept the sharp utility knives.

He let out a howl of pain and she heard something hit the floor. His gun? Had he dropped it? She could hear him moving the silverware around on the hardwood floor. He was searching for something. She could hear the clink of the silverware she'd thrown mixed with his curses.

She felt hope soar but quickly tamped it down.

Even if he couldn't find the gun, she was still in mortal danger. Nor could she give him time to find the gun.

Pulling out another drawer, she felt around, frantic to find a sharp knife. Her father must have moved the knives. Not her father, she realized. Allie. Monte had always kept them in a drawer. It would be just like Allie to buy him a knife block. All that whipped through her mind in an instant.

She grabbed the other kitchen utensils in the drawer and froze.

He must have heard the rattle of the silverware drawer because she realized that he'd stopped searching. Like her, he must have been holding his breath, because she couldn't hear him breathing, either. A chill rocketed up her spine. Had he found the gun? Was he just waiting for her to make a sound before he fired?

When she thought she couldn't hold her breath any longer, she heard him move, shoving the couch aside, knocking over the other end table. The matching lamp hit the floor, the bulb shattering, the sound lost in his curses as he came storming toward her.

Fingers shaking, she hurled the utensils in her hand. She had to find a weapon that would stop him. *Think!* What was on the island or the kitchen counter that she could use? She felt around madly, knocking something that hit the floor and broke.

She heard him crash into the kitchen island and curse, low and hoarse. She closed her hand around the handle of the blender and threw it in his direction. He let out a cry, but the container wasn't heavy enough to do any damage—just like the silverware.

Blaze picked up the base of the blender and jerked the cord free as she heard him moving around the end of the kitchen island. He sounded as if he'd hurt himself and, like her, was limping. She wanted to run, but she knew there was nowhere to run to, to get away.

She stood stone still, telling herself that she had to wait until he was close enough because she would get only one chance.

She heard her cell phone begin to ring from inside the bathroom.

As soon as Jake had reached his pickup, he'd called Blaze. The phone rang and rang. He tried the number again, fighting panic. He'd told her to keep her phone handy, but if she was in the bath… Still, no answer.

Jake drove as fast as he could through the pouring rain toward the ranch. He tried Blaze again, leaving a message that she was to call the moment she heard his voice mail. Rain pelted the pickup so loud he feared he wouldn't be able to hear his phone when she did call. If she called.

All his instincts told him that something was wrong. He shouldn't have left her alone. Fear had his heart racing. He tried to think about anything but what could have happened to her. He told himself that if she'd gotten into the tub and forgotten her phone in the other room, he would never forgive her.

He tried to concentrate on his driving, to think

about anything but what kind of trouble could have found her.

He thought about what Herb had told him. LJ was a bully. He liked to hurt women. He'd once hurt Blaze, even though she'd never told him. LJ had hurt Tawny, his fiancée. If the deputy thought that Frank had taken his rifle, he would have gone out to the man's ranch to get it back before Frank had a chance to pawn it. They would have argued. LJ would have left with the rifle, but as he drove out of the Anson Ranch, his anger would have grown.

By the time he reached the county road, he could have looked back and seen Frank out in his pasture. He could have stopped and, not seeing any traffic, gotten out, laid the rifle over the hood of his truck and taken the shot. He would have taken a second one to make sure Frank was dead. That would be the shot that whizzed past Monte as he hurried toward the fallen man.

Jake almost missed the turn into the ranch, the rain was coming down so hard, the night so dark. By the time he drove under the arch, it had begun to snow.

HER CELL PHONE stopped ringing and then began to ring again. The man stood as frozen as she was. Blaze realized why. He didn't know exactly where she was in the dark kitchen. She stayed perfectly still, holding her breath, afraid to make a sound. Had he found his gun? He hadn't fired since she'd heard him drop something. She hoped that meant he no longer had it.

But he could have picked up something else to use as a weapon. Just as she had. Or he might just kill her with his bare hands. He sounded angry enough.

She waited for him to take a step. He was breathing hard from exertion or fury or pain…or excitement? She tried to think rationally and not let her terror force her to make a mistake that would cost her her life.

The base of the blender was growing heavy in her hand. She wasn't sure how much longer she could hold it still. But the moment she moved, he would hear her. If he had the gun… She couldn't think about that. She focused on the sound of his breathing, gauging the distance between them.

Take a step, she willed him. *Just one step*. Then he would be close enough that if she swung the blender base at the spot where she could hear him breathing…

He took a step.

CHAPTER TWENTY-FIVE

BLAZE COULD ALMOST feel his breath on her face as she swung the base of the blender. It struck him in the head. She felt spittle spray across her face and heard his scream of pain. He grabbed for her, his fingers locking down on her arm. She struck out at him with her fist and connected with something hard. She heard a snap and another scream as he released his hold on her and stumbled back.

She turned and tried to run. The floor was slick with something. His blood? She careened around the corner and started down the hallway.

Behind her, she heard his lumbering footfalls. She heard him crash into something. The hallway wall? She told herself that if she could reach her father's den—just as she thought of the loaded handgun her father kept in the bottom drawer of his desk, she remembered that the sheriff had taken all of his guns again.

All hope fled as she was struck in the back and felt herself falling. She wouldn't have been able to reach the den and the gun anyway, she thought as she went down. The air rushed from her lungs even before he fell on her. Deprived of oxygen, she still fought to escape, kicking and crawling as she tried to get him off her.

He grabbed a handful of her hair, jerking her head back as he fought to get a better grip on her. "Bitch!" he spit as her foot found his groin in a hard kick.

His arm looped around her throat, cutting off the air she'd only just been able to suck into her lungs again.

Then his voice was next to her ear. "You couldn't leave well enough alone. You had to keep pushing, didn't you? I knew the moment you saw me with that rifle that you would put it together. I thought if I could hide the rifle I'd taken in the back of LJ's pickup and then make an anonymous call to one of the other deputies as to where they could find the murder weapon… But then you saw me. I knew you would have come forward and told. The only way is to shut you up for good." He leaned harder on her, fury in his every ragged breath.

"Frank deserved to die. I did it for Sandra. For our baby. Frank would have never left us alone. He would have bled us dry with his blackmail."

Surprise shot through her as she recognized the voice so edged with anger and what could have been regret.

Lonny Dean.

JAKE ROARED UP to the ranch house and leaped from his pickup. He stopped for a moment, breathing hard. The house was dark. Blaze's pickup was parked out front. Nothing seemed amiss.

And yet he couldn't shake the bad feeling he'd had
in town. His heart pounded with the fear that had
sent him racing back to the ranch. Snow fell around
him, a wonderland of white. Grabbing his gun and
his flashlight, he climbed out. He heard nothing but
the crunch of his boots on the fallen snow as he
reached the front door of the house. Locked.

He quickly stepped around to the back door. As he
neared the door, he saw that it was standing slightly
ajar. The wind? If Blaze had forgotten to lock it…

Stepping closer, he quickly eased the door all the
way open. He felt the hair on the back of his neck
rise. Something was wrong. He could feel it. He
started to step in when he heard a grunt from down
the hallway. He moved toward the sound, his gun
drawn, a large flashlight in his other hand.

OVER THE MAN'S ragged breaths, Blaze thought she'd
heard the sound of a vehicle roaring into the yard.
Jake? Lonny had heard something, too. He swore
and tightened his hold on her as he dragged her to
her feet.

She could feel his frustration. He'd come this
far. He had to finish what he started even if he was
caught. Even if he had to kill more people.

She thought of Jake. He might not even realize
anything was wrong and go straight to the bunkhouse. Even if he tried the front door, he would find
it locked. He would think she was in bed, asleep.

That had been him she'd heard, hadn't it?

As Lonny jerked her to her feet, holding her up

with the arm around her throat, she felt a sob work its way up her throat but willed herself not to cry.

The house was still pitch-black inside. But outside she could see snow falling in a white shroud. Had she seen movement outside? She tried to scream Jake's name to warn him.

But little sound came out as Lonny's gloved hand clamped over her mouth. She struggled, but her kicks and jabs with her elbows did little more than make him angrier.

"Shut up!" he whispered hoarsely.

He dragged her toward the living room. The falling snow outside the windows cast a little light into the room. She realized he was looking for his gun. He dragged her toward a spot where she could see the sparkle of silverware on the floor. She could hear him muttering to himself.

Blaze told herself that if he found the gun, he would kill her and then Jake if that had been him returning. She couldn't let that happen. He would have to let her go to pick up the gun. It would be her only chance.

THE LIGHT IN the hallway was dim. Jake listened. He could hear movement in the living room and that same grunting sound he'd heard before. All his instincts told him that Blaze was in trouble—and she wasn't alone.

He wanted to race down the hallway to her. It took all of his willpower not to do just that. Seconds could count. If he didn't get to her soon enough…

Jake shook away the thought as he carefully worked his way down the hallway. He had to know what the situation was. Going in guns blazing could get the woman he loved killed. If she was still alive.

His heart told him she was. He had to believe that. He couldn't lose her. He paused at her bedroom door. The room was dark like the rest of the house. But her curtains were open, the snowfall outside providing a little light. He didn't want to turn on the flashlight. Not yet. He could make out her bed. She wasn't in it, just as he'd known she wouldn't be.

He kept going, cringing when a step made the floorboards creak. Just a little farther and he would reach the end of the hallway, where it opened up into the kitchen and living room.

BLAZE HEARD THE creak of a floorboard in the hall. She didn't think that Lonny had heard it, though. He was breathing hard from exertion since she continued to fight him, hoping for one of her kicks or elbow jabs to loosen his hold on her. Nor did she want him to find his gun.

Was it just the old house settling? Or had Jake come back and was he now coming down the hall-way toward them?

She thought of the words she'd withheld from him. If only she had told him the truth. She didn't want to die. She wanted that happy ending Jake had talked about. She wanted Jake with all her heart. If only she had said those three little words. She might never get to tell him. Unless that was him in the hallway, unless they could somehow both get out of this alive, he would never know how she felt.

Blaze fought harder, only to have Lonny tighten the arm around her neck, lifting her off her feet and cutting off her oxygen. She dug her nails into his arm, but he didn't relent. He was going to kill her and there was nothing she could do. He was too strong and she could see black dots forming in front of her eyes. She desperately needed oxygen. Her lungs screamed for another breath.

She felt panicked as Lonny let out a triumphant sound. He'd found his gun. She'd hoped that this would be her chance. But even as she thought it, she felt her vision go dark and her body start to go limp.

As she did, she realized that she'd thrown Lonny off balance. She was falling to the floor, but she was bringing him with her.

JAKE COULDN'T BELIEVE what he was seeing in the dim light. He snapped on the flashlight as he raised his gun. For a moment, Lonny Dean had a headlock on Blaze. He saw her go limp in his arms as the man appeared to be reaching down to pick up something from the floor littered with silverware.

The sudden light startled Lonny, blinding him. Jake could see that he was trying to keep his grip on Blaze, but was losing his balance. He let go of Blaze. She started to fall to the floor. But the movement had taken Lonny with it. He fought to get his feet under him, costing him only a few seconds, but it was enough for Jake to get the upper hand.

Lonny tried to turn toward the blinding light, the gun appearing in his hand as he struggled to stay on his feet. Jake fired, then dived to the side. He already knew that Lonny was a crack shot. He wasn't surprised that the man managed to get off a round. The bullet hit the wall only inches away, sending Sheetrock dust and particles into the air.

Jake fired a second time as he was diving to the side. He heard Lonny grunt a few moments before the man dropped to knees on the floor next to Blaze. He saw Lonny trying to hold the pistol in his hand steady as he swung it around to point it at Blaze's head.

Firing as he rushed the man, Jake got off three shots, all of them hitting their mark. Lonny's head snapped back, the pistol falling from his bloody fingers, an instant before he fell face-forward on the floor.

Jake kicked the man's pistol. It skittered across the floor only a few feet away as it got hung up in the silverware littering the floor. But Jake wasn't worried about Lonny going after it. Lonny Dean wasn't going anywhere but the morgue.

Jake dropped down beside Blaze, terrified that he'd been too late, terrified that she was already dead. But as he lifted her, he heard her gasp for air and try to sit up. "It's all right," he kept saying as she struggled for breath. He could see the reddened skin around her throat. Her chest heaved and her eyes filled with tears as she looked up at him.

"I'm here," he said. "I'm here."

"Jake." The word came out in a hoarse whisper. "I love you."

"Oh, baby," Jake whispered against her hair and she began to sob as he held her tighter. "Oh, baby. I was so afraid that I'd lost you."

CHAPTER TWENTY-SIX

THE REST OF the night was a blur as sheriff's department vehicles again roared up in the yard, followed by an ambulance and the coroner's van. Jake insisted Blaze be taken to the hospital to make sure she was all right. Her throat was bruised and her ankle was sprained, but it was hard to tell if she had other injuries since so much of Lonny's blood was on her.

He rode in the back of the ambulance with her. He had no intention of letting her out of his sight. She'd said she loved him. But he wanted to hear her say that when he wasn't in the process of saving her life.

The sheriff came to the hospital emergency room to take down their statements. Jake hadn't thought he could admire Blaze more, but he'd been wrong. He listened to her harrowing account of what had happened after Lonny had cut the power to the house and begun to stalk her. Jake couldn't imagine how terrified she'd been and yet she'd managed to stay alive through her wits alone.

Things could have gone so differently had Lonny succeeded in killing her. Jake had no doubt that the man would have been waiting for him. Jake would have never seen it coming and he and Blaze would both be dead.

"That's quite a story," Bud said when Blaze finished. "Have you heard from your father?"

"Sheriff, Blaze was almost killed tonight and all you're interested in is her father?" Jake demanded.

Bud shot him a warning look. He hadn't wanted Jake in the room when he'd taken her statement, but there was no way Jake was going anywhere.

"I guess we don't have to worry about Lonny Dean right now," the sheriff said. "You kind of took care of that. Now I have to drive over and tell his pregnant wife and then his in-laws. But Frank Anson isn't the only murder on my books right now."

"I just told you," Blaze said in a whisper. "Lonny confessed how he stole your son's rifle to kill Frank. If I hadn't seen Lonny trying to hide the rifle in the back of LJ's pickup—"

"Don't strain your voice," Jake told her. "He's got your statement and mine. His deputies took photos of the scene at the ranch house. They back up everything you told him. He was planning to frame your son for Frank's murder and maybe our deaths, as well. If I hadn't gotten there when I did…"

Bud nodded as he put away his video recorder and stood. "If you're expecting me to thank you… Just let me know when you hear from Monte." With that, the sheriff turned and walked out.

Jake felt his hands ball into fists. Blaze touched his arm and he let his anger go as he turned to her. "I'm so sorry I wasn't there."

"You were when I needed you most."

BUD FELT OLD as he went back to his office. The building was nearly empty except for the dispatcher and one of the deputies taking his break. He walked down the hall, his legs feeling lead-like. Not bothering to turn on the light in his office, he entered and closed the door behind him.

The snowfall outside lit the room enough that he didn't stumble over the furniture as he plopped down in his chair. If what Blaze McClintock said was true, Lonny Dean had killed Frank. He'd been wrong. He swore under his breath. The evidence at the scene backed up her story.

Turning to face the window, he watched the snowfall. He should retire. The thought felt as heavy as his heart right now. He'd always thought that being a lawman was at least something he was good at. But here, in the dark of his office, he could admit that he hadn't seen this one coming. He'd been so sure Monte had killed Frank…

Well, at least he would get Monte on Bethany's murder. He had that to look forward to and then maybe it was time to hang up his star. Maybe he would take up golf and go to Arizona for the winter months after all.

He'd always told himself that he was too young to retire. That he had a lot of good years left. That Saddle Butte and the county needed him.

Now it felt like a lie. He'd been so focused on getting Monte… He shook his head and at the sound of his door opening behind him, turned to see his son standing in the doorway.

"Why are you sitting here alone in the dark?" LJ asked as he snapped on the light.

Bud blinked at his son. LJ was still healing from his accident. He was facing assault charges. Jake hadn't filed them. Bud had. He couldn't let his son get away with this. He couldn't have people saying he played favorites. He told himself he was doing it for his son.

His phone rang. He motioned for his son to come in and close the door. He took the call from the crime lab. He could use some good news.

"Tell me you have something definitive from the car so I can make the arrest stick," he said without preamble. He noticed that LJ was walking around his office, seemingly lost in his own world and not paying any attention to the call. That worried him because he knew something was on his son's mind. He realized he hadn't been paying attention to the crime lab tech on the other end of the line. "I'm sorry, I didn't catch that."

"There was multiple DNA evidence left by the killer, so we had an easy time of getting the results you asked for."

Music to his ears. He couldn't help but grin. Maybe he wouldn't retire. The last thing he wanted to do was learn to play golf. "Just tell me we have a match." Monte's DNA was in the system from his arrest for Frank's murder. Wrong or not, they had it and now it was just a matter of tracking the rancher down and—

"It matches a man by the name of Frank Anson."

"What?" He must have heard wrong. "That's not possible." He realized they weren't talking about the same case. "This is evidence from Bethany Mc-Clintock's car, right?"

"That's correct. You asked for a rush on the results. That's why I'm calling you tonight. We got lucky. Blood from both the victim and her attacker was found on a rag in the trunk along with the remains. Frank Anson's DNA was already in our system."

"That's because he was murdered recently." Bud felt sick. "What about the husband, Monte Mc-Clintock?"

"There is no evidence that he was involved in the homicide."

Bud felt as if his feet had been kicked out from under him. Monte hadn't killed her. Frank Anson killed Bethany? He looked at his son and felt his heart drop. "You're sure?"

"There isn't any doubt. The DNA on the bloody rag found in the trunk of the car with the remains matched both Bethany McClintock's and Frank Anson's. The test was conclusive. The killer took no precautions when it came to leaving his DNA behind." He'd been careless. Frank Anson hadn't realized he was leaving conclusive evidence that would lead the law right to him.

"I'm sending you the results," the crime tech was saying. "I already sent it to your county prosecutor."

Bud thanked him even as he was swearing silently to himself. If Dave had the same evidence he did, he would demand that the BOLO be called off against

McClintock and his pregnant girlfriend. Bud wondered how things could get worse.

LJ finally quit moving around the office and took a chair across from Bud's desk. "You heard the news?" he asked his son. LJ looked pale under his cuts and bruises, and he could tell that he was still in pain.

"I never liked Lonny Dean," his son said. "Now it turns out that the bastard was the one who stole my rifle to frame me for not just Frank's murder but Blaze and her...boyfriend's? I heard Blaze put up one hell of a fight."

He couldn't miss the admiration in LJ's voice. He should have known his son would have talked to the deputies at the scene after he heard the call on the scanner. He wanted to ask LJ how things were with his fiancée, but he held his tongue. He figured that situation wouldn't improve until Blaze McClintock was long gone out of the county again.

"I'm afraid that isn't all the news," Bud said, still shocked by the lab's findings. "That call I just took? It was from the crime lab about Bethany McClintock's car."

"Good news?"

Bud chuckled at that. "The good news is that the killer left a lot of DNA evidence in the car with the remains." That dumbass Frank. "It wasn't Monte." He was watching his son, wondering if he knew that Frank was his father. "Frank Anson killed her."

"No shit?" LJ shook his head. "I wasn't expecting

that. You were so sure it was Monte. But the lab said it was definitely Frank?"

"Definitely." Bud knew the evidence had been there all along. He'd ignored the flat tire in the back seat just as he'd ignored the suitcase next to it. The clues had all been there, including the bloody tire iron in the trunk along with the remains. He'd been blinded by his hatred of Monte.

Now that he saw everything clearly, he could easily imagine what had happened. Bethany McClintock had packed a suitcase, planning to send for the rest of her things once she was settled, just as Monte said. She'd left late at night.

It was hard to say how far down the road she'd gotten before she had the flat. Knowing her, she would have tried to change it herself rather than call Monte to help her.

Who knew why Frank was on the road that night, but he would have seen her and stopped. Bud imagined him coming upon her car in the road after she had the flat. She would probably have been happy to see someone who might offer to help. Until she realized it was Frank.

Bud doubted Frank liked Bethany any more than he did Monte. Bethany had befriended Frank's wife, Allie. That meant Bethany knew all his secrets. She knew the way he treated his wife. There would be no love lost between Frank and Bethany.

And there they were alone on the road in the dead of night, no one for miles. Had they argued? Or had Frank seen a way to get the woman out of his and his wife's lives forever? Bethany had been leaving for good, but Frank wouldn't have known that.

He started to tell his son about it, but realized LJ wasn't listening.

"I have to ask you something," his son said, looking young and vulnerable. "Is it true?"

For a moment, Bud feared what LJ was asking. He felt his heart bang against his ribs and hoped he didn't have another panic attack. "Are you asking if Lonny Dean killed Frank Anson? According to Blaze, he admitted it."

"No, not that." LJ put his head in his hands for a moment. Bud felt sweat run down his back. He'd known this day was coming. With Frank having killed Bethany, it would only be worse if Bud told LJ the truth.

"Pastor Westlake says evil can run in a person's genes." LJ raised his head to look at him.

Bud found himself unable to breathe for a moment. He knew he had to say something. "I don't think—"

"The pastor says that if a man finds God, though, he can overcome his genes and fight his weaknesses." His son looked so hopeful, Bud felt his eyes burn with tears. He desperately wanted to tell him that there was no evil in his genes. He wanted to tell him that he was his son—not Frank's.

But when he opened his mouth, he found he couldn't speak. He knew nothing about genetics. But the truth was, LJ had inherited his father's temper and maybe worse.

His son dropped his head again to stare at the floor. "Pastor says that a man can choose to be whatever he wants to be—with God's help."

Bud took a breath, then another, as he tried to still his pounding heart. He'd never wanted to believe anything more in his life. He wiped at the sweat on his forehead with his sleeve and stood on trembling legs to move around the desk to lay his hand on his son's shoulder. "What kind of man do you want to be?"

LJ lifted his head to look up at him. He saw so much anguish in the young man's eyes that he felt his heart break. "I want to be just like you, Dad."

CHAPTER TWENTY-SEVEN

BLAZE LOOKED UP to see her father and Allie come into her hospital room. Her father rushed to her bedside. She opened her mouth to speak but burst into tears instead. Monte took her in his arms and she cried against his shoulder as she had as a girl.

When she stopped crying, she pulled back to look at him and Allie. "Have you heard? They found Mom."

Her father nodded. "I'm so sorry, Blaze. I would have been here sooner but Allie and I... We eloped."

She smiled as her gaze went to Allie and the diamond band on her left hand. "Congratulations."

"Terrible timing," her father said. "We headed back as soon as we heard the news."

Blaze looked to Allie. "You know about...Frank?" She nodded. "I'm so sorry about all this."

"We both are," her father said as he reached for Allie's hand. "It was such a shock. Even though I knew your mother had to be dead all these years... But even more of a shock was Lonny Dean trying to kill you."

Blaze felt a shudder at the memory of the dark house and Lonny tracking her. She wondered how long she'd have to sleep with a light on before she could forget the horror of it. "But I'm fine now." She smiled at the two of them. "It's finally over, huh."

Her father nodded. "We have to go down to the sheriff's office, but then that should be the last of it. With Frank dead, there won't be a trial to drag things on forever. The doctor said you are going to be released this morning."

"Jake is picking me up."

"Then we'll see you at the ranch." Her father squeezed her hand. "I'm so glad you're all right. Maybe…" He shook his head. "Never mind, it can wait until later."

She watched them go, wondering what could wait until later. Would her father stay on the ranch now that he and Allie were married? Or would they leave for a fresh start somewhere else? What would happen to the ranch?

Before she could consider how she felt about all of it, Jake stuck his head in the door. She'd never been so happy to see anyone.

JAKE STOPPED JUST feet from her bed and took in her amazing smile. She'd been through so much and yet she'd come out the other side smiling. He couldn't help smiling himself as he moved to the bed and leaned down to kiss her.

She put her arms around his neck, pulling him closer. He heard her sigh against his lips and sat back to look at her.

"How are you?"

"Now that you're here? Happy. I know I shouldn't be, having found out about my mother only hours ago, but—"

"The not knowing had to be the worst."

She nodded. "I knew she was gone, but now I know why she didn't come back for me. I've spent a lot of years angry at her and my father and myself. Am I awful for feeling…freed?"

He shook his head as he cupped her cheek for a moment. "You've been dealing with a lot since the night your mother left. Now you have the answers that have haunted you for so long. I just saw your father and Allie leaving…"

"They eloped. That's why they left. To get married. I think Dad was worried that he'd be arrested again," she said. "It's been years since he's looked that happy."

"Marriage does that for some people," Jake said and met her gaze.

She chuckled. "Is that so? What are you—"

"Blaze McClintock," he said as he dropped to one knee beside her bed.

Leaning over the side of the bed, she looked down at him, her eyes wide. But he didn't see fear in them anymore.

"I've thought of dozens of romantic ways to ask you this." He chuckled as he reached into his pocket and pulled out the small velvet box. "It doesn't matter where I do this, I realized. We don't need candlelight and soft music. It's what's in our hearts. Will you marry me?"

BLAZE COULDN'T HELP but laugh at the sight of him down on one knee beside her hospital bed. She could hear a doctor being paged over the intercom and a squeaky wheelchair moving slowly down the hallway outside her room.

But her gaze was on Jake Horn and the look in those green eyes of his. She knew what was in her heart. "You really want to marry me?"

He blinked. "You are going to seriously ask me that right now?"

She laughed again, then smiled down at him. "I thought you would never ask."

Jake shook his head. "You are an impossible woman, you know that, Blaze?"

She did. And he knew it as well, and yet he wanted to spend the rest of his life with her. For someone who didn't believe in happy endings, she definitely liked the thought of this one.

He rose from the floor to take her left hand and slip the most beautiful ring she'd ever seen onto her finger. "I chose agate because it is one of the oldest healing stones. It protects the wearer from storms and calamities." She chuckled at that. "Also because it is a stone of many colors that forms in the spaces other rocks leave."

"It's beautiful," she said on a breath, her eyes filling with tears. "It's our story, isn't it?" He nodded. "And the story of our children. Oh, Jake."

She would have said more, but the doctor came in then with her release papers. She felt as if she was floating on air as she looked at her ring and at her future husband.

"I should get you home," Jake said.

Home? "If you mean the ranch, my father and Allie will be there."

He rubbed his neck for a moment, his gaze locking with hers. "You have a better suggestion?" She nodded. "You sure you're up for this?"

She laughed and said, "Just get me out of this hospital."

"I'm not making love to my fiancée in some cheap motel," he said.

"Of course not. Why would you when you have a perfectly good pickup?" Jake opened his mouth, but she didn't give him a chance to argue. "Oh, come on. It wouldn't be the first time. Or, hopefully, the last," Blaze said. "I want you, Jake Horn. And I'm damned tired of waiting."

He laughed and shook his head. "You are one contrary woman."

She smiled. "You know me so well."

BUD HEARD A tap at his door and looked up from his desk to see Monte and Allie standing in the hallway.

"We heard you were looking for us," Monte said.

A little late, Bud thought but waved them in. "Have a seat. I'm tying up loose ends on your wife's murder," he said to Monte. "My condolences, by the way. I assume you've already heard." The man nodded solemnly. He didn't look surprised that his wife was dead. He just looked sad.

Bud sat back down and pulled out his notebook and pen. He no longer needed this information, but this time, he wanted to cross all his *t*'s and dot all his *i*'s. He'd planned to put in for his retirement, but LJ had talked him out of it. "You're too young. What would you do?"

He'd seen the wisdom in staying on, but only if he could leave a better legacy in this town for his son. He was determined to change.

"The night Bethany left, do you remember where your husband might have been?" he asked Allie.

"Frank had gone into town that night," Allie said and stared down at her hands in her lap. "I thought it was odd at the time because when he came back he said he'd never made it that far. He said he'd gotten a flat that he had to change. He didn't return until almost daylight and his clothes were dirty and he had a scratch on his face. He told me it was from a wild rosebush beside the road where he'd changed the tire."

"Did Frank know that Bethany as leaving that night?" Bud asked.

Tears welled in her eyes. "He might have suspected. I was heartbroken, afraid I couldn't go on without her as a friend. I'd promised her I would leave Frank but without her nearby, I feared that I wouldn't have the courage. As it was… I didn't."

"Frank's DNA was found in Bethany's car on a bloody rag. It appears that she had a flat tire as she was leaving. Frank must have come up on her on the road."

"He hated her," Allie said, her voice breaking. "I'm sure he blamed her for me being unhappy. Said she was bad for me. I figured he'd be glad she was leaving, but he must have found out about my plans to join her later with Blaze." Allie began to cry. Monte put an arm around her.

The sheriff looked at Monte. "Seems you're off the hook." He cleared his throat, finding this harder than he'd even imagined. "I need to apologize. I was wrong."

"I appreciate that, Bud. I know how you felt about Bethany."

The man's words took him by surprise. He looked away, swallowed and pushed to his feet. "By the way, I heard congratulations are in order."

JAKE PARKED IN a spot overlooking the valley. He left the pickup engine running and heater going since it was winter in Montana, but made a point of engaging the emergency brake before turning on the radio to the local station. A country song came on as they climbed into the back of the king cab. He pulled her into his arms. "You're really going to be my wife?"

Blaze snuggled into him. "You best believe it." She kissed him. "I like the sound of *Mrs. Jake Horn*."

"Blaze Horn," he said. "I like the sound of that, too." His gaze met hers and held it. She knew what he was looking for. He was afraid that she might change her mind about him. Not a chance.

"I love you, Jake Horn."

He smiled. "You know what that means. Till death do us part."

"If this pickup rolls off this mountain it could be sooner than later," she joked and then turned serious. She'd needed this man for so long. She couldn't bear waiting another minute. "Make love with me, Jake Horn."

She didn't have to ask him twice. He cupped her face in his hands and kissed her deeply. Blaze felt heat rush through her veins to her center. She wanted this man. She'd always wanted Jake, but on her terms, not his.

But after almost dying, she'd realized how foolish she'd been. She loved him. Wanted to be his wife. Wanted his children. On *any* terms. She'd been afraid to love too deeply for fear of being devastated like she had when her mother had left and hadn't come back for her.

She was seeing a lot of things more clearly, she thought as Jake trailed kisses down her throat and slowly began to unsnap her Western shirt. She couldn't bear another moment without being naked in his arms. She grabbed his shirt and pulled each side, making the snaps sing, making him chuckle as he did the same with the last few snaps on hers.

"So that's the way you want it," he said, grinning.

She laughed as she shrugged out of her shirt and jeans and he did the same. He pulled her to him, unhooking her bra and peeling it off before pressing his warm, hard chest against her aching breasts. She groaned with pleasure. As he laid her back on the seat, his mouth dropped to one breast and then the other as he laved them with his tongue. His hand slipped beneath her panties. She was wet and aching and when his fingers caressed her, she came at once, crying out as she clung to him.

She reached for him, guiding him into her, and lay back as he leaned over her, their gazes locked in a silent bond as he took her even higher before they both collapsed in each other's arms.

"Next time in a bed," Jake said as he pulled on his clothes.

Blaze chuckled knowingly as she struggled into her jeans. "If we can make it that far."

CHAPTER TWENTY-EIGHT

BLAZE WAS RIGHT about her father and Allie waiting for them. She felt like a teenager as she and Jake entered the house, both of them flushed and too happy. But Monte and Allie only congratulated them when Blaze showed them the engagement ring.

"If you want a big wedding…" Monte began, but Blaze cut him off.

"I want to elope like you two did," she said and looked at Jake. "Tomorrow will work." He laughed but nodded. He'd give her anything she wanted and she knew it.

They hadn't been at the ranch long before neighboring ranchers and their wives began to stop by with food and condolences and ultimately congratulations. If anyone thought it strange, they didn't show it. Actually most everyone seemed relieved that as somber as the occasion could have been, there was good news, as well.

The Garrisons, along with their son, Ty, who still had his arm in a cast, stopped by with a freshly baked pie. As more and more people showed up, the atmosphere took on that of a party for a while. When everyone had left, Blaze saw her father's pleased expression and the tears in Allie's eyes. The community reaching out to the two of them had come as a surprise, but a pleasant one.

"What are your plans now?" she finally asked them after the four of them sat down in the living room.

"Well, now that you mention it," her father said with a guilty smile, "I was hoping that one day you would come back here and take over the ranch. You and Jake."

"You aren't really going to try to talk me into raising buffalo, are you?" she asked him with a laugh.

"Actually, to be accurate, they're bison. The American buffalo was misnamed."

She gave him an impatient look.

"And I'm not raising bison just to upset area ranchers."

"But it's a plus, right?" Blaze asked, grinning.

Her father gave her a wry smile. "I'm trying to be serious here."

"Sorry, please continue."

"Bison have more protein, more iron, more of the good fatty acids and less fat, less cholesterol and fewer calories."

Blaze laughed. "I've heard this."

He smiled at her. "Then I don't have to tell you about the other benefits of bison, all the vitamins it contains."

She shook her head. "You can save your sales pitch."

"I'd be interested in raising bison," Jake said and grinned over at Blaze. "I've actually looked into it down in Wyoming, where I have a small herd of Black Angus."

Blaze didn't know which of the men surprised her more. She turned to her father. "You really didn't just start raising bison out of spite?"

He gave her a disbelieving look. "I'm a businessman, as well as a rancher, my lovely daughter. Because the bison market is so small, it's quite beneficial financially to raise them. I'm not a fool, Blaze."

She shook her head as she studied her father. He was a lot of things, stubborn, obstinate, mule-headed, opinionated, but mostly strong and intelligent. She looked from him to Allie. Her father was finally happy. She could see the two of them together for a very long time.

"I was so angry with you, believing that you had run my mother off," she said and met his gaze. Jake reached over and took her hand. "You were really going to let me go."

"I knew I had to," her father said. "You were so miserable and you'd started getting into trouble. As much as I love you, I wanted the best for you. And that was your mother." He shook his head, tears filling his eyes again. "I loved your mother." He squeezed Allie's hand. "Allie knows how hard it was on me when she left. I loved her so much that I thought if she loved me..." He shook his head. "I tried to keep her here. It was wrong. I could see her fading, like a rose denied water. I couldn't do it anymore. It broke my heart but I knew she had to leave. I loved you both too much to deny either of you any longer. Your mother wanted to introduce you to ballet and opera and Broadway shows. She talked about culture as if it was fine crystal."

Blaze studied her father. She might look like her mother at this age, but she was her father's daughter. She felt at home here on the ranch. She would have hated urban living and she suspected her father had known that.

When she'd first told him about her mother being found, he'd taken it hard. He'd looked broken in a way he hadn't, even facing life in prison. But the closure seemed to have done him good. He'd bounced back with the help of his new bride.

She smiled at the two of them, happy for them and sad about the years she'd lost with her father as well as her mother.

"I'm sorry, Dad," Blaze said and swallowed. "I'm sorry I mistrusted you on so many levels." She reached over to cover his large, weathered hand with her own.

He shook his head, a large, shaggy head reminding her of the bison he raised.

Blaze looked to Allie. "You were my mother's best friend, her only friend. I can't imagine what you've gone through, as well. It must have been hard when she didn't come back for either of us."

Allie met her gaze. "I knew something had happened to her. She'd promised to help me. She was going to contact me as soon as she was settled. She'd actually thought that you and I could travel together. She wouldn't have broken that promise unless she was dead."

"You were going to leave Frank?" Blaze asked. "But then you changed your mind?"

Allie looked away for a moment. "When I didn't hear from Bethany… Then Frank's mother died and he begged me to stay. He was so lost…"

"Did he know you were going to leave him?" Monte asked.

"I think he suspected because of what we know now. He knew I wasn't happy. Maybe that's why he was better for a while. Or maybe it was guilt over what he'd done." Tears filled her eyes. "I'm so sorry, Blaze. I had no idea."

She moved to the woman and hugged her. "We can't undo the past. You and my father have such a bright and happy future." She pulled back to look down at Allie's ever-growing stomach and smiled. "And a baby on the way."

Allie wiped at her eyes. "It's a girl."

"A girl?" she said and turned to her father. "Are you disappointed? I always thought you would have been happier with a son."

"Where do you get those ideas?" he asked, shaking his head. "You are my pride and joy. I'm delighted to have another daughter."

"Well, the past is over now." She cocked her head at him as she removed her hand from his. "You don't have any more skeletons that will be falling out of the closets, do you?"

He laughed. It was a wonderful sound. She realized she hadn't heard that hearty laugh of his in years. Not since she was a girl. "Not that I know of."

Blaze looked over at Allie. "So you're staying here?"

"We thought about leaving, starting over somewhere else, but after everything that has happened..." She looked to her husband.

"We're going to stay here and run the ranch until the two of you decide you've had enough of the private detective life and want to come back and raise your children here. Then we'll build ourselves a place on the ranch to give you space."

"Dad—"

"Or maybe you won't want to come back here," he added quickly. "Then we'll see. We'd probably sell the ranch and move closer to you and my grandchildren."

"That sounds like a threat," Jake joked. He turned to Blaze. "They are going to spoil their grandchildren rotten."

"You'd better believe it. I also want our daughter to be close to her family," Monte said. His gaze seemed to take in the room and the ranch beyond it. "I think this ranch will be good for the two of you," he said, his gaze taking in Jake. "If the two of you decide to come back. You'll take care of my daughter?"

"I will, sir."

"No more *sir*. It's Monte. Or...Dad. We plan to have Christmas here," her father continued. "I was hoping the two of you would come back. This house wouldn't be a bad place to get married, if you haven't already eloped."

Blaze looked at Jake, who smiled and nodded. "I'll think about it."

Her father got to his feet and helped his new bride to hers. "In the meantime, we need to go back over to Allie's. We have some packing to do, so this place is yours as long as you want to stay."

"Thank you, but we need to make some decisions, as well," Jake said. "No matter what we decide, we have to return to the lives we left, at least for a while."

AFTER MONTE AND Allie left, Jake asked, "Did you call the judge yet?"

She nodded. "You know him. He'd already heard most everything." She grinned. "Except for the part about us being engaged. He wished us well."

Jake chuckled. "I bet he did." He saw how exhausted Blaze was. "If you want to take a hot bath, we could watch a movie. I'd make popcorn," he suggested.

She stepped to him, wrapping her arms around his waist and pressing her inviting curves against him. "There's a bed in my room."

"I've noticed that," he said with a grin. "But let's see how you feel after your bath, okay?"

"That sounds wonderful. Join me?"

"I will for the movie. I'll bring the popcorn and candy. Wait for me in bed?"

"Where are you going?" she asked drowsily. He could see that it would be a while before she was her old self again, as hard as she tried to hide it. All of this had taken a toll on her, not to mention she'd fought off a killer not that many hours ago.

"There's something I need to take care of. I promise I won't be gone long. You have your phone?"

She nodded and smiled. "Hurry back."

He kissed her and promised he would. There'd been something nagging at him, and as he'd told Blaze, he didn't like to quit until he'd finished what he'd started. He drove into town to Pastor Westlake's house only to find that the pastor was still down at the church. When he walked in, he found Wilber writing furiously on a sheet of paper.

"Sorry to bother you," Jake said, making the man look up, startled. "You really should lock your door. Anyone could come in when you're working."

"It's a church. We welcome anyone," the pastor said, smiling.

"Even a man like Frank Anson? He came to see you to apologize, didn't he?"

"You missed my sermon Sunday. It was about forgiveness."

Jake nodded. "Was that meant for your parishioners or for you? I suspect that when Frank apologized, you did forgive him."

"Of course. The man had a tormented soul."

"I'm sure he did. Pastors are like priests right? They can bare their souls and you keep their secrets."

"I'm sorry, what is it you're trying to ask me? If there is something you'd like to unburden yourself of, I'd be happy to listen."

"I'm thinking it was you who might want to unburden yourself, Pastor. You were the sheriff's anonymous caller. You were smart enough to know that a person wouldn't give up that kind of information without asking for something. But you didn't want the five hundred dollars for yourself. I saw that you're raising money for a new roof."

The man rose from his chair. "That's quite a theory."

"I think I know what happened. Frank bared his soul and then worried you would tell, threatened you. No," Jake said, "he threatened your *daughter*. So for sixteen years, you never told his secret—until now." Jake took a step toward the door, then turned to look back at the man. "I heard you finally have enough money for that new church roof. God does work in mysterious ways, doesn't he?"

TRUE TO HIS WORD, Jake wasn't gone long. As he came into the house, he smelled the bath salts that Blaze loved and heard the television on down the hallway to one of her favorite movies. The thought made him mentally shake his head. How could a woman who fought a romantic happy ending so hard love them so much on the screen?

He promised himself that he would move heaven and earth if that was what it took to give her one of those happy endings as he made the popcorn just the way she liked, dumped the candies into the bowl with it and followed that alluring scent down the hallway to her bedroom.

As he peeked in, he saw that the television was on to the Christmas movie, candles burned on the nightstands and Blaze was curled up in the bed—sound asleep.

He tiptoed in to blow out the candles. She didn't stir. Not even to the smell of buttered popcorn. That alone told him how exhausted she'd been.

He carefully climbed into the bed beside her and began to watch the movie and eat the popcorn and candy. He couldn't remember the last time he'd felt so alive, so happy and so content.

Looking down at his beautiful sleeping fiancée, he wondered if Blaze already knew that they would be coming back here to take over the ranch, buffalo and all. He'd noticed how sad it had made her when she'd thought about selling the ranch. She'd once been happy here. He knew she would be again. This ranch, this life had always been calling her. She might even like raising buffalo. Or not, he thought with a chuckle.

It didn't matter. He could see the future etched in the landscape as their children grew up here and they continued her father's legacy.

When the movie ended, he put the bowl of half-eaten popcorn aside and turned off the television. Curling up next to his soon-to-be wife, he breathed her in and closed his eyes. Blaze stirred just enough to nestle in his arms and whisper, "I love you, Jake Horn."

He'd never get tired of hearing those words, he thought as he whispered back, "And I love you."

* * * * *

Look for Heartbreaker, *the next book in*
New York Times *bestselling author B.J. Daniels's*
Montana Justice series from HQN Books.

HER EYES FLEW OPEN, her fight-or-flight response already wide-awake. She jerked up in the bed, blinking wildly, terrified and yet unable to believe what she was seeing. Three hulking black forms appeared out of the dark shadows of the large bedroom. One of them tripped over her duffel bag on the floor where she'd dropped it. He swore. She realized that must have been what had awakened her as she tried to banish the men back to the nightmare they must have climbed in from.

This couldn't be happening, because their being here tonight made no sense.

But before she could open her mouth to speak, the largest of the three reached her side of the king-size bed, pushed her back and clamped a gloved hand over her mouth. Any hope that this was only a dream vanished as he roughly held her down. This was real.

She tried to scream, but the gloved hand over her mouth muffled the sound. Not that it would have done any good if she had screamed to bloody hell. There was no one else in the house to come to her rescue—let alone nearby.

Frantically, she shook her head as she met the man's eyes, the only feature not hidden by his black ski mask, and tried to communicate just how wrong this all was.

"Don't fight me," the man said in a hoarse whisper as he renewed his efforts to hold her down. "We don't want to hurt you."

But she did fight, because they were making a terrible mistake.

Panic rocketed through her system. Her heart banged against her rib cage, her thundering pulse deafening in her ears. She fought to pull the gloved hand from her mouth. Failing that, she struck out with her fists as her legs kicked wildly to free themselves from the covers until he pressed his body weight against her chest with his forearm, taking away her breath.

"Did you find it?" the man holding her down demanded of the other two. They'd produced flashlights and were now searching the room. She could hear one of them at the dressing table knocking over bottles of expensive perfume and rejuvenating skin creams.

Moments later, she saw the smaller of the men motion that he'd found something as she tried to breathe. "Got it." He pocketed what appeared to be a cell phone before the men turned to her.

Hope soared. They'd found whatever they'd come for. Now maybe they would leave the way they'd come in, like phantoms in the night. It wasn't as if she'd seen their faces. Nor was she going to report this, but they didn't know that, did they?

Her slender thread of hope died as she heard the man holding her down say, "Help me with her." The words sent a fresh stab of fear coursing through her. She fought even harder. Kicking free of the covers, she got a leg out and struck the smaller of the men in his masked face as he tried to grab her legs. She got his nose with her heel, and it gave a loud pop. He let out a wounded cry as he backed off.

"Dammit," the first man said. "I need help here."

The other man who'd been searching the room earlier climbed onto the bed, crawling across the mattress toward her. She caught him in the jaw with her fist before he pinned her arms down as he climbed on top of her.

She struggled to breathe from the weight of him, gagging at his smell. What had he eaten tonight? Pizza with anchovies? She tried to turn her head away as she bucked in an attempt to throw him off her, but he was too heavy. All she could do was heave and squirm under him, terrified at what these men now planned to do with her. *To* her.

"Come here," ordered the man who still had her mouth covered. The one she'd kicked in the face appeared off to her side, still holding one of his gloved hands over his bleeding nose. "Cover her mouth."

She caught the angry glint in the man's pale eyes before the men made the switch. She tried to tell them about the mistake they were making, but before she could get out more than a word and a breath, the broken-nosed man covered her mouth roughly with his bloody glove. She gagged at the smell and feel of the warm fluid on her lips. But it was the look in his eyes that sent her heart rate off the charts.

He would kill her if he got the chance.

Panic had her gasping for breath through her nose as she watched the first man pull a syringe from his coat pocket. She fought with all the strength she had left in her. But even as she did, she knew it was useless. She had no chance against three men. She felt him jab the needle into her neck as she continued to fight until her body went limp.

As she lay like a rag doll, helpless on the bed, she heard a sound that turned her blood to ice. Someone was tearing duct tape into strips.

"Who's in the house?" he asked.

Another head shake from Laney. "A man. I didn't see
his face."

Not that he needed it, but Owen had more confirmation
of the danger. He saw that Laney had a gun, a small
snub-nosed .38. It didn't belong to him, nor was it one
that he'd ever seen in the guesthouse where Laney was
staying. Later, he'd ask her about it, about why she hadn't
mentioned that she had a weapon, but for now they
obviously had a much bigger problem.

Owen texted his brother again, to warn him about the
intruder so that Kellan didn't walk into a situation that
could turn deadly. He also asked Kellan to call in more
backup. If the person upstairs started shooting, Owen
wanted all the help he could get.

"What happened?" Owen whispered to Laney.

She opened her mouth, paused and then closed it as
if she'd changed her mind about what to say. "About

ten minutes ago, I was in the kitchen with Addie when the power went off. A few seconds later, a man came in through the front door and I hid in the pantry with her until he went upstairs."

Smart thinking on Laney's part to hide instead of panicking or confronting the guy. But it gave Owen an uneasy feeling that Laney could think that fast under such pressure. And then there was the gun again. Where had she got it? The guesthouse was on the other side of the backyard, much farther away than the barn. If she'd gone to the guesthouse to get the gun, why hadn't she just stayed there with Addie? It would have been safer than running across the yard with the baby.

"Did you get a good look at the man?" Owen prompted.

Laney again shook her head. "But I heard him. When he stepped into the house, I knew it wasn't you, so I guessed it must be trouble."

Again, quick thinking on her part. He wasn't sure why, though, that gave him a very uneasy feeling.

"I didn't hear or see a vehicle," Laney added.

Owen hadn't seen one, either, which meant the guy must have come on foot. Not impossible, but Owen's ranch was a good half mile from the main road. If this was a thief, he wasn't going to get away with much. Plus, it would be damn brazen of some idiot to break into a cop's home just to commit a robbery.

So what was really going on?

Don't miss
A Threat to His Family *by Delores Fossen,*
available January 2020 wherever
Harlequin® Intrigue *books and ebooks are sold.*

www.Harlequin.com

Don't miss the second book in the highly
anticipated Montana Justice series from
New York Times bestselling author

B.J. DANIELS

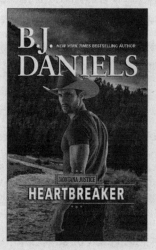

"Daniels is a perennial favorite on the romantic suspense
front, and I might go as far as to label her the cowboy
whisperer." —*BookPage* on *Luck of the Draw*

Preorder your copy today!

HQNBooks.com

PHBJD1219